Mrs Hudson & She

CW00499351

A
SPIDER'S
WEB

LIZ HEDGECOCK

WHITE
RHINO
BOOKS

Copyright © Liz Hedgecock, 2021

All rights reserved. Apart from any use permitted under UK copyright law, no part of this publication may be reproduced, stored in a retrieval system, or transmitted, in any form or by any means, electronic, mechanical, photocopying, recording or otherwise, without the prior written permission of the copyright owner.

This is a work of fiction. Names, characters, businesses, places, events and incidents are either the products of the author's imagination or used in a fictitious manner. Any resemblance to actual persons, living or dead, or actual events is purely coincidental.

ISBN-13: 979-8482221402

For Stephen—
We made it!

CHAPTER 1

Dr Watson sighed as I took the top off my boiled egg. 'Doesn't Holmes have a new client this morning?'

'He does,' I replied, scooping out the white of the egg with the tip of my spoon. 'But not until ten o'clock.' I smiled encouragingly at Dr Watson. 'I'm sure he will tell you all about it when you return from work, John.'

'That's if he remembers,' grumbled the doctor. He finished his piece of toast and dabbed his moustache with a napkin. 'By then he could have embarked on a new monograph, or have been summoned to the Yard by Lestrade or Gregson.'

I couldn't help a grin. 'It's possible. I'll get the details if I catch him before you do.'

'Thank you, Nell.' He scrutinised me. 'I take it you're off to the Excelsior Hotel this morning. Your dress tells me as much.'

'I am indeed,' I said. 'You have learnt from the master.'

Since the number of cases coming my way had increased, and to save wrangling with Sherlock over access to the consulting room, I had taken to meeting my clients in a select range of hotels. I met my more well-heeled clients at the Corinthian, those who were clearly of straitened means at the Mansfield, and everyone else at the Excelsior or the Queen's Hotel. For my own safety, and also to decrease the risk of an embarrassing encounter outside working hours, I also adopted a different hair colour and style of dress in each venue. Today my hair would be dark brown and pulled back in a no-nonsense bun, but that would take place after breakfast.

The door creaked and Sherlock entered, still in his dressing gown.

'Really, Holmes!' spluttered Dr Watson.

'Good morning, Watson,' said Sherlock, grinning. 'Shouldn't you be on your way to the hospital by now?'

'Shouldn't you be dressed by now?' countered the doctor. 'I assume you aren't planning to receive your client dressed like that.'

Sherlock mused. 'It would save on the laundry bill,' he said, and laughed at Dr Watson's expression. 'It would not affect my deductive capabilities one jot, Watson, and you know it.'

'Professional is as professional does,' said Dr Watson, wiping his moustache again. 'What sort of case is it today?'

'I'll find out when my client arrives,' Sherlock added nonchalantly, as Martha set a plate of bacon and eggs before him. 'He was circumspect in his letter, so I am afraid the grisly details will have to wait.'

'And then…?' prompted Dr Watson.

'Monograph,' said Sherlock firmly. 'The recent glut of cases has forced me to neglect it, and I want to finish the draft this week.' He smiled at Dr Watson's downturned mouth. 'I thought you would be glad of a rest, Watson. You're always complaining that you haven't time to write up my cases, and here is a golden opportunity.' He turned to me and his eyes narrowed. 'Isn't today one of your shop days, Nell?'

'It is,' I said, 'but I have a meeting first. It shouldn't take more than an hour, and I shall go on to the department store afterwards. I've wired Evie to let her know.'

'On that note,' said Dr Watson, rising, 'I shall leave you two busy bees alone. Good hunting to both of you.' He pushed his chair in and strode off with the air of a man who has his own important business to attend to.

'Good hunting?' Sherlock murmured, his eyes wide with amused delight.

'Don't be hard on John,' I murmured reprovingly. 'He has our best interests at heart, and he supported us when things were much more difficult than they are now.'

'I know,' said Sherlock, loading his fork with egg and bacon. 'But the idea of us as intrepid hunters in the vast jungle of London – especially you, dressed like that – is amusing, to say the least.'

'Camouflage, my dear,' I said, leaning across and kissing his cheek. 'Camouflage.'

***

Half an hour later I was in a hansom and approaching my destination. The cab slowed and I got my purse out. An unexpected wait due to an overturned carriage at Hyde Park Corner meant I would have to hurry if I were to be my usual five minutes early.

'Here we are, ma'am,' said the cabbie, and winked. 'Enjoy your coffee.' I had travelled with him many times, in a variety of guises, and while I was reasonably sure he was unaware of the nature of my business, I felt he wished me well.

'Thank you,' I said, and put the fare into his hand. I consulted my watch: four minutes early. It would have to do.

As soon as I entered the quiet, sparsely populated room where morning coffee was served, I saw my client waiting for me, clutching her napkin in both hands. Mrs Taylor was in her early twenties, carefully dressed, with big dark eyes that formed a startling contrast with her neatly coiled blonde hair.

'Good morning,' I said, smiling pleasantly. 'It's a lovely day, isn't it? Are you well?'

'I have barely slept for worrying,' she replied. 'Please, Mrs Hudson, tell me the worst. I can bear it.'

'In that case,' I said decisively, 'I shall tell you that it is not what you feared.' A waiter hovered at my elbow. 'Could I have a cup of milky coffee, please,' I said to him.

'Of course, madam, and a cake?'

'Not today; it is not so long since I had breakfast.'

'Don't let me stop you,' said Mrs Taylor. 'Could I have a black coffee, please. Nothing else for me.'

The waiter still hovered, looking hopefully at me, though he knew I never ordered cake in the morning. I had grown tired of being fed treats when I had returned from a month-long undercover case a year before. Even now, the sight of a chocolate eclair revolted me.

4

The waiter gave up and disappeared, and I took out my notebook and opened it. 'As I said, Mrs Taylor, things are in no way as bad as you feared. At least, that is my opinion.' I turned to my initial notes on her case. 'You came to me, having been married for six months, and told me you were worried that your husband was . . . straying. Your grounds for this suspicion were that he was finding more and more reasons to spend his evenings from home. He said he had joined a theatre club, yet was vague about the plays he had seen and what he thought of them, and moreover would never attend the theatre with you though it is a passion of yours. He also said he had joined a gentlemen's club, yet could say little of what he did there except that he conversed with other members. Apart from this, you said he was a model husband.'

Deliberately noisy footsteps announced that the waiter was returning with our coffee.

'That's right,' said Mrs Taylor, when he had departed. 'You're sure it isn't – that?' She bit her lip. 'Oh dear. I feel terrible.'

I smiled. 'I am sure. I have shadowed your husband over the past week, and on three of the four nights when he went out, he was at the music hall.'

Mrs Taylor's spoon clattered in her saucer and she goggled at me. 'The music hall?' she said in a shocked whisper. 'He promised he wouldn't. He knows how I hate it!'

I suppressed a frown; this was not quite the reception of my news that I had anticipated. 'On each occasion that Mr Taylor attended the music hall, he behaved impeccably,

5

was not rowdy, did not speak to any women, and indulged in no more than two pints of beer.'

Mrs Taylor wrinkled her nose. 'Not beer.'

'I'm afraid so,' I said. 'On Thursday, Mr Taylor met with two friends at a chop house.' Mrs Taylor looked ready to swoon. 'They played cards after their meal for small stakes, and Mr Taylor came out the winner. From my observations I would say that he is possibly a regular but controlled gambler, and I do not think you have anything to worry about on that score.'

'My life is ruined,' said Mrs Taylor, staring past me and no doubt visualising all sorts of horrors.

I sighed; I had not thought she would take it so badly. 'Mrs Taylor, your life is not over.' I laid a hand on hers. 'Far from it. You said yourself that in other respects your husband is exemplary. All this means is that his taste in amusements differs from yours, and that rather than upset you by insisting you attend events you do not enjoy, he has decided that pursuing his entertainments in secret is the only option.'

'It's so low!' she said, and she was close to tears.

'That is your opinion,' I said firmly. 'Plenty of people enjoy the music hall, regardless of what you think, and perhaps they would consider your liking for the theatre equally strange.'

'I should have known when he told me he was going to see *Coriolanus*,' she said, in a low, bitter tone.

Under the table, I dug my fingernails into my palm to keep from laughing. 'I agree, Mrs Taylor, that he should not have deceived you, but you left him little choice other than to be bored and miserable.'

Her eyes met mine. 'I don't want him to be bored and miserable. I just want him to enjoy the same things as I do.'

'Perhaps that will come with time, and also with trying things together that are new to one or both of you. A Gilbert and Sullivan opera, perhaps?'

'Perhaps,' she echoed, and looked brighter. 'But what do I do about – you know?'

I sipped my coffee. 'What I would suggest,' I said, 'is for you to mention that a friend saw him at the music hall the other day. Don't accuse him; just make the observation. Then say that you don't mind, but you would like to go out with him sometimes too, and suggest a light play or a concert he might enjoy.'

'He doesn't mind paintings,' said Mrs Taylor thoughtfully. 'We could go to the National Gallery on Saturday, then out to dinner.' She sighed. 'I have been terribly selfish, haven't I? Especially when he works so hard.'

'Marriage is a compromise,' I said, smiling, as Mrs Taylor called the waiter back and said that actually, she would have a cake after all. *I'm so glad that, comparatively speaking, I am independent,* I thought. I ordered another coffee to be companionable, and turned to the page of my notebook which set out my fee.

CHAPTER 2

Once Mrs Taylor's worries were eased she proved surprisingly loquacious, even while eating cake, and it was a good half hour more before I was able to bring our meeting gently to a close. I strove not to mind, for she had heaped praise upon me, paid my fee in cash without a single quibble, and stated that she would recommend me to any of her friends who found themselves in a predicament which might require a detective. A good morning's work, indeed, but it did not alter the fact that I would have to hurry. As soon as I left the hotel, I set off at a fast walk towards the nearest branch of my bank.

My usual custom following the successful resolution of a case was to visit the bank and pay in my fee, minus anything under a pound. This ensured that if I were attacked by a robber, they would come away with little. It had never happened, but I felt it best to take precautions. I kept a stock of money at home for emergencies and unexpected outgoings, of course, but I much preferred the idea of travelling light as I went about my daily business. In case someone did attack me, I invariably secured my hat with a long, sharp pin which would make any miscreant think twice – and I was prepared to use the self-defence skills which I had persuaded Sherlock to teach me.

My other habit on completing a case was to visit Marylebone post office to see if there were any letters for me. When I had first resolved to take the plunge and set up on my own behalf, I tested the waters by taking out a small, inexpensive advertisement in an evening newspaper: *Female detective. Discretion assured in all cases. Fees moderate. References available on request. Correspondence to Mrs Hudson, care of Marylebone Post Office, London.*

Dr Watson had been utterly horrified when he spotted the advertisement and realised what I was up to. He had gone as far as to bang on the door of my sitting room, burst in the moment I replied, and thrust the newspaper under my nose, jabbing at the offending words with his forefinger. 'Nell, I must protest. You cannot advertise yourself in a newspaper like a purveyor of patent medicine or a fortune teller! What were you thinking?'

I counted to ten before I answered, since I could already feel my gorge rising at his tone. 'John, no one will seek out my services if they don't know I exist. While Mr Poskitt and Inspectors Lestrade and Gregson all said that they intended to put business my way, the fact remains that so far, to misquote Mr Micawber, nothing has turned up.' I paused for breath, and spoke more gently. 'I believe there is a place for a female detective in London, and I intend to be that detective.'

Dr Watson regarded me, still breathing hard. 'What does Holmes think? Does he know about this?'

'He knows,' I said. 'In fact, he helped me write the advertisement, and he is interested in the outcome.'

'I am surprised at you both,' snapped Dr Watson, and left, shutting the door none too gently behind him.

I smiled as I hurried past a postbox, remembering my first trip to the post office following the placing of the advertisement. I had left it three days, on the grounds that someone might have written by then. If they had, a prompt reply would be appropriate. On the other hand, if I had received no letters, then three days was no time at all, when you thought about it. That, at any rate, was what I told myself. Waiting those three days was agony, and there had been several occasions when I had had to set my jaw and march myself past the post office in the course of running another errand.

I had chosen to make my expedition at four o'clock, when I believed the post office would be comparatively quiet. I was correct in my assumption, as it was almost deserted, but this did not make things any easier. I still had to approach the counter and address the stern-faced clerk, who was already eyeing me as if he knew I would be a nuisance.

'My name is Mrs Hudson,' I said, leaning forward and speaking quietly, though no one was near.

'What?' he barked. 'Can't hear you, madam.'

I tried again, a little louder. 'My name is Mrs Hudson, and I wondered if there were any letters for me, care of the post office.'

He looked at me as if I must be under a delusion, then walked to a row of pigeonholes behind the counter, each marked with a letter of the alphabet. He reached into *H* and brought out a small bundle of perhaps five or six letters. My heart leapt before I remembered it was quite possible that none of them were for me.

The clerk peered at the bundle he was holding, walked through the letters with his first two fingers, then pulled one out and approached me. *Someone has answered my advertisement!* I beamed at him, which had no effect whatsoever.

The clerk reached the counter, put down the bundle of letters and pushed them towards me. 'Your letters, madam.'

'Good heavens,' I murmured, looking at the array of envelopes. Two white, two blue, one lavender. What lay within? I wanted to rip them open and devour them then and there. Instead I took a deep breath, murmured 'Thank you very much,' and in a fit of optimism, bought ten postage stamps.

And so my career as a female detective truly began. Sherlock was pleased and also astounded when I burst into the consulting room waving my letters (of course I had first checked with Martha that he was not busy with a client). 'This is quite something, Nell,' he said, as I plumped myself down and ripped open the first envelope.

Even Dr Watson managed a grudging 'Well done' when I told him at dinner that I had had five replies to my advertisement and intended to take three of the cases, although he qualified his congratulations with the pronouncement that I must be careful, not accept any case that might put me in danger, and make sure I was paid

11

promptly in cash. I decided to take this as a sign that he was concerned for my welfare, rather than that he thought I was completely incompetent. Naturally, the day on which I solved my first case and received my first fee was sweetest of all. I celebrated by buying myself a silver letter opener, in anticipation of the business to come.

I reached the imposing stone building that was the nearest branch of the London and Westminster Bank, and the doorman tipped his hat to me. I entered, produced my bank book, and made my deposit with the minimum of fuss and ceremony, though the bank clerk seemed inclined to chat, and on a normal day I would have indulged him. My business concluded, I smiled at the increased total in my bank book, emerged into the crisp autumnal air, and hurried to Debenham and Freebody, which was only a few more minutes' walk away.

My position at the department store had undergone a change since I first worked there as a 'lady detective'. In those days I had had to negotiate hard with Mr Turner, the sceptical manager of the store, to receive a wage above that of a normal shop assistant. However, I had soon earned him back my salary and more through apprehending pilferers and preventing thefts.

When I had forsaken my position to take on a special assignment, the shop assistants, led by my friend Evie, had performed the role turn and turn about in my absence and achieved considerable success, so that on my return I assumed there would be no work left for me.

However, in Mr Turner's case my absence had made his heart grow fonder, and he proposed that I return for a few hours a week, at a very respectable fee, as a sort of mentor for his assistants. As Evie had already secured a pay increase for every assistant who took on detection duties, I was only too happy to accept.

'Morning, Mrs H,' said Alf, raising his peaked cap and opening the door. He had seen me in so many different outfits that my frequent changes in appearance did not faze him one bit.

'Good morning, Alf,' I said. 'How are things?'

He considered. 'Plenty of people through the door,' he said, at last. 'Although Evie's been rather exercised this week. I daresay she'll tell you.'

I laughed. 'I'm sure she will.'

Once inside the store I checked my watch and was pleased to find that I was two minutes early for my meeting with Evie. My pace slowed as I strolled through the various departments, smiling at the assistants standing at their counters ready to serve, noting who was masquerading in plain clothes as a customer today, and of course, admiring the merchandise. I rarely admitted it to myself, but the other reason why I banked my fees as soon as possible was so that I wasn't tempted to spend my hard-earned money on silk stockings and accessories. I had had a terrible weakness for gloves ever since returning to Baker Street, as it had taken several months of loving care until my hands were fit to be seen in polite company.

I tore myself away from a beautiful pair of cream kid gloves with navy-blue embroidery at the wrists, and made for the door at the back of the store which led to Mr Turner's office. *Business before pleasure*, I thought –

though if I got the chance in the course of my work today, I might well enquire the price of those gloves.

CHAPTER 3

I was rather surprised when I entered Mr Turner's office and found him alone, sitting behind his huge desk. As a rule, Evie was punctual to a fault, and Mr Turner took the opportunity to head out of his office for a break of sometimes inordinate length.

'Good morning, Mr Turner,' I said, trying not to look disappointed to see him. 'How are you?'

'Tolerable,' he growled, 'all things considered. If you want Evie, she was here two minutes ago and then she dashed out. Something about an upset stomach.' He scowled. 'I daresay she's been eating too many sweets again. Ever since we started stocking confectionery she's been unable to resist.'

I raised an eyebrow. Tall, elegant Evie was, in my opinion, far too conscious of the fit of her clothes to indulge in wanton snacking. 'Will she be long?' I asked.

'Shouldn't think so,' said Mr Turner. 'Put it this way, I hope not.'

A timid knock sounded at the door. 'Speak of the devil,' he said, in a voice intended to reach whoever was on the other side. 'Come on in, then.'

Evie entered, and while she wore a professional, calm expression, and her cheeks were as rosy as ever, I had the distinct impression that was due to rouge rather than natural good health.

Mr Turner rose from his chair, decreasing slightly in height as he did so. 'I'll leave you ladies to it,' he said. 'Mrs Turner has given me an errand to do, so I may be some time.'

I fought the urge to raise my eyebrows again. In all the time I had known him, Mr Turner had never mentioned that he was married. I had assumed that he lived for his job – perhaps he did – and this sudden admission of a life outside his department store disconcerted me.

I moved around the desk and perched on his high chair. 'Do take a seat, Evie,' I said, smiling. 'You look like a naughty girl pulled up in front of the headmistress.'

Evie managed a small smile and lowered herself carefully onto the chair opposite me.

'Are you sure you're all right?' I asked. 'You're rather – I won't say green, but—'

'Please don't,' said Evie, pulling a handkerchief from her sleeve and putting it to her mouth. 'I'll be all right in a moment,' she added, her eyes squeezed tight shut.

I thought of suggesting that she go home for the rest of the day, but kept quiet, since I knew perfectly well that would mean a corresponding deduction from Evie's pay at the end of the week. She and her husband had managed to rent a tiny flat for themselves, by dint of living frugally and a little help from her mother, and money was tight. I took my diary from my bag and pretended to be absorbed in it until Evie was ready to face me.

'Too many sweets,' she said, grinning and looking about as jolly as a corpse.

'Are you sure?' I scrutinised her. 'As far as I remember, you've never had a sweet tooth.'

'Oh, I have,' she said, and produced a small bag from her petticoat pocket. 'I've just kept it under control until now.' She shook the bag, which rattled. 'Would you like one?'

My stomach made a small but distinct noise. 'Yes please, if you don't mind,' I said. Evie held out the bag and I peered in. Boiled sweets, of many colours. I selected a red one, on the grounds that it was least likely to be an unpleasant surprise, and popped it into my mouth. It turned out to be strawberry flavoured. 'Very nice.' I sucked the sweet and eyed her, then leaned across the desk. 'Evie,' I said in a low voice, 'is there anything you'd like to tell me?'

Evie's eyes were fixed on me as if I might leap at her. 'About the shop?' she quavered.

I rolled my eyes. 'No, Evie, about you.'

'Please don't tell Mr Turner,' she muttered, looking down at her lap. 'I've been sick every morning this week. I can't face breakfast. Anyway, I'm only a bit late, so it might not even be that.'

'I know,' I soothed, 'but it's possible.'

'It's not that I don't want a baby,' she said, all at once. 'I just didn't expect one yet. When Mr Turner finds out, he'll sack me. He'll have to. The boiled sweets help a bit, but not enough.'

'Does your husband know?' I asked.

Evie nodded. 'He saw the face on me, and I had to tell him. He's pleased as punch.' Her hands twisted in her lap. 'But I don't know how we'll manage. I'm hoping Mum will help, and then maybe I could come back, but I haven't said anything to her yet in case it doesn't take…'

I came round the desk and crouched beside Evie. 'Try not to worry,' I said, laying my hand on hers. 'I'm sure everything will be all right.'

She swallowed. 'I hope so.' She put away the bag of boiled sweets. 'Anyway, we aren't here to talk about – that. I'm afraid we've had a few incidents. That's why Mr Turner looks so sour.'

Since Evie seemed determined to be businesslike, I resumed my seat behind the desk. 'What sort of incidents?'

'The only sort we mind,' said Evie. 'Thefts. Two of the girls have reported missing stock in their departments. Several pairs of stockings and two bottles of perfume.' She grimaced. 'I'm in such a state that I can barely see what's going on under my nose. Mr Turner will fire me for sure.'

'You can't be everywhere at once, Evie,' I said. 'When did they report the missing stock?'

'The stockings went on Monday and the perfume on Tuesday,' said Evie. 'Whoever did it, they're crafty. Most shops don't count everything in until the end of the week, but Mr Turner's so particular…'

'Have any of the girls noticed anyone behaving strangely?' I asked. 'Hanging around, loitering…'

'Gladys said she'd had a woman asking a lot of questions at the glove counter,' said Evie. 'But you know how shortsighted Gladys is. She thought it might be you in one of your disguises.' That made her smile for a moment.

'So a woman of fairly average height and build, then.' I frowned. 'That doesn't give us much to go on. Did she say anything else?'

Evie looked pained. 'She might have, but I had to dash off to the lavatories.'

I wondered how long it would be before Evie's condition was common knowledge. 'Evie, I'll organise a pot of tea and some plain biscuits; why don't you sit here while I talk to Gladys? That will do you good.'

Evie nodded, too washed out to argue, and I made myself busy in the tiny staff kitchen before sallying forth.

'I thought it was you,' said Gladys as I approached. 'Of course, it helps that it's your day. I could have sworn I saw you on Tuesday.' Her gaze followed mine to the cream kid gloves. 'Would you like to try them on?'

'I would,' I said, 'but I have something to ask you first. When you thought you saw me on Tuesday, how did I look?'

Gladys's eyebrows drew together. 'Now you're asking. I see that many people…' She chewed her bottom lip and squinted into the distance. 'She was young, and she had bright gold hair, very striking it was, rather like one of your dos.' She eyed my severe dark-brown bun. 'One of the fancy ones, I mean. She was wearing a black jacket, and a little black hat turned just so, and she was interested in all the gloves. She must have tried on five pairs, but she said they were too large for her.'

'So she had small hands,' I said. 'Was she petite?'

'She was,' said Gladys, eyeing me critically. 'Not as slim as you. What they call a pocket Venus, I'd say.'

'And she was smartly dressed. Was that smart-for-a-servant-or-shop-girl smart, or young-lady smart?'

'Oh, she wasn't rich,' said Gladys at once. 'But she made the best of what she had.'

'Was she pretty?'

Gladys thought. 'She was quite pretty, and she acted like she was pretty.'

'I see,' I said, forming a mental picture.

'Am I in trouble?' asked Gladys.

'No, not at all,' I said. 'Only Evie told me some stock had gone missing – not gloves – and that someone was behaving oddly at your counter.'

The corner of Gladys's mouth turned up. 'Has she said anything to you?' she asked, with a mischievous glint in her eye.

I put my nose in the air. 'I have absolutely no idea what you mean, Gladys,' I said, and Gladys winked as a customer approached.

***

I sauntered around the store, looking at this and that and keeping my eyes open for a smart golden-haired woman, but none appeared. I enquired at the counters that were quiet, but none of the other assistants remembered her. I asked them to be vigilant and report any sightings to Evie, and noted their guarded expressions when I said her name. *It's a good thing they're all friends, or Mr Turner would know at once.*

I returned to Mr Turner's office to find Evie sipping tea

with a half-nibbled biscuit in her other hand and appearing noticeably brighter. 'I have a description,' I said, 'and I've warned everyone to watch out for the golden-haired thief.'

Evie giggled. 'That sounds like a penny dreadful. You know: the mysterious, attractive young robber who gets away with it every time.'

'Not if I have my way,' I said. 'I'm happy to be an extra pair of eyes on the shop floor for the next couple of hours, if you want.'

Evie's eyes widened. 'Oh, would you, Nell? I can manage when I'm stood at the counter, but when I'm on the lookout, moving my head turns my stomach.'

'Of course.'

The door opened and Mr Turner stuck his head round it. 'Having a nice chat, are we, ladies?'

'We have a possible pilferer,' I said. 'I've made all the other assistants aware and I shall conduct a personal patrol this afternoon.'

'Glad to hear it,' said Mr Turner. He gave Evie a significant look, and she jumped to her feet and scurried out.

I got up from Mr Turner's chair and he resumed his place. I noted that he was carrying a small flat parcel which he put in his top drawer. 'I'll get to work, then,' I said.

'Before you do, Mrs Hudson…' He beckoned me closer. 'Has Evie told you she's…'

I stared at him. 'You mean you know?'

'Course I do,' said Mr Turner. 'I wasn't born yesterday.'

'She admitted it,' I said. Then I smiled. 'The poor

thing's terrified you'll find out and sack her.'

Mr Turner moved his chair closer to me. 'As long as she can get herself into the shop and leave more or less on time, I'll keep her on. I can't be seen to play favourites, but she's a good worker.' He glared at me. 'You're not to breathe a word, understand? Now go and do your job.'

I grinned at him and left, and spent the next two hours searching for a golden-haired, light-fingered woman with a particular interest in gloves. But she remained elusive, and it was only once I had resumed my normal appearance in the staff lavatory and caught a cab that I realised I had forgotten to ask about the cream kid gloves.

CHAPTER 4

I spent the first part of my journey to my mother's house wondering whether I could perhaps make Evie a small present of money. I doubted she would take it, though; while she would accept help from her mother, Evie was too proud to receive charity from a friend. I had once practically had to force a piece of cloth on her, so money was probably out of the question. Perhaps an anonymous donation? I could put money in an envelope and deliver it myself, so that it wouldn't be lost in the post...

Then it dawned on me that I had been so taken up with Evie's financial difficulty that I had completely forgotten to give her my congratulations. For a moment I felt guilty, then reconsidered. Evie had been so very clear that her pregnancy was a predicament that the excitement of bringing forth a new life seemed to have completely passed her by...

I winced as a long-buried memory forced itself to the front of my mind: that brief time when I, too, had been expecting a baby. I had been full of plans, full of wishes – and it had come to nothing.

It felt like a lifetime ago. That baby had been with my

then husband, Jack, and I had never had the chance to tell him about it. I was planning to on the day that he vanished, never to be seen in England again, and the shock of his disappearance had made me lose the baby. I had been so happy that day, buying treats for dinner, never realising how tenuous, how fragile human life could be, until it was all dashed away. I wrapped my arms around myself and stared out of the window at the London traffic. Anything was better than closing my eyes and reliving it.

I thought of it less and less these days; I had so many other things to think about. My career as a detective; running the house; Sherlock. But occasionally the memory bubbled up to haunt me, though I could usually push it back down. *And what if you hadn't lost the baby*, I asked myself. *You would have had to raise a child by yourself, without a husband, in very difficult circumstances. Or perhaps the child would have been taken from you. Would that have been worse, or better?* At least I had not had to face that trial. Still, sometimes I thought of who that child might have been, and my heart ached. Although if he or she had taken after Jack, it would have been a different trial together.

We were on the outskirts of Clerkenwell, not far from my mother's house. Automatically, I glanced at my watch. I was perhaps a quarter of an hour later than usual, due to my delayed start at Debenham and Freebody. In my heart I was rather glad, since my flashback had left me in no mood for company. Perhaps I could plead a dinner engagement and leave early. I put my hands to my cheeks to cool them. At least I had not cried. I had become quite good at not crying, having spent time in situations where crying would only get you into more trouble.

The cab began to slow. 'Here we are, madam,' called the cabbie.

'Thank you,' I said, and took my time getting my purse out of my bag. What a change from my earlier journey, when I had been so ready to leap from the cab and begin my day. Then I rebuked myself for my attitude. It wasn't my mother's fault that I had been overcome by emotion, and if she had known she would have been more than understanding. It was more the thought of taking afternoon tea in my sister's company. *You must do your best, Nell*, I told myself. I climbed out of the cab, paid my fare, and knocked once, twice at my mother's trim front door, with its polished brass knocker.

Mama herself answered. 'I was beginning to think you weren't coming, Nell,' she said. 'You're after your usual time.'

'Sorry, Mama,' I said. 'I started a little late today, and so I am running slightly behind.'

Her eyes took in every detail of my appearance. 'Well, come in and sit down. All that rushing around will do you no good.'

'Is she here at last?' called a voice from the parlour, and I resisted the urge to roll my eyes. No need to ask if Sally was here, then.

'Couldn't she have come to the door?' I asked.

Mama's lips tightened a fraction. 'Apparently your sister is not quite herself today. Although that hasn't stopped her from putting away several sandwiches and two slices of cake,' she added, with a gleam in her eye. 'You'd better come in before the cupboard is bare.'

I followed her into the parlour. I spent much more time there as a weekly caller than I ever had when I was living at home, barred from it except on high days and holidays. It was a stiff, uncomfortable room, with high-backed chairs so stuffed with unforgiving horsehair that sitting down too hard caused a painful rebound. I would have preferred to sit in the kitchen and eat stew, but now that my siblings had grown up and left home, we had advanced to the parlour, finger sandwiches and sponge cake.

My sister Sally was partly responsible for this change. Once I had left to marry Jack she came out of my shadow, decided that she wanted to be known as Sally, not Susan, since it was more fashionable, and as she put it, married well. Her husband, who was perhaps fifteen years older than her, was a merchant of some kind, and she had two small children whom she talked about constantly, though they stayed home with their nanny rather than coming to tea. They were, of course, the most charming, pretty, and clever children that ever lived, but while I could forgive Sally her maternal pride, her opinion of me as a dismal old maid was exceptionally galling. It was hardly her fault, since as far as she knew I was housekeeper for two bachelor gentlemen, with no interest in changing that situation. But sometimes, just sometimes, I wished Sally were my younger sister Susan again, who worshipped me and did my chores in exchange for help with her sums.

'Good afternoon, Sally,' I said, taking a seat in the most comfortable of the remaining armchairs, which wasn't

26

saying much. 'Are you well?'

My sister sniffed. 'I barely slept,' she said. 'Poor dear Barney is suffering from colic, and Nanny was up with him in the night, walking. She has such a heavy tread.'

'Oh dear,' I said. 'Have you tried medicine to soothe it? Or doesn't that work?'

Sally opened her eyes very wide. 'I couldn't possibly give some drug to my child,' she said, looking at me as if I were a monster. 'Who knows what might be in it? You hear such terrible stories.' She sighed. 'So I lay awake, listening to Nanny's footsteps. It's so worrying when a child is unwell. Of course, you wouldn't understand.'

'Of course,' I said. 'Is Amelia well?'

'Oh yes,' said Sally, 'she is bursting with health. Although I worry that she will outgrow her strength. She is so tall for her age...' She proceeded to discourse on her children while I poured cups of tea and helped myself to a couple of ham sandwiches, as one plain biscuit was not much of a lunch, really.

Sally broke off and gazed at me sadly as I bit into my sandwich. 'If you aren't interested—'

'Oh no, I'm very interested,' I said, as soon as I was able to speak without being rude. 'Only I haven't eaten much since breakfast.'

Sally gave me a severe look. 'You work yourself to skin and bone, Nell, and for what? Two elderly gentlemen who no doubt are making you do far more than is appropriate.' Her eyes narrowed. 'How many servants are there, besides you?'

'Just two,' I said, 'but they are both hard workers, and

most diligent.'

'Have you ever thought of going back to teaching? I mean, it must be hard work, but surely it would be more rewarding than doing menial tasks.'

I thought of the visits to the music hall I had made the previous week in the course of my job, and smiled. 'It is not such hard work as you think, Sally. After all, you run the house, and you have children to care for.'

'Oh, but that's different,' said Sally. 'That is part of my duty as a wife and mother.' She regarded me speculatively. 'It was a terrible shame about Jack, but would you ever consider marrying again? You're still in your twenties, just.'

'I'm happy as I am,' I said, hoping that would be the end of it.

'What about children?' pressed Sally.

'Who would like more tea?' asked Mama, getting up and lifting the large brown earthenware teapot. 'Sally?'

'Oh no, thank you,' said Sally. I could feel her gaze though I was staring at my plate, eating my second sandwich and trying to contain myself. 'Nell, surely you—'

I dropped the sandwich onto my plate and faced her. 'I lost a baby, Sally, while I was married to Jack. Can we please talk about something else.'

Sally drew back as if I'd slapped her. 'You never told me that.'

'It didn't come up in conversation,' I replied. 'But now you know.' I turned to my mother. 'Have you read any interesting books lately?'

My mother, bless her, launched into a description of her

latest borrow from the circulating library. She was an enthusiastic and voracious reader, but not a patient one, and had a tendency to read the volumes of a novel out of order depending on which was available first. It didn't seem to bother her in the slightest, but it made some of her descriptions distinctly peculiar.

We stuck to pleasantries for the next quarter of an hour, then Sally took her leave pleading a dinner engagement. I wasn't sure whether I believed her or not.

'Don't think too badly of her,' said Mama, once she had gone. 'She doesn't mean to be unkind.'

'I know,' I said, 'but it is difficult to bear.'

'You're usually able to rise above it.' She scrutinised me. 'Have you had a difficult day? Is all well with Mr Holmes?' Mama was much better informed of my true situation, though there were still things I kept from her.

'Oh yes, he's keeping busy.'

She smiled. 'That wasn't what I asked, Nell.'

'Yes, we are still getting along together,' I said, smiling back. 'And no, I still haven't accepted his proposal. One day, but not yet.'

Mama leaned across and put her hand on mine. 'At the risk of sounding like Sally, make sure you put your own happiness first. I won't say more than that.'

I pondered her words as I jolted through the London streets towards home. At least my mother had been more circumspect than Sally. But what was my own happiness, exactly? Wasn't I happy already? What more did I need? And their words niggled, no matter how hard I tried to dismiss them.

CHAPTER 5

I let myself into the house with my latchkey and heard Billy's footsteps on the kitchen stairs. He stood to a sort of attention when he saw me. 'Good afternoon, ma'am,' he said, trying not to look disappointed. Billy was always crestfallen when I chose to open the door myself rather than knock and wait for admission. He enjoyed the drama of getting to the door, preparing himself, then opening the door just enough to see who was beyond. I had seen him do it so many times.

'Good afternoon, Billy,' I replied, removing my hat and putting the hatpin in my bag for safekeeping. 'Is Mr Holmes in?'

'He is, ma'am, but he asked, if you wouldn't mind, that he is not disturbed until fifteen minutes before dinner time.' Billy leaned forward as if to impart a secret. 'Writing,' he said, in a tone of deep reverence.

'I see,' I said, laughing. 'In that case, I shall leave him to it. Between Mr Holmes and Dr Watson, we shall soon be running a literary salon.'

'Ooh,' said Billy, clearly impressed.

I took off my coat and gloves, then followed Billy down

to the kitchen to request a pot of tea. Sally's preference was for weak China tea, and I felt a strong Indian brew would do much to restore my humour.

I found Martha cutting vegetables for dinner. 'Good afternoon, ma'am. Dinner will be ready for seven. Roast chicken, roast potatoes, carrots, and parsnips.'

I frowned. 'Didn't I say boiled potatoes?'

Martha met my gaze with a blank expression. 'I believe you did, ma'am, but you know how Dr Watson feels about boiled potatoes.'

'And you know how I feel about roast potatoes at almost every meal,' I countered. 'As I plan the menu each week, I would appreciate it if you inform me of any changes.' Martha wore a hurt expression, and I knew exactly why. 'Could you do a dish of both? I know it is more trouble, but we are eating roast potatoes three or four times a week at the moment.' Martha's expression didn't change. 'I'll have one roast potato if you stop looking so wounded.'

That made Martha smile. 'Very well, ma'am,' she said, with a long-suffering air.

Having put in my order for a pot of tea, I told Martha I would be in my sitting room and proceeded upstairs. On the first floor I paused, and listened. I could hear faint mutterings from the consulting room. By my estimate, Dr Watson would not be home for another half hour at least. I tiptoed to the door and put my ear against it.

'Where are my notes on hobnail patterns? I know I put them somewhere relevant… Perhaps the index?' A book was pulled from the shelf. 'Aha!' Pages rustled and I

31

tiptoed away, careful to avoid the creaky floorboards. Sherlock was clearly enjoying himself.

I went to our bedroom and pulled a house dress from the wardrobe. It was only an hour until I would need to dress for dinner, but I wished to be comfortable, and also to wear something which allowed freedom of movement. That task accomplished, I climbed the stairs to the second floor and my sitting room.

There, I took a small key from a secret drawer in my desk and unlocked the large cupboard which stood in the corner. From it, I took out a metal water can which, when full, could fill a sink. It was a relic from the days before I had installed a reliable hot-water system in the house, when we had carried cans of water upstairs for washing and shaving. It had been gathering dust in the attic until I found a new use for it. I took it to the bathroom, half-filled it with cold water from the tap, returned to my room, and locked the door. 'Now then,' I said to the can, grasped the handle with my right hand, and lifted. 'One . . . two . . . three…' Once I had managed fifteen lifts with each hand, I put the can in front of me and lifted with both hands, aiming to touch my chin with the handle. As I lifted, images from the day floated back to me: Mrs Taylor's excitement when she fixed on a course of action, Evie's frightened, wary expression, Sally's tight, smug little smile…

Water slopped over the rim of the can and I huffed. If I got a cloth to mop it up, it would break my rhythm. Sally had already made me lose concentration. I took a deep breath and started again. 'One . . . two . . . three…'

I was ready for dinner at five to seven, and entered the dining room to find Dr Watson already seated. 'Nell,' he said, rising.

I waved him back down. 'How was work, John?'

'Much as usual,' he replied. 'A couple of variations on the theme, but nothing that would make anyone sit up and take notice. Is it a special occasion?'

I smoothed my navy silk dress. 'Not that I know of. I felt like wearing something different.'

'Well, you look very elegant,' said Dr Watson gallantly.

'Perhaps I should tell Martha that it is in honour of her roast chicken.'

'Ha ha! Very good.' Dr Watson paused. 'Is Holmes dressing up, too? He is normally here by now.'

'I doubt it. When I came down he was only just changing. Work, you know.' I said it lightly, but I had been disappointed when a quarter to seven came and went and the consulting-room door remained closed. I had thought of knocking, but experience had taught me that disturbing Sherlock when he was in the throes of something was never a good idea.

He had dashed in as I was leaving, kissed me, said, 'You look lovely,' then flung open the drawers of the tallboy in a quest for a clean shirt.

Martha appeared in the doorway and eyed Sherlock's empty chair. 'Shall I serve, ma'am, or shall I wait?'

'If you could give him two more minutes,' I said. 'I'm sure the chicken won't mind waiting.'

Martha rolled her eyes at the grandfather clock in the

corner, then bobbed and withdrew.

'So, um, what have you been up to today, Nell?' asked Dr Watson. 'May I help you to a glass of water?'

'Yes, please,' I said. 'I concluded a case this morning, and the client was satisfied. I banked my fee and did some surveillance work at the department store, then visited my mother and sister for afternoon tea.'

'Excellent, excellent,' said Dr Watson, setting down the carafe. 'Ah! Here he is.'

Sherlock opened the door a crack, peeped in, then whipped round it and took his seat, shaking out his napkin. 'Terribly sorry,' he said. 'I was working out a formula for calculating a man's weight from the depth of the imprint his boots leave in various compositions of soil.'

'Of course you were,' I said.

Martha came in with a carafe of wine, which she placed on the table. 'Leek and potato soup to start,' she announced, and left the room.

'Yes,' said Sherlock. 'There really is a remarkable difference between clay, sandy and chalky soils. The thought came to me early this afternoon, so I spent time visiting different parts of London and testing my theory. Of course, the dampness of the ground will have an effect, so I shall have to factor that in.'

'Tell us about your new case,' said Dr Watson, as Martha and Billy brought in the soup tureen and the bowls.

'Oh, that.' Sherlock turned to address him and leaned an elbow on the back of his chair. 'A missing pedigree dog, of all things. My client was convinced a jealous rival must have stolen his new dog, which he plans to show, and held up a piece of rope as Exhibit A. Well, the rope was frayed in a manner that suggested it had been chewed through, not cut. Adding the information that the dog had been kept on strict rations, as the owner judged him overweight, it was not difficult to form the hypothesis that the sagacious dog had escaped and quite possibly returned to his breeder. The client wired me an hour ago to say that I was correct and he would bring a case against the breeder, from which I deduce that he is not the most humane of men.'

'Not worth writing up then, Holmes?' asked Dr Watson, with rather a desperate expression.

Sherlock laughed. 'Not unless you wish me to specialise in recovering lapdogs and getting cats out of trees.' He picked up his spoon. 'I shall ask you about your days shortly, but I must admit I am fearfully hungry.'

My stomach growled in agreement and I began my soup, wondering if Martha had managed to hide a potato in the pudding too. Dr Watson sighed, applied pepper liberally to his bowl, and fell to.

Martha was removing the bowls when the doorbell rang. She paused, a bowl in either hand. 'Shall I go?'

'Let Billy answer it,' I said, and soon we heard running feet, a sort of skid, emphatic throat-clearing, and finally the scrape of the bolt and the click as the door was unlocked.

'Good evening, sir,' said Billy, sounding rather surprised. 'Everyone is at dinner.'

'Oh,' said Inspector Lestrade's voice. 'I can wait a few minutes, but if you wouldn't mind asking.'

The door closed. 'Of course, sir,' said Billy, and burst into the dining room. 'Inspector Lestrade's here, and he looks as if he's got something to tell you.'

Martha rolled her eyes.

'In that case, Billy,' I said, 'please show him in and place an extra chair. Martha, serve the chicken. If we are required urgently, we shall need sustenance; if not, I daresay the inspector will not mind a dinner invitation.'

'Very good, ma'am,' said Martha and bustled off, clearly relieved.

Billy dashed off and returned with the inspector, who was settled at the table with a glass of wine just as Martha came in bearing a glistening chicken.

Sherlock leaned back in his chair. 'So, Inspector, to what do we owe the pleasure?'

The inspector gave Sherlock what I characterised as one of his looks from beneath his eyebrows. 'A case, of course.'

CHAPTER 6

'Well, come on then, Lestrade,' urged Sherlock, as Billy came in with a dish of roast potatoes.

'I would rather wait,' the inspector responded, eyeing the servants.

'Shall I carve?' asked Martha.

'Yes please,' I said. Martha could portion a bird quickly and efficiently, possessing an almost surgical skill where poultry was concerned, whereas if Dr Watson did it, we would receive a lecture on anatomy in the process.

Martha set to, detaching the wings and the drumsticks then slicing the breast thickly. 'I'll let you decide what you're having while I fetch the vegetables,' she said, and fled. I was pleased to note that Billy had brought in a dish of boiled potatoes and set them towards my end of the table while Martha was operating.

'So,' said Sherlock, filling our glasses. 'What has brought you to Baker Street at this hour of the day, Lestrade? I assume it isn't normal police business.'

'Perhaps we should fill our plates first,' said the inspector, who was eyeing the chicken with barely suppressed longing.

'What a good idea,' I said, and began to serve the chicken while the other dishes circulated the table. I served myself last and thereby secured a medium-sized helping, rather than the extra spoonful that Martha invariably added after I had said I had enough. 'Inspector, the floor is yours,' I said, taking my seat.

The inspector set down his knife and fork, looking disappointed. 'As you surmise, Holmes, this is a delicate matter, and requires careful handling. I have received intelligence of a series of frauds perpetrated predominantly in Mayfair and Belgravia.'

'That's not your usual patch,' I observed.

The inspector actually blushed. 'I was co-opted.' He cut a piece of chicken breast and popped it into his mouth. 'Because of my connections.'

Sherlock raised an eyebrow. 'Would that be me?'

'You are one of those connections, yes,' said the inspector. 'And while the person who approached me is unaware of the fact, so is Mrs Hudson.'

Sherlock smiled. 'Tell me more.'

'Do you recall the collapse of the Latimer Brothers investment firm a few months ago?' said the inspector.

'Of course,' Sherlock and I said together.

'Then you will be aware that after the collapse, several people said they had been mis-sold shares with promises of high yield and speedy return which, once the facts came to light, could never have been fulfilled.' The inspector loaded his fork with roast potato. 'Something similar may be happening again, but on a smaller scale and with a range of companies. Two promising new financial businesses have folded in the last month without warning, and when the news broke, the board of directors was nowhere to be found.'

'What does this have to do with us?' I asked.

'A couple of my back-room men have been looking for patterns to see if they can spot the next crop of failures, with help from government statisticians when they can get it. Today they informed me that among the companies they are investigating, around a third have a name in common on the board of directors: a certain Humphrey Montagu.'

'Not a name I know,' said Sherlock, 'which in itself is interesting. What do you know of him, Lestrade?'

'Precious little. He lives in Mayfair, he is a member of several clubs, and presumably, therefore, is a wealthy man. He is also married, and Eliza Montagu is an interesting woman in her own right. Before her marriage she was Eliza Davenant, the musical-comedy actress.'

'Good heavens,' said Dr Watson. 'An actress.'

'Indeed,' said the inspector. 'And from what I understand, Mrs Montagu is active in London society.'

'So where do we come in?' I asked.

'I want you to shadow the Montagus,' said the inspector, spearing another piece of chicken. 'Follow them, discover their habits, which clubs they belong to, what they do in the evenings. If possible, befriend them – not as yourselves, of course. And if you can, get them to spin you a yarn about business.' He put the piece of chicken in his mouth and chewed aggressively.

I glanced at Sherlock. His previous languor had disappeared completely. He was leaning forward, bright-eyed, drinking in the inspector's words.

'For how long, exactly?' I asked.

The inspector waved his fork. 'As long as it takes. I'm sure it won't take you too long to find something which will enable me to bring them in and search their residence from top to bottom.' His eyes gleamed.

'What are you proposing to pay?' I asked. 'You are asking that we both devote our time to pursuing your targets.'

The inspector stared at me. 'We don't usually discuss that.'

'In that case, Inspector, I am afraid I must decline,' I said. 'I have work scheduled and I can't drop my clients to fulfil your request, especially when you can't even tell me how much you propose to pay me for it.'

The inspector opened his mouth, closed it, then opened it again. 'We agreed I would give you work to do!'

'We did, Inspector.' I prepared a forkful of chicken and boiled potato. 'But in the months I spent waiting for you to do that, I found work of my own, and I have more than enough. In fact, I daresay that when I call at the post office tomorrow I shall find more cases for my attention.'

'This is real police work,' said the inspector. 'Not stocking thieves and lost rings, or whatever it is you do.'

I set down my knife and fork with a clatter. I ought to count to ten, at least, but I was in no mood to curb my temper. 'Inspector, you have no idea what I do, and I'll thank you not to insult and belittle my work in my own house. I have worked hard to establish myself, and you ought to respect that.' The inspector studied his half-full plate. 'I was disinclined to accept your offer of work before, and now I am completely unprepared to consider it.' Feeling better for letting off steam, I picked up my cutlery and continued eating. Inspector Lestrade's pettishness was no reason to waste a perfectly good meal.

The inspector was silent for perhaps half a minute. Then he turned to Sherlock. 'Are you prepared to assist me in this case, Holmes?'

Sherlock glanced at me, his expression a curious mixture of eagerness and caution. He picked up his wine glass and sipped. 'There may be something I can do,' he said, eventually. 'I think we should discuss it once we have finished dinner. Perhaps in my consulting room, over a brandy.'

'An excellent idea,' said the inspector, giving me a triumphant look. I smiled back at him and cut into my roast potato. I felt I had earned it.

***

Will he ever go? I thought, as I lay in bed and listened to the laughter downstairs.

The rest of dinner had been a comparatively brief affair due to everyone's reluctance to prolong it, and I had excused myself from coffee, saying that I had work to do.

Martha brought me coffee in my sitting room as I looked through my accounts and calculated what remuneration I might expect in the coming month.

'Thank you, Martha,' I said, pushing away my account book and gratefully accepting the steaming cup with a shortbread biscuit tucked into the saucer.

'Are you all right, ma'am?' Martha asked. 'I hope you

don't mind me asking, but I heard raised voices. It isn't like you to go upstairs so early.'

I sighed. 'I'm quite well, Martha. The inspector expected me to drop my clients for some wild-goose chase, and I'm not even sure he intended to pay me for it.'

Martha's lips tightened. 'I hope you told him what to do with that suggestion.'

'Almost.' I smiled. 'I was rather forthright, and I don't think he was expecting it. In fact, I think I was supposed to be grateful.'

Martha snorted. 'You stick to your guns, ma'am.' She leaned forward confidentially. 'Is that what they're talking about downstairs?'

'I expect so,' I said.

'You tell me when you wish to go to bed, ma'am, and I shall ask them to move downstairs if the inspector hasn't gone by then.' Martha nodded firmly and whisked out.

I read for a while, and on the stroke of ten I went to the kitchen for hot milk. Soon afterwards, feet clattered downstairs. Three pairs, if I wasn't mistaken. *I might have known John would be in on it. This sort of caper is exactly the kind of thing he likes to write up.*

It was around half past ten when the inspector left, and another half hour until the men came upstairs. I frowned as I heard the dressing-room door open. A charitable person might have concluded that Sherlock did not want to disturb me in case I was asleep, but I was not feeling particularly charitable.

Eventually he came in and slipped into bed beside me without a word. I turned over to signal I was awake, but

42

that elicited no response.

'So you're doing it,' I said.

There was a pause before Sherlock replied. 'Yes, I am,' he said. 'As you know, I get much of my work through Lestrade. Though who knows whether the endeavour will be successful, or how long it will take, since you have refused to participate.'

'So I should desert my clients to please a man who has no respect for me,' I said. 'You may work for praise if you like; I prefer money. So does the bank.'

'He does respect you, Nell,' said Sherlock. 'And you didn't have to be rude to him.'

'I wasn't rude,' I said. 'I merely pointed out the facts of the situation. He was rude for insulting my work.'

'Watson thinks you were rude, too,' said Sherlock. 'He's surprised at you.'

'Because I didn't smile sweetly and jump at the inspector's offer, I suppose,' I said. 'Frankly, I have better things to do with my time. If you don't, that isn't my problem.' I paused. 'It must make a nice change from lost dogs. Goodnight, Sherlock.' And with that, I rolled over. Sherlock might be in Inspector Lestrade's pocket, but I had no such obligation. I was my own woman, free to do as I chose. And I smiled to myself as I settled down for a good night's sleep.

CHAPTER 7

I woke early; the light that found its way round the edges of the curtains was still a dull wintry grey, without a hint of warmth. But when I stretched my hand out, Sherlock was gone. I told myself not to read anything into it, shrugged on my dressing gown, and went downstairs.

'Everyone's early this morning,' said Martha, getting up and taking the kettle to the tap.

'I take it you've seen Mr Holmes, then,' I said, sitting opposite Billy at the kitchen table. He was busy polishing Sherlock's best black shoes.

'About an hour ago, ma'am,' said Martha. 'I was barely down myself.'

'How was he dressed?'

Martha set the kettle on the hob. 'Scruffy, and he hadn't shaved. He went out through the back door.' She faced me. 'He said that if anyone was interested, he was visiting Wiggins.'

'I see.' I listened to the gentle, insistent rubbing of Billy's cloth on the leather, and the ticking of the kettle as the water heated. I was fairly certain of the reason for Sherlock's expedition. He would hire Wiggins and possibly

44

some of his friends to watch the Montagus, then move in once he had intelligence he could act on. I had to admit that it was a sensible plan, showing considerably more foresight than Lestrade's order to shadow the pair indiscriminately. If the Montagus were as sharp as all that, one or both of us would have been spotted before we discovered anything useful. I presumed Billy's polishing of the shoes was in case they were required at short notice, and suspected that if I went into the dressing room I would find a variety of dress outfits pulled out for inspection.

'Here you are,' said Martha, handing me a large mug of tea. 'As it's early, I thought you might need a big one.'

'That I do,' I said. 'Thank you.'

'What are you doing today, ma'am, if you don't mind me asking?'

I sipped my scalding tea while deciding how to phrase my answer. 'I shall call in at the post office for my mail,' I said, 'then do fact-finding on my current cases.' Despite my indignant words to Inspector Lestrade the previous evening, I had nothing pressing. My two other cases were progressing nicely, requiring a small amount of research which I could fit around other commitments. But it was the principle of the thing.

Martha ruminated on my words for a moment. 'When would you like breakfast?'

I considered. I had not planned to get up so early, but Sherlock's industry had galvanised me. 'I had better get on, so just some toast and jam, please, as soon as you can; perhaps you could bring it to my room.' I paused. 'I am sure Dr Watson will require his usual spread at the usual hour.'

'I daresay,' said Martha, and opened the bread crock.

I took the tea to my sitting room, and was looking over my case notes when I heard loud rapping at the front door, followed by an indignant 'Do you mind?' from Martha. That was almost certainly the telegraph boy, whose knock set Martha's teeth on edge. *Probably an urgent summons for Sherlock.* His cases tended to involve telegrams, dashing about in hansom cabs, and lying in wait for people at the dead of night. It was all very dramatic. So I was surprised when I heard Billy's footsteps pelting upstairs, followed by a tap first at our bedroom door and then, after a further ascent, mine. 'Telegram, ma'am,' he called.

I took the yellow envelope, sat down, and picked up my silver letter opener. The wire was from Mr Poskitt, Mycroft Holmes's secretary.

Would appreciate a visit from you soonest to discuss delicate matter STOP At Somerset House today STOP Your assistance would be most welcome STOP Poskitt.

A smile spread over my face. Now I felt last night's refusal was entirely justified. I could not shadow some actress turned socialite day and night, for I had been called to an urgent meeting about what could well be government business. For good measure, I resolved to call at the post office on my way to Somerset House; there might be letters waiting for me to further prove my argument. I fell into a pleasant daydream of describing the day's events to a weary and dispirited Sherlock that evening, which was only disturbed by the arrival of my toast.

I set out forty-five minutes later, well breakfasted, smartly dressed, and for once, in my own person. The day had warmed up considerably since that chilly start, although it was getting to that stage of the year when a thicker jacket was required.

I was slightly disappointed to find just three letters waiting for me at the post office; normally I could count on six or seven, especially after a few days' gap between visits. *Who knows what lies within, though.* I put them in my bag, thanked the clerk, and went outside to summon a cab. While I was always curious about my post, the letters could wait until I had seen Mr Poskitt.

The roads were no more crowded than usual, and I arrived at Somerset House at a quarter to ten. 'I have an appointment with Mr Poskitt,' I told the clerk, and was directed to his new, larger office. Gone were the days when I had had to sneak into the building and meet him in one of the attics. I was sure none of the Somerset House clerks had any idea what I was doing there, but it was nice to feel legitimate.

I knocked on the door and Mr Poskitt's secretary, a deferential young man called Mr Harris, answered it. 'Good morning, Mrs Hudson,' he said. 'Mr Poskitt is speaking on the telephone, but he will meet with you as soon as he has finished, if you wouldn't mind waiting.' He opened the door wider and waved me to a seat in the corner, beside a low table with various periodicals.

A few minutes later, Mr Poskitt came out of the inner office. 'My dear Mrs Hudson,' he said, beaming. 'How nice to see you, and thank you for coming at such short notice. Do come in. Harris, could you arrange tea, please.'

I looked at the telephone curiously as I took a seat. I had seen drawings and photographs, but this was the first time I had seen one in the flesh, so to speak. It was an imposing device of wood and metal, with sinister wires poking out.

'I imagine you're wondering why I have summoned you,' said Mr Poskitt, taking a seat behind his desk.

I smiled. 'I was, rather.'

'As I said in my telegram, it is a delicate matter, and as such, you are exactly the person to undertake it.' Mr Poskitt looked nervous, and I wondered what I was in for.

'Oh no, it is nothing unpleasant,' he hastened to assure me. 'Nothing like last year. However, it needs careful handling.'

'May I ask what needs careful handling, Mr Poskitt?' I was used to his roundabout way of approaching the point, but I dearly wanted to know what he had in mind.

'We would like you to interview Emmett Stanley,' said Mr Poskitt. He seemed relieved to have got it out.

'Emmett Stanley?' I asked. 'But why me? Surely I am the last person you would ask.'

One of my first cases as Sherlock's then assistant had involved getting close to Emmett Stanley's wife. I had done so by befriending her over afternoon tea at a hotel: in disguise, of course. As a result, I had intercepted a letter with a secret message about a planned robbery of the Bank of England, and her husband had been caught red-handed. Subsequently, Stanley had been abducted from prison and tortured, so my reticence was justified.

'I believe I'm right in thinking that on both occasions when you met the Stanleys, you were in disguise.' Mr Poskitt looked at me expectantly.

'I was,' I said, 'but I still don't see—'

'His health is much improved,' said Mr Poskitt. 'His physician assures us that he is quite capable of conducting a conversation.'

'I'm extremely glad to hear that,' I said.

'But he stressed that it must be a gentle conversation, not a cross-examination. The police, for example, would be completely inappropriate. I telephoned Mrs Stanley and she is in agreement, provided her husband is not overtired or distressed in any way.'

'I take it that you wish me to obtain information—'

A tap at the door announced Mr Harris, bearing a tea tray with three cups and an impressive array of biscuits. 'Ah, thank you, Harris.' Given the number of cups, I assumed Mr Poskitt would invite him to join us, but he gave no sign, and Mr Harris withdrew.

'Are you expecting someone, Mr Poskitt?'

'In a manner of speaking,' he murmured. He got up and approached a door in the shadow of the bookcase that I had not noticed. He knocked gently, then called, 'Mr Holmes, tea has arrived.'

I heard a sort of grunt, and a couple of minutes later the door opened and Mycroft Holmes walked in. He had grown since our last meeting. While he had never been as thin as his younger brother, he was now positively portly, and his second chin had grown more prominent.

'Ah, Mrs Hudson. Jolly good.' He sat down in the chair nearest the tray, poured himself a cup of tea, and put two biscuits into the saucer. 'Have a biscuit, do. You look as if you need sustenance.'

I poured cups of tea for myself and Mr Poskitt, and to be polite, took a biscuit. Sherlock and I saw little of Mycroft these days. He had been badly shaken by his brief and unjust fall from grace the year before, and tended to divide his time between work, his club, and his rooms.

Mycroft made short work of his first biscuit. 'So,' he said, 'Poskitt will have explained your mission, but has he told you why?'

I stirred my tea. 'Not as yet, Mr Holmes.'

'Ah.' The second biscuit went the way of the first, followed by a deep draught of tea. 'We've been doing a bit of work on what I shall call the Jasmine Gang, and on Moriarty in particular. We couldn't do more than clip his wings at the time, given his government connections, but that doesn't mean we can't dismantle things in the background.' He reached for another biscuit. 'Though we have been hampered by one of our chief witnesses being incapacitated.' He waved the biscuit to emphasise his point. 'Now he's in a better state of health, we can see what he remembers. And as I recall, you got on well with his wife.'

I grimaced. 'Don't remind me.' I was not proud of my role in obtaining the letter which had imprisoned Emmett Stanley, especially as I was convinced that his wife had known nothing of what she was carrying.

'Be that as it may,' said Mycroft. 'You'll be able to chat

to them in a friendly manner and remember enough of the conversation to report back afterwards. You won't be able to take notes, you see. Nothing official whatsoever.'

'No,' said Mr Poskitt. 'Mrs Stanley and I agreed you would visit them at home for lunch.'

'Our usual rates would apply,' said Mycroft. 'Given that there will be some preparation, and also travel to and from Ealing, we would pay for a full day plus travel expenses. In advance.'

I raised my eyebrows. Payment in advance was not usual.

'So you'll do it?' Mycroft Holmes held out his fleshy hand, and after a moment, I put mine into it. 'Excellent. Poskitt, I'll let you attend to the details. Delightful to see you, Mrs Hudson.' He heaved himself out of the chair, refilled his cup, picked up the plate of biscuits, and disappeared through the connecting door.

'Is that all right?' asked Mr Poskitt.

I laughed. 'I'm not sure I had a choice.' But it was rather thrilling to be summoned at short notice as *the* person to interview Emmett Stanley. *Wait till I tell Sherlock*, I thought, but my sunny mood was chilled by the realisation that Sherlock, most probably, would not want to know.

CHAPTER 8

I left Somerset House with my fee burning a hole in my purse. I knew exactly what I would spend it on – but not yet.

I walked down to the river and strolled along the Embankment. It was mid-morning, and comparatively quiet. I found a bench, then took my letters from my bag.

Dear Mrs Hudson,

Please help me. I am engaged to a commercial traveller and we are due to marry next April. While he is often away on business, he has always written to me regularly – at least twice a week. I have had no letters from him for three weeks, and I am beginning to wonder whether something is wrong…

Dear Mrs Hudson,

I would appreciate your assistance in a delicate matter. A valuable opal tiara has gone missing, and while I have my own ideas about what may have happened, I would welcome a professional view…

Dear Mrs Hudson,
Are you in contact with the spirit world?

I grimaced and shoved that letter into its envelope. The other two, though, looked distinctly promising. And there was no reason why I could not reply to my prospective clients and offer a meeting, since Mr Poskitt had yet to arrange a date for my visit to the Stanleys. I put the letters away, resolving to reply as soon as I got home. First, though, I had an appointment to keep in Wigmore Street.

Debenham and Freebody was busy. Women were everywhere, bright and fashionable, alone or in twos and threes, chattering, laughing and comparing items. I smiled; it was lovely to see them enjoying themselves. I remembered how excited I had been to return to the department store after my month working undercover and luxuriate in hats and underthings and perfume. I had been giddy with pleasure. *Speaking of pleasure...*

I strolled to the glove department, where Gladys was superintending. She frowned as I approached. 'It is you, isn't it?' she said, peering at me. 'At this rate I won't know which day is which.'

'No, I suppose not,' I said absently, my attention fixed on the display case. 'Gladys, I saw a pair of gloves here the other day. Cream, with navy embroidery.'

'Oh yes, I know the ones you mean,' said Gladys. She gave me a sly smile. 'I sold them not an hour ago, and you'll never guess who to.'

'Was it my doppelgänger?'

Gladys looked confused. 'She didn't say what her name

was.'

'I meant the young fair-haired woman we're all interested in.'

'That's the one,' Gladys said, her expression lightening. 'Of course, practically every assistant in the store was watching her, just in case.'

'And did anything untoward happen?'

'Not a thing. She tried on the gloves, paid in cash, and went straight out of the store. Perhaps she was in a hurry. Evie was terribly upset; she is rather up-and-down at the moment.'

'I imagine she is,' I said. 'Though that's not surprising. Is she about?'

'She's on shawls,' Gladys replied. 'The smell of the perfume counter makes her ill, and she can't bear handling the stockings. She says it gives her shivers down her spine.'

I looked at the relevant counter and saw Evie leaning on it glumly. I had a feeling that even a kind word would set her off. 'You don't have another pair of those gloves in stock, do you?'

'I can find out.' Gladys turned to the shallow drawers behind her and rummaged. 'Aha!' she cried, shaking the gloves at me so fast that they were a blur. 'They mayn't be the right size, mind.'

'Let's see,' I breathed. I pulled on first one, then the other, and admired them. 'They're lovely. How much are they?'

Gladys found her price list and named a figure a little higher than I had expected.

They're so pretty...

Where on earth will you wear them?

I have money in hand—

'I'll take them,' I said, before I talked myself out of it. I pulled the gloves off and handed them to Gladys to wrap, then took out my purse. It was fortunate that I had not banked Mr Poskitt's fee, since I did not have enough loose change for the gloves.

Gladys's eyes widened as I handed her a sovereign. 'I say,' she said. 'We *are* fine.'

'Money well earned,' I said, and smiled at her as she gave me my change and the parcel.

From the department store it was a pleasant walk home. I gave Billy the satisfaction of letting me in, hinted that I had had a most productive morning, and said I had letters to write upstairs. 'Is Mr Holmes back yet?' I asked, as if it were an afterthought.

'Not yet, ma'am,' said Martha, who had come up too. 'He didn't say when he'd return, but I've prepared lunch for two.' She grimaced. 'It was meant to be a cold chicken salad, but as all the chicken got eaten yesterday, it's a ham salad now.'

'I'm sure that will be just as nice,' I assured her. 'I don't want anything yet, but I may ring for tea in a little while.' I took the letters from my bag as if I couldn't wait to get started on my correspondence.

I noticed a letter for Sherlock on the post tray, printed and unstamped. *Sherlock Holmes, Esq., 221B Baker Street, London.* Perhaps a note from a client who lived nearby, and had asked their servant to deliver it. I was sure it would keep until his return.

I went upstairs, then paused on the first-floor landing and listened. Nothing. Dr Watson would be safely at work. Then I crossed to the consulting-room door and peeped through the keyhole. It appeared empty. I turned the knob and applied gentle pressure to the door, which opened.

I could have entered the room without any need for stealth. There was no reason why not, since officially it was a room for both Sherlock and me to use. In practice, however, Sherlock occupied the consulting room far more than I did. His books and his scientific equipment lived there, and he invariably met his clients and did his thinking within its four walls. I occasionally visited to look for a snippet of information in Sherlock's extensive collection of reference works, or to discuss something with him, and even then I felt like an interloper. However, the purpose of my visit today was different.

Gently, carefully, I pulled open the drawers of the bureau, alert for traps and giveaways such as a hair across the opening or a sprinkling of dust. None of the drawers contained what I was looking for. I moved to the bookshelves, pulling out a volume here and there and checking behind it. My search was in vain. I investigated the sofa and the armchair, and sighed with relief.

Then I had a thought: the dressing room. I kept my disguise paraphernalia there too, but there were drawers and cupboards which only Sherlock used, in which a small object or two could easily be hidden. I glanced around the room to make sure everything was as I had found it, then opened the connecting door and began another careful search. But I did not find what I sought: a small morocco case and a vial of cocaine.

You ought to trust him, I told myself. *John said he had given up the habit, and he shows no signs of it. It's been well over a year since—*

Trembling hands. Forgetfulness. Euphoria, followed by depression, irritation and blame. Nights when he rocked in the corner of the consulting room until I thought he would surely snap.

I do trust him – but I want to be sure.

A creak downstairs made me jump. Hastily I put everything in order and moved speedily through the two connecting doors to the bedroom, where I changed into a house dress. Then I went upstairs, arranged my letters and writing case in a way that suggested I had been hard at work, and rang the bell twice, the agreed signal for tea.

It did not take me long to compose my letters, as I had prepared a set of stock replies for the most common enquiries, which I could then copy out, adapting as necessary. Sherlock had once joked that I should consider purchasing a typewriter, to which I replied that my clients preferred the personal touch of a handwritten letter, not to mention the additional reassurance that I dealt with my own correspondence and their confidentiality would be maintained. I told him that – and I believed it – but I also felt that if Sherlock and Dr Watson heard me bashing away at a typewriter on a regular basis it would give the impression that I was a clerk or typist, not a professional detective. It was a small thing, but I wished to defend my status.

I stamped and addressed my envelopes, then checked

my watch. *Not long until lunch.* There was a postbox close by, and if I buttoned a jacket over my house dress and hurried, I might be able to catch the next collection. I snatched up my letters and ran downstairs.

'I'm going to the postbox,' I called down the kitchen steps. 'I won't be long.' But as I took my jacket from the hall stand footsteps ascended from the kitchen, and I recognised their cadence.

He went out through the back door.

I thrust my arms into the jacket, but the footsteps were growing louder. I assumed what I hoped was a neutral expression. In another second, I was face to face with Sherlock.

CHAPTER 9

Sherlock looked a mess. He was unshaven, his hair uncombed and mostly on end, and I wasn't sure whether he had washed that morning. His clothes were shabby and mud-spattered and his boots down at heel. However, his eyes were bright and he was smiling. 'Good morning, Nell – or is it good afternoon?'

'It is afternoon, just,' I said. 'I was about to post some letters.'

'Ah,' said Sherlock. 'More cases? I would offer to accompany you, but I doubt you'd have me, and I probably shouldn't be seen going out of the front door like this.'

I smiled. 'Perhaps not. And I'm not sure what Martha will say if you present yourself at the lunch table looking like that.'

'True.' He inspected himself in the small mirror we kept in the hallway and grimaced. 'I can't say I'd blame her. You go and post your letters, and I shall make myself fit to be seen. We can discuss our respective mornings over lunch.'

I finished putting on my jacket, opened the door, and hurried to the postbox. I saw the postman approaching and broke into a fast walk, then a run. 'Please wait!' I called.

He paused with the key in the postbox door, shaking his head good-humouredly. I made to hand him the letters, but he shook his head and pointed to the slot in the postbox.

'But you'll open it in a minute anyway,' I said.

'We must observe the rules of the mail,' he said, and waited until I had dropped my letters in the box. Only then did he open the postbox door with a flourish, as if revealing the crown jewels. Given that he had waited for me, I felt obliged to stand and watch as he collected the post. 'Yes, ma'am, I am sure that your letters are in there,' he said smugly, then closed up the postbox, and went on his way.

I returned home and entered the dining room, since lunch was minutes away. Shortly afterwards Sherlock joined me, well-scrubbed, hair combed, and in clean clothes, though still unshaven.

I looked him over. 'I suppose you'll do,' I said, with a smile.

'You're too kind.' He poured me a glass of water, then one for himself, and drank deeply. 'Do we know what is on the menu today?'

'Ham salad, I believe.'

He wrinkled his nose. 'I hope that is more filling than it sounds,' he said. 'I have had a busy morning, and I do not expect this afternoon to be particularly quiet.'

'Oh yes?' I asked. 'What have you been doing?'

'I expect Martha has told you that I went to see Wiggins first thing,' he said.

I nodded, remembering the curt message he had left.

No doubt he had felt slighted after our exchange at bedtime, but his bad temper was completely gone now.

'Much to my surprise,' said Sherlock, toying with his fork, 'Wiggins had heard of Humphrey Montagu. He knows someone who knows someone who works in the Montagu household, which is uncommonly good fortune. I enquired further, of course, but couldn't get much out of him except that Montagu was, in his words, quite a swell.'

'In Wiggins's opinion,' I said.

'Don't underestimate him,' said Sherlock, wagging his fork at me. 'Considering that he lives in a slum, Wiggins has a sophisticated understanding of the different gradations of class in our great city. That comes from having to read people quickly, in order to work out whether they are more likely to tip you a penny or take their whip to you.'

Martha came in with a bowl of dressed salad and a plateful of sliced ham and set them down. 'There are hot rolls and butter to come,' she said, 'and I can bring cheese and biscuits afterwards if you wish.' Her face wore a polite but closed expression, and I suspected she had heard Sherlock's comment about the salad.

'Very good, Martha,' I replied. She bobbed to me and withdrew.

'Am I in trouble?' Sherlock stage-whispered.

'Not yet. Anyway, what else have you been doing? You can't have spent all morning chatting to Wiggins.'

'Chatting, indeed,' said Sherlock. 'We spent time discussing recent developments around London, particularly among the criminal underclasses.'

'In other words, chatting,' I said.

Sherlock rolled his eyes. 'We agreed our terms, then Wiggins excused himself to rally his troops. I have asked that they keep the Montagu residence under observation as much as possible, including late into the evening and first thing in the morning, and obviously that takes some arranging.'

'Won't that be expensive?' I asked.

Sherlock shrugged. 'I won't be paying. Lestrade wants results, and I believe this is necessary, so he will have to put up with it.'

Martha returned with the rolls and butter. Sherlock waited until I had taken one, then took two, put one on his side plate, and began eating the other, pausing every so often to continue his narrative.

'Do excuse me, Nell, for I am as hungry as a hunter. Since Wiggins was busy I undertook the first watch myself, and proceeded to the Montagu residence. Luckily they live in a street with plenty of comings and goings, so nobody noticed one more scruffy man loafing about. I imagine they assumed I was hoping for an easy job, and indeed I did earn a couple of pennies for holding horses and, on one occasion, carrying a lady's parcel to her door. Sadly she was not Eliza Montagu, but it enabled me to exchange pleasantries with her coachman and footman, and as she lives two doors away from the Montagus, they could be valuable acquaintances. I shall endeavour to cultivate them, and also inform Wiggins of my new friends.'

He took another bite of his roll. 'The Montagu household itself seems well regulated. The staff answered the door promptly, looking spick and span in their uniforms, and the house itself is a model of propriety. Mr Montagu left in his carriage at a quarter past nine precisely, with the *Times* under his arm, while Mrs Montagu had not appeared by the time that I left. Presumably she was dealing with her correspondence or some household business.'

'I daresay,' I said, picking up the tongs. 'Would you like salad?' My stomach had been growling through much of Sherlock's speech, and I had been desperate for a lull in his narrative.

'Please,' said Sherlock, helping himself to two large slices of ham. I added salad to his plate and mine, then took a slice of ham for myself. 'And what have you been doing?' he asked, glancing at my house dress. 'A quiet morning, I presume.'

'Not as quiet as I anticipated,' I said. 'I received a telegram from Mr Poskitt first thing this morning, summoning me to Somerset House. He wants me to interview Emmett Stanley to see if he can shed any more light on the Jasmine Gang, as he calls them.'

Sherlock raised an eyebrow. 'Stanley?' He cut his ham. 'I thought they'd got all they could out of him.'

'It seems not,' I said evenly, 'and your brother and Mr Poskitt think I am exactly the person to draw him out. Mr Poskitt will arrange a date, and I shall travel to Ealing.' I ate some salad. The dressing was rather sharp: too much vinegar. I would have to speak to Martha. 'After Somerset House I called at the department store to enquire about a person of interest, and I also called at the post office to

63

collect my mail.'

'Oh yes,' said Sherlock, looking a little less pleased than before. 'I take it that the letters you were posting are related.'

'That's right,' I said. 'Just three today, but two are potential cases, and interesting ones at that. I answered them as soon as I got home.'

'Always so keen,' he commented, spearing a lettuce leaf.

'It is professional to be prompt,' I said, then put a large forkful of salad into my mouth. I did not wish to say any more on the subject, and I could feel myself growing nettled. I counted to twenty as I chewed, and by the time I had finished, I had thought of a diversion. 'That reminds me,' I said, when I was able. 'There was a note for you on the hall table; it must have come while we were both out. Hand-delivered, by the look of it.'

'Oh, really?' said Sherlock, in the manner of someone vaguely interested. 'I must remember to pick it up after lunch.' His pace of eating increased, and I feared for his digestion.

'Actually,' he said a couple of minutes later, laying his knife and fork on his empty plate, 'I may fetch it now. I am planning to smarten myself up and pay a visit to various doormen at the London clubs this afternoon, to glean more intelligence about Humphrey Montagu.' He put his napkin on the table. 'Please excuse me.'

I congratulated myself on remembering the note as he pushed his chair back and strode to the door. I was in no mood to engage in verbal sparring with Sherlock; I was far too busy for that. Besides, we were two grown people. Teasing each other was one thing, sniping quite another.

He came in with the envelope and flung himself down in his chair. 'Ready gummed,' he said, 'and no seal. Common black ink, printed by a right-handed person, almost certainly a man, and of an optimistic bent, at least when he wrote the address.'

'The lines slope upwards, I take it,' I said.

'Indeed they do,' said Sherlock. 'Let us see what my hopeful correspondent has to communicate.' He worked his thumb under the flap of the envelope and ripped it open, then extracted a single sheet of white paper and unfolded it.

'What does it say?' I asked, putting more salad on my fork. When I looked up, Sherlock was staring at the piece of paper, his jaw slack. 'Sherlock, what is it?'

His eyes met mine. 'It is a threat,' he said, 'but not a threat against me. Someone has planted a bomb in London, and I have less than ninety minutes to find it.'

CHAPTER 10

I stared at Sherlock. 'A bomb?' My mouth had gone dry.

'Yes. Look.' He came round the table and put the note in front of me.

Dear Mr Holmes,

I have heard much lately about your great skill as a detective. Here is a riddle for you.

My first and last are in bee but not in wasp, though the sting you would feel from me is far greater.

I have a hasty temper – some might say a short fuse – and if I am not calmed down by two o'clock this afternoon, I shall make my displeasure known.

You will find me in London, near a venerable seafaring friend who had cause to resent the operation of gunpowder. I am not at the obvious place, though. That would be far too easy.

I do hope you find me.
Yours,
An Admirer

I looked up at Sherlock. 'You are right,' I murmured. 'It

must be a bomb.'

'And I assume that this person has not informed the police, or I would have received a wire by now,' said Sherlock. He opened the dining-room door. 'Billy!' he bellowed. 'Come here, right away.'

We went into the hall as feet thumped up the kitchen stairs. Billy appeared, panting and wide-eyed. 'What is it, sir? Have I—'

'Billy, I need you to send some telegrams with the utmost urgency. Come with me.' Sherlock took the stairs two at a time, and I followed them into the consulting room. Sherlock sat down at the bureau, took paper and pen, and consulting the note, wrote rapidly, reading aloud as he did so. 'Bomb threat received STOP Will explode at two STOP Location unknown but in London STOP QUOTE Near venerable seafaring friend who resented gunpowder but not obvious place UNQUOTE STOP Working on this with NH STOP Holmes.'

He handed the sheet to Billy. 'I want you to send that to Lestrade and Gregson at Scotland Yard and also to Mycroft Holmes at Somerset House and Whitehall.'

'That's a long telegram,' murmured Billy.

'It is necessary,' said Sherlock. He felt in his pocket and handed Billy two sovereigns. 'Wait for ten minutes, then come back and tell me who has answered.' Billy stood there, mouth open. 'What's keeping you?' snapped Sherlock. 'Go, Billy! This is a matter of life and death.' Billy fled, and presently the door slammed downstairs.

Sherlock looked at his watch. 'It is ten to one now. Just over an hour to work out where it is, get there, and disable

67

the bomb.' His eyes were wild, and he was breathing quickly. He loosened his tie and undid the top button of his shirt.

'We must think rationally,' I said. 'This person has left us clues, and all we can do is try to solve them. A venerable seafarer—'

'Nelson,' said Sherlock.

'That fits,' I said. 'And his injuries would mean that he was no friend of gunpowder. Nelson's Column!' I imagined the huge plinth shattering in an explosion, chunks of stone flying across Trafalgar Square, the giant column swaying, then crashing to the ground like a felled tree—

'No,' said Sherlock. 'The note says it isn't at the obvious place.' His brow furrowed. 'But where is it?'

I sat down in the armchair. 'There must be public houses and streets named after him. Did he have a house in London?'

'There are probably a dozen public houses named for Lord Nelson,' said Sherlock. He ran his hands through his hair. 'Streets, though... I don't know.' He strode to the bookshelves and pulled out a London street directory. 'Nell, get my index and see what you can find on Nelson.'

I found the index and searched under N, but there was nothing. I tried H, just in case, but drew a blank. 'I'm sorry, Sherlock,' I said, closing the book. 'There is no entry.'

'Why would there be?' he said bitterly. 'Why would I have written an entry on a sailor who died about seventy years ago?'

'Have you found anything in the street directory?'

'Too many things,' said Sherlock, closing the directory and tossing it aside. 'I don't think it is a street.'

'I agree,' I said. 'A street is too large to search, especially when there are several in London. This person is playing a game with you: a game with rules. One rule would have to be that it is possible to find the bomb, so it must be in a specific location, linked to a specific thing.'

'Yes,' said Sherlock, 'but what?'

'Are there any other statues of Lord Nelson?'

'Again, I have no idea. Probably. Wait! Nelson's tomb in the crypt at St Paul's Cathedral!' Sherlock's eyes lit up, then dulled. 'Too obvious, and not public enough. This is impossible.'

'It isn't impossible,' I said, 'just very, very difficult.' I closed my eyes and thought of Lord Nelson in his uniform, his empty sleeve pinned— 'A portrait?'

Sherlock turned to me, and there was a glimmer of hope in his face. 'Yes, a portrait would work,' he said. He smacked the surface of the bureau. 'Where would you find a portrait of Nelson? Why, surely at the National Portrait Gallery.'

'There are other galleries.'

'Yes, but that one is the most likely, and if we draw a blank, perhaps they can tell us where other portraits are located.' He sprang out of his seat and hurried to the door. 'Come on, Nell.' A slight furrow appeared between his eyebrows. 'You are coming, aren't you?'

'Of course I'm coming,' I said. 'I wasn't sure if you'd want me to.'

69

'I may well need your help,' said Sherlock. 'This may surprise you, but I've never disarmed a bomb before. If I can't do it, at least you'll be a witness that I tried.'

'You'll do it,' I said, hoping against hope that I was right.

We went down to the kitchen. 'I have my penknife,' said Sherlock. 'What else would help?'

'It might be hidden behind or under something,' I said. 'Perhaps a crowbar, or a hammer.'

'I have a crowbar upstairs,' said Sherlock. 'Martha, do we have a hammer, or any other tools?'

'Billy keeps a toolbox in the scullery,' said Martha, looking extremely confused. She hurried out and returned with a large, battered metal box.

'Excellent,' said Sherlock, taking it from her and setting it on the table. He opened it and we gazed at an assortment of chisels and screwdrivers, some pliers, a small saw and a hammer. 'Just the thing.'

Billy erupted into the kitchen and gaped at us. 'What are you doing with my toolbox?'

'We're going to disarm a bomb, Billy,' Sherlock replied. 'Any answers?'

'One from Inspector Lestrade, sir. He says he'll put men on the case.'

'No bright ideas there, then,' said Sherlock. 'Billy, get a cab and hold it at the door. Once we've gone, wire Lestrade and tell him we're going to the National Portrait Gallery. Nell, get your hat and boots on. I'll fetch the crowbar.'

***

The drive to South Kensington seemed interminable. Sherlock had promised the cabbie a sovereign if he could reach the gallery in half an hour, but at that time we were only at the head of Exhibition Road. 'Come on,' Sherlock urged, gripping the handle of the toolbox, knuckles white.

At long last the cab reached the gallery. Sherlock jumped out, helped me down, and paid the cabbie.

'Aren't you waiting for your change?' said the cabbie, looking at the coin as if he'd never seen anything like it.

'Hang the change!' cried Sherlock, and we ran to the gallery.

'Excuse me, sir.' A uniformed doorman stepped in our path. 'What's in that box?'

'I have reason to believe a bomb has been planted in the gallery,' said Sherlock. 'Tell me where the portrait of Lord Nelson is.'

The doorman drew himself up. 'A bomb, sir? In an art gallery? I don't think so.'

'I don't care what you think,' said Sherlock, and poked him in the stomach with the crowbar.

The man doubled over and we ran past. I heard shouting. I only hoped we could reach the painting and disarm the bomb before the whole place went up.

Suddenly Sherlock caught my arm and drew me aside. 'Nell, ask an attendant where the portrait of Lord Nelson is. Look as calm as you possibly can.'

I smoothed my clothes and glanced about me. An attendant stood by the door to the next room, and I approached him with a polite smile. 'Excuse me, but could you tell me where I might find the portrait of Lord

Nelson?'

He beamed down at me. 'Certainly, madam. It is in the next room, at the end. A fine portrait by Lemuel Abbott.'

'Thank you so much.' I hurried to the next gallery, where ten or so people stood in various attitudes of contemplation. As I walked, the portrait came into focus; the gold braid and epaulettes, the Star of the Bath, the brass buttons—

'Keep walking,' Sherlock murmured. 'I may need you to cover me.' As he passed, he handed me a small chisel and a screwdriver, which I slipped into my bag.

Sherlock strode to the painting, peered at the frame, then stepped back. A wrought-iron ventilation grille was set beneath the painting, just above the skirting board. Sherlock crouched and opened the toolbox.

'There he is!' The doorman was standing behind us. One hand clutched his stomach; the other pointed at Sherlock.

A policeman ran forwards and seized Sherlock's arm. 'Now, sir, you had better come with me.' The doorman, who seemed to have forgotten his injury, seized Sherlock's other arm, and they led him away.

I consulted my watch: a quarter to two. Gritting my teeth, I waited until the hubbub had died down, then dropped my handkerchief and knelt in front of the grating. It was held by four screws. I retrieved the screwdriver from my bag.

The screws were new and bright, and moved easily. I caught the first one as it was about to fall and placed it on the floor. The second and third followed.

Then I heard raised voices, and looked round to see two people talking to an attendant and pointing at me. He advanced towards me at a rapid walk. I turned my attention to the final screw and as he reached me, the grating clattered to the floor.

'Madam, I must ask you to leave,' the attendant said firmly.

There was nothing for it. I plunged my hands into the opening and they closed around a metal box. Holding my breath, I drew it out.

'What the—' The attendant took a step forward as I opened the box, revealing a bundle of cardboard tubes attached to a short length of something like waxy string, with a glowing tip. 'It's a bomb!' he shouted, then turned and ran. Everyone in the room made for the door, jostling each other aside in their haste to get through it.

I studied the bundle. If I pulled the fuse away – but would the friction detonate it? I ran to the door of the gallery. The attendant was talking to the policeman, who stood with his arms folded. 'I knew that workman was up to no good this morning,' he was saying. Sherlock stood in handcuffs, fuming.

'Come quickly, Sherlock!' I shouted. 'I've found it, and I don't know what to do.'

Sherlock held his wrists out. 'Get these damn cuffs off,' he said to the policeman, 'or people will die.'

'Help me!' I shouted, tears running down my face. 'There really is a bomb, I swear it!'

That, for some reason, moved the policeman, and finally he released Sherlock. I ran back to the bomb, and a few seconds later Sherlock was beside me. 'Please be careful,' I murmured, as if talking too loud would set it off.

'I shall,' he said. 'You see the fuse?' He touched the dark, thick string. 'We must cut off the bit that is alight, then our troubles are over.' He produced his penknife. 'Hold the fuse taut, Nell.'

I took the fuse between finger and thumb of both hands, wincing as I did so, and Sherlock sawed at it. 'It's a sort of safety fuse,' he said. 'Like a slow match, but coated in something to make it more durable. And harder to cut, damn it.' He clenched his teeth with the effort. 'It is starting to fray,' he said, a moment later.

'Don't stop,' I said. 'The end of the fuse is getting closer.' I felt heat on the side of my finger and thumb. I stared at the blade of Sherlock's knife as the threads of the fuse sprang up, until one strand held it together.

'Ah!' I cried as the tip of the fuse burnt my thumb.

'There,' said Sherlock, and the two halves of the fuse separated. 'Drop that piece, Nell.' I obeyed gladly, and Sherlock crushed it under his heel. 'We should be safe,' he said. 'But let's get out of here, just in case.'

We hurried through the gallery, retracing our steps to the entrance. It was only when we stepped outside and found the street deserted that I realised the enormity of what we had done, and what could have happened. My knees wobbled, and Sherlock steadied me. 'Take my arm, Nell, and stand tall. We have beaten the enemy.'

I looked up at him as we walked towards the crowds gathered at a safe distance. 'We have beaten him – for now.'

CHAPTER 11

Sherlock had just opened his mouth to reply when a cry of 'Holmes!' rang out. Inspector Lestrade hurried towards us. 'Have you disabled the bomb?' he enquired, in a low voice.

'We have,' said Sherlock. 'We severed the live end of the fuse, and extinguished it for good measure.'

'You're sure?' said the inspector.

'Quite sure,' said Sherlock. He consulted his watch. 'If we had not, you would have heard the bang by now.'

'Good work,' said Inspector Lestrade, in that same low voice, and clapped Sherlock on the arm. 'I wasn't sure if we would get here in time, but I knew you would have the situation under control.' I looked past him and saw a cluster of policemen chatting with the crowd. 'Men, come forward!'

The policemen peeled themselves away and marched over. 'Sir,' came the ragged chorus.

'It appears the bomb is no longer live,' said the inspector. 'However, I wish you to proceed with the utmost caution.' He turned to Sherlock. 'Where is the bomb?' he muttered.

'On the floor in front of the portrait of Lord Nelson. I daresay an attendant can direct you, if you can find one willing to re-enter the building.' Sherlock made no attempt to disguise his amusement.

'Very good.' The inspector scanned the spectators, then beckoned over a man in the gallery uniform and explained his requirements. After murmured negotiation, during which I heard the words *this far and no farther,* the attendant nodded.

Inspector Lestrade addressed the crowd. 'Everyone stand back!' he shouted, spreading his arms wide to reinforce his point. Though everyone was a good hundred feet from the building, they all shrank away. 'Men, go with this attendant, find the bomb, ensure that it is disabled, and remove it from the building.' He glared at a policeman in the act of lighting a cigarette. 'No smoking!'

The officer, with a disgusted look, pinched the tip of his cigarette out and was about to stick it behind his ear when Inspector Lestrade snatched it from him and ground it under his boot. 'Have you no sense, man?'

The men approached the gallery with considerable reluctance until finally one of them decided to get it over with and marched boldly forward, at which point the others quickened their pace, not wanting to be left out.

'I'm surprised you weren't leading from the front, Lestrade,' said Sherlock.

'I am here to direct operations,' said the inspector. 'And to talk to the press,' he added, as a sharp-faced man with a notebook hurried over.

'Lewis Andrews, from the *Messenger*,' he said. 'Are

you sure it's a bomb, Inspector?'

The inspector drew himself up. 'As sure as we can be,' he said. 'We received an anonymous tipoff, and immediately hastened to the scene. It is only thanks to quick thinking, and of course the actions of the gallery's staff, that no lives were lost.'

'Did your tipoff say who was responsible?' asked Mr Andrews, his pencil moving at lightning speed.

'They did not,' said Inspector Lestrade. 'But it's obvious that it's the Fenians again. They have already planted several bombs in London, and I have no doubt that this will not be the last.'

Sherlock and I exchanged glances, and in his I detected a distinct warning to keep quiet.

'Fenians,' murmured Lewis Andrews, still scribbling. He leaned forward confidentially. 'Once your men have the bomb and it is pronounced safe, would we be able to photograph it?'

The inspector considered. 'Provided a safe distance is maintained, I see no reason why not.'

'Excellent.' Mr Andrews turned and let out a shrill whistle, and a minute later a man with a camera slung around his neck, carrying a portable tripod, came hurrying over as best he could. 'Perhaps here,' said Mr Andrews. 'Would you mind being photographed, Inspector?'

Inspector Lestrade drew himself up. 'It would be a pleasure. I suppose you will require a few official words from me.'

'That would be most kind, sir,' said Lewis Andrews. 'Was this young man involved in the discovery? I saw—'

'I was merely passing,' said Sherlock. 'I stopped to speak to the inspector, whom I know through an unrelated matter.'

I tried not to look reproachful. Sherlock and I had done all the work of the case, and Inspector Lestrade would take all the credit.

Mr Andrews frowned. 'I could have sworn—'

'The young lady, likewise, has no part in this,' said Inspector Lestrade, so smoothly that I almost doubted my own experience. He gave a satisfied nod, then as Mr Andrews moved aside to speak to his photographer, shot me an unmistakable warning glance. 'I suggest you both take your leave,' he said. 'My men may be some time, and I daresay there will be little to see. You will be able to read about it in Mr Andrews's paper later.'

Mr Andrews turned at the mention of his name. 'The *Daily Messenger*, available at news stands throughout the city.' He smiled at us, then returned to conferring with the photographer. Presently they called the inspector over, and the three of them had a fine time settling on a background for the inspector's portrait, adjusting the angle of his hat, and murmuring about the light. In the midst of it, Sherlock and I quietly took our leave.

'Shall we get a cab?' I asked, indicating a nearby rank where several hansoms were waiting.

'Would you mind if we walked a little first, Nell?' asked Sherlock. 'I am lightheaded, and fresh air would allow me to collect my thoughts.' He studied me. 'How do you feel? You are as involved in this as I am.'

I slipped my arm through his while I considered my

answer. We passed the doorman, who was holding forth to a small crowd on his part in the proceedings. 'Wild-eyed he was, like a madman, and he knocked the breath fair out of me.' Clearly he perceived Sherlock as the villain of the piece.

'I am rather shocked,' I said. 'For such a thing to come out of the blue…' My mouth twisted in a wry smile. 'Not that you or I will see any benefit from it, if Inspector Lestrade has his way.' I looked up at Sherlock. 'Are you keeping out of it to please the inspector, or do you have another reason?'

We travelled perhaps fifty yards before Sherlock replied. 'I am not sure of the inspector's motive in declaring this the work of the Fenians,' he said. 'As far as I know they have never given a warning, preferring to let the bombs speak for them. And why would they send a warning to an obscure private detective? Surely they would make as much noise as possible.'

'I think you are right,' I said. 'We must speak to the inspector and see if he will divulge his motives, or if we can work them out for ourselves.' I paused. 'He was very keen to keep me out of it, too.'

Sherlock squeezed my arm. 'For the same reason, I am sure.'

'Probably.' We continued for some time in silence. 'He did give me an odd look, though.'

Sherlock laughed. 'He doesn't want you stealing his thunder.'

'No, it wasn't that.' I couldn't put my finger on what it was about the inspector's look that had impressed me, only that he had not looked at Sherlock like that. Sherlock had distanced himself from the case almost immediately, though. Then I realised Sherlock had not answered my question. 'So why don't you want to be associated with this case?'

We walked towards Hyde Park, our pace brisk but not hurried. 'Part of it,' said Sherlock, 'is that I am concerned that if the true facts of this case were reported, I might be deluged with all sorts of threats from would-be copycats. You know the sort of thing.'

I knew only too well what he meant. When the newspapers reported a lurid murder or a particularly gruesome suicide, a host of similar attempts would follow. Inspector Lestrade had warned me of the phenomenon. 'You said part of it,' I said, to distract myself from the unpleasant train of thought. 'What else?'

Sherlock was silent, and when I glanced at him he was looking straight forward, his mouth set firm, as if determined to say no more on the subject. 'Whatever it is, Sherlock, tell me. I promise to breathe a word to nobody, if that is what you wish.'

'I know I can trust you, Nell,' he said, patting my hand. 'That is absolutely without question. Indeed, it comes from what you said not half an hour ago.'

I tried to recall my words. 'What did I say?'

'You said that we had beaten our adversary for now, and you were absolutely right. Someone who plants a bomb and sends a warning will not stop at one attempt. I have no doubt that they will try again and again.' He winced. 'I shall have to tell Watson about this, since Martha and Billy are bound to say something, and he will be desperate to write it up, and annoyed when I refuse to let him.'

'Why won't you let him?' I asked. 'You could forbid him from publishing it anywhere, and I am sure that he would respect your request.'

Sherlock's jaw clenched for a moment. 'If I allowed Watson to write an account of this, it would be a small step to giving an interview to the newspapers and becoming a public figure. I would become some kind of hermit, watching the letterbox for another communication from my adversary, and unable to think of anything else. The papers would follow my every move, and rejoice every time I – that is, we – diffused another bomb. The person behind this, no doubt, would redouble their efforts in the hope of catching me out. Inevitably, one day he would succeed, and I would fail. Blood would be on my hands. I would never forget it, and I would never be allowed to forget it.'

'Oh, Sherlock.' We were at the Serpentine, and the ducks paddling about and having arguments with each other seemed most incongruous against the enormity of what we were dealing with. 'What shall we do?'

He sighed, and some of the tension left his shoulders. 'We shall continue our walk home, if you are in agreement,' he said. 'There I shall peruse our adversary's note and take down its particulars, in case the inspector requires it as evidence. Then I shall make myself tidy and pursue my original plan of conversing with as many doormen of exclusive London clubs as I can, in an attempt to take my mind off this. Oh, and I have a task for you, Nell, if you wouldn't mind.'

'Of course,' I said. 'Anything.'

His mouth quirked up at the corner. 'I'm glad you said that. Would you mind wiring the inspector and asking him to send Billy's toolbox to Baker Street? We shall be in trouble with the servants if it is lost, not least because after all that, we disabled the bomb with a screwdriver and my penknife.'

I laughed for the first time in what felt like a long time. 'In the words of Inspector Lestrade, Sherlock, it would be a pleasure.'

CHAPTER 12

The front door of 221B Baker Street opened before we had reached it. 'Well?' demanded Billy.

'We found it,' said Sherlock.

'And…? I mean and, sir?'

Sherlock smiled. 'We disarmed it. Inspector Lestrade and his men are tidying up.'

'Did you use my toolbox?' Billy's gaze fell to Sherlock's hands, then mine, then the step.

'Of course,' I said. 'We have had to leave it at the crime scene, but I shall make sure we get it back. I hope we won't need it again, but you never know.'

An expression of immense pride spread over Billy's features. 'To think…' He threw the door wide open. 'I'll get Martha to make tea.' He ran down the kitchen stairs, clearly bursting to tell her.

'I'm glad someone is pleased,' said Sherlock. 'Now, to this note.' He pulled it out of his pocket. 'I should perhaps have told Lestrade that I had it with me, but I can make better use of it than he can. He will be far too busy.' He grinned. 'Let us go to the consulting room.'

It was odd to open the door and see the street directory

on the floor, the index sticking out of the bookshelf, and the paper and pens lying on the open bureau. We had been in such a rush a couple of hours ago. Comparatively, it felt as if we had all the time in the world.

Sherlock placed a chair for me near the bureau and sat down beside me. 'So, this note. Hand-delivered, so no postmark or stamp, unfortunately. Although given the puzzle we were set, I am sure the writer would have contrived to send us on a false trail if he had posted it.'

'You say *he*,' I said, 'and earlier you said the note had probably been written by a man. What makes you think that?'

'A certain rigidity about the writing,' said Sherlock. 'I have observed that men's writing is often less neat than women's, particularly for those individuals who are not required to write neatly as a condition of their work. The stiffness of this penmanship suggests that this is an educated person, not a clerk or secretary or tradesman, who is striving to disguise the fact by printing his missive.'

'Could it not be a woman doing the same?'

'It is possible, but how many women would be interested in planting bombs? It seems a very male crime.' He scrutinised me. 'Do you think it might be a woman, Nell?'

I considered. 'As you say, Sherlock, it is possible. And there is something odd about the phrasing of the letter. Would a man write, "I do hope you find me"?'

'Mmm,' said Sherlock. He held the letter up to the window. 'The paper is thin and has no watermark. It could have been bought anywhere cheaply.'

'There is no way to narrow that down, then. Is the envelope of the same type?'

Sherlock peered at it. 'It appears to be. There are no stains or fingermarks on the envelope or the note which would help us. I said the correspondent was in an optimistic frame of mind when I first saw the envelope, and the upward trend of the lines in the note bear this out. Presumably the writer was confident that they would beat me.' His lip curled for an instant. 'The printing is regular, if cramped, with no particular distinguishing traits.' He brought the paper to his nose. 'No scent is detectable.'

A shiver ran down my spine as I recollected a note perfumed with jasmine from the year before. At least that danger was past.

'Now, the ink.' Sherlock took a magnifying glass from a cubbyhole in the bureau and peered at the note. 'It looks like Stephens' ink to me.' He put the magnifying glass away, took a razor blade from a drawer, and scraped at a small section of the address until he had separated some tiny fragments of inked paper. 'I daresay this will tell us nothing, but it is best to be sure.' He slid the fragments into a fresh envelope and put it in a pigeonhole.

'That might have been easier if the ink had been left to dry naturally,' I commented. 'The colour indicates that it was blotted, and from the small amount of smudging, it was blotted quickly.'

'That is hardly surprising,' Sherlock replied, 'given that the writer was working to a specific time.'

'They could have written the note long before and kept it until it was needed. This indicates that the matter was executed in a rush.'

Sherlock turned to me. 'Do you know, I believe you're right.' He laid his hand on mine. 'I'm so glad you're here, Nell.'

'I'm glad I could help,' I replied, and a warm glow spread through me. On impulse, I leaned forward and kissed him.

He smiled at me, and a merry light danced in his grey eyes. 'There is that, too.' He got up. 'I had better get on with my other work. There is more thinking to do, but I think best when I am on the move.' He looked at the note, then at me. 'Nell, would you mind making a copy of this? I do not mean imitate the writing, but a word-for-word copy, with the words on the same lines. It may come in useful if Lestrade takes the note.'

'Er, yes, I suppose I could—'

'You will remember to wire Lestrade, won't you?' Sherlock kissed the top of my head. 'Thank you so much. I shall go and reacquaint myself with my razor.' He left the room, and I heard whistling as he climbed the stairs.

I sighed, took a fresh sheet of paper, and drew the letter towards me. Making a copy would take a few minutes; what irritated me was Sherlock's assumption that it was a job for me to do. I wrote rapidly, blotted the paper, and set it aside. Then I took another sheet of paper: *Please could you return toolbox and contents left at gallery STOP Hudson.*

I counted the words, pointing with the nib of my pen. Twelve: excellent. While we could certainly afford not to worry about sending long telegrams, I had not yet shaken the habit of phrasing my wires to avoid paying extra whenever possible.

I looked at my dress, which I had never contemplated leaving the house in, and decided to change before going to the post office. I would not want the clerks to think I had fallen on hard times.

A quarter of an hour later, in my day dress and smartly hatted and gloved, I set out for the post office.

'Do you wish to wait for a reply, madam?' asked the clerk.

'No, not on this occasion,' I replied. I thought it extremely unlikely that Inspector Lestrade would see the wire until much later, and certainly would not think it worth a prompt reply in comparison with the important business he was handling. I imagined his chest puffing up as he gave a statement to Lewis Andrews of the *Daily Messenger*, and no doubt any other newspaperman who would listen.

The clerk was gazing at me expectantly, and I realised I had not paid him yet. I put the money into his hand and he took my message into the back room, passing in front of the pigeonholes. Of course – I could check my correspondence while I was here.

But should I? What if another bomb were planted, and we had to race around London again?

But then, what if we didn't? It couldn't hurt to ask.

He returned two minutes later. 'Your telegram is on its way, madam.'

'Thank you. Could you check if any letters have come for me, please? Mrs Hudson.'

He looked at me as if to say that he knew perfectly well who I was, and turned again. This time he had just one letter in his hand, and I tried not to feel disappointed. 'Here you are, madam.'

I thanked him, put the letter in my bag, left the post office, and walked in the direction of home. After a few steps, I paused. Of course I was perfectly within my rights to open my own letter in my own house, and no one could stop me.

But what would Sherlock think if he saw? What if he entered my sitting room to bid me farewell and caught sight of the letter? Of course I could hide it, or wait until he had left the house, but that suggested I was hiding something. Which I was, though I had no reason to. And he was going out specifically to undertake other work…

A man jostled me from behind. Once he had passed, he glared at me for being in the way.

'Sorry,' I said automatically. Then I turned and walked towards Regent's Park. A few minutes later, I had found a vacant bench. I took the letter from my bag, looked around once more, and opened it.

It was a reply to one of the letters I had sent only a few hours before, from a Mrs Farintosh. I consulted my watch. She must have pounced on my letter as soon as it arrived, dashed off a reply and caught the next post. Or – no. The letter was unstamped; it had been hand-delivered to the post office. The address at the top of the letter was in Mayfair, which was not far away; clearly she had not been able to wait. That settled, I perused the letter.

Dear Mrs Hudson,

I am delighted you think my case worthy of your attention, and would be most willing to meet with you at the Corinthian Hotel. May I suggest tomorrow morning (Friday) at 9 o'clock? I wish to bring this matter to a speedy conclusion, and hopefully, recover my tiara. To that end, I am willing to reward you handsomely if you succeed in the case.

Yours sincerely,
Mrs Edwin Farintosh

I frowned. Of course my client would be keen to recover a valuable opal tiara, but I had not expected things to proceed at such a rate. *What will Sherlock think?* Then my eye fell on the phrase 'reward you handsomely'. *There.* Since there was no guarantee that Sherlock would be paid anything for his current work, it was my duty to take the case. I put the letter away, then walked back to the post office, composing my wire to Mrs Farintosh in my head. And as we were meeting at the Corinthian Hotel, a very smart dress and my new gloves would be entirely appropriate.

CHAPTER 13

I had no doubt that anyone who saw me descend from my cab and ascend the steps of the Corinthian Hotel would have thought me fortunate indeed: just another well-dressed lady with nothing to do but meet her friends and gossip. But despite my serene expression, my heart was heavy.

Sherlock had come home from his expedition full of plans. 'Humphrey Montagu frequents the Athenaeum and the Criterion,' he said, 'and I have it on the doorman's authority that he will be at the Criterion tonight by nine o'clock, if not sooner.' He stiffened suddenly, glanced at the post tray, and seeing it empty, relaxed. 'I take it nothing has come.'

'No,' I said, 'nothing has come.' I thought for a moment. 'It would be useful for both of us to know the other's whereabouts, as far as possible, in case we need to make contact quickly.'

'If we can.' Sherlock made a face. 'This is perhaps the worst part of the business: the uncertainty. A communication may come at any time.'

'We cannot live our lives based on the whims of a

villain,' I said. 'Nor the vagaries of the post.'

'What a thought,' said Sherlock.

'I take it you are planning to visit the Criterion tonight,' I said. 'Are you a member?'

'I am not,' said Sherlock. 'But it would not matter if I were, for I do not intend to visit in my own person. Luckily I have a friend of few scruples who is a member, and he is prepared to vouch for me under whichever identity I choose to assume. I have already wired him to that effect, and I shall be a gullible young chap with money to burn. Just the sort of fellow to appeal to Mr Montagu, I hope.' He glanced at me. 'You don't mind, do you?'

'No, not at all,' I said. 'It will take your mind off today's events. In any case, I shall be in bed betimes. I have an early start tomorrow.'

Sherlock's eyebrows lifted. 'Oh yes?'

I smiled. 'A small matter of an opal tiara.'

'In that case,' said Sherlock, 'shall we ask Martha to bring dinner forward half an hour? I would welcome time to dress, and Watson would not mind. He is generally home by six, so it's no inconvenience to him.'

'I shall go and speak to Martha,' I said.

Dinner was duly brought forward to half past six, and Sherlock and I were both seated in the dining room five minutes before, but of Dr Watson there was no sign. 'Of course, he would be late on the one day when it matters,' said Sherlock, fidgeting.

Martha entered with the soup tureen and started upon seeing only two of us. 'Shall I wait another five minutes?'

I was about to assent when we heard the rattle of a key

and the creak of the front door, followed by Dr Watson's heavy tread. 'I'll go and tell him dinner is early,' said Martha, and left the room, still holding the tureen.

Sherlock and I exchanged glances as Martha explained the situation. Dr Watson merely said, 'I see.'

His footsteps approached, and he put his head around the door. 'I shall wash my hands, then I shall be with you directly.' However, he did not smile, and showed none of his usual urbanity.

'Oh dear,' I murmured.

'I shall explain, Nell, and I am sure that he will be perfectly satisfied,' said Sherlock. 'It is but for one night.'

When Dr Watson returned and soup had been served, he listened to Sherlock's explanation in stony silence. 'So you propose to go without me, Holmes,' he said, at last.

'I am afraid it is necessary, Watson,' Sherlock said gently. 'I shall not be in my own person, and it is too great a risk. What if, in a momentary lapse, you addressed me by my name? What if an acquaintance of yours recognised you?'

'I could disguise myself,' said Dr Watson, and I made an effort to keep my face perfectly straight. It was so difficult to imagine John Watson as anything other than he was.

'Of course you could,' said Sherlock. 'But I would worry about you, and that would distract me from Humphrey Montagu.'

'You would have no need to worry about me,' said Dr Watson. He picked up his spoon. 'I see your mind is already made up. I shall speak no more of it.'

We got through dinner as best we could, and despite the excellent quality of Martha's tomato soup and lamb cutlets, I do not believe that any of us appreciated them. In some ways it would have been easier if Dr Watson had shouted. But no, he brooded, and that was much harder to address.

When dinner was finished, he went straight to his sitting room with a brief goodnight, and I knew the rift would remain unhealed at least until morning. I helped Sherlock dress for the club and wished him luck, then went to bed with a book feeling that I had had quite enough.

I woke early to find Sherlock asleep beside me, which was a relief. I ran my hand down his arm and he stirred. 'How did it go?' I whispered.

Sherlock sighed and rolled over. He was still wearing the side whiskers and moustache I had affixed the night before, which was unusual, and was pale to the point of greenncss. 'I can confirm that Montagu has an extremely good head for drink,' he murmured, and put a hand to his forehead.

'He didn't find you out, did he?'

Sherlock managed a smile. 'Don't be ridiculous, Nell. There is an aspidistra at the Criterion that will never be the same again.'

'Did you discover anything?'

Sherlock shook his head, then winced. 'He seems an uncommonly pleasant chap, full of lively conversation which, when you look back on it, has no substance at all. We parted on good terms, and I sincerely hope to see him again.' He closed his eyes. 'But perhaps not tonight.'

I giggled, gently peeled away one of his side-whiskers

and stuck it on his forehead. 'I'm glad to hear it.'

'Give my apologies at breakfast,' murmured Sherlock. 'Perhaps a tray later.'

When I went down to breakfast Dr Watson was already there, stabbing a soldier into his boiled egg. 'Good morning, John,' I said, taking a slice of toast from the rack. 'Sherlock is indisposed at present, but I'm sure he will be glad to talk to you later.'

Dr Watson gave me a cold stare. 'I shall leave for work directly after breakfast, Mrs Hudson.' And that was all he said.

***

I put a smile on my face as I entered the foyer of the hotel. I hated discord, especially when I had not caused it and could do nothing to dispel it. I pushed it to the back of my mind, lifted my chin, and walked into the coffee room.

As soon as I entered, I knew I was being watched. I kept my countenance and looked calmly around me until I located the source of my scrutiny: a well-dressed woman of about forty with dark eyes and dark-brown hair. I had found Mrs Farintosh. I advanced, our identities were confirmed, and I took a seat opposite her.

'No doubt you are wondering why I have not called in the police,' said Mrs Farintosh. 'The fact of the matter is that I do not wish to cause a scandal, and I am confident that the problem lies within my own household.'

I wondered why Mrs Farintosh needed me, since she seemed to think she already had an approximation of the truth. 'So you believe that it is either a member of your family or one of the servants.'

'I do not think it is a member of my family,' said Mrs Farintosh. Her tone indicated that that was, of course, ridiculous.

'So you want me to concentrate on the servants,' I said.

'I do.' She stirred her tea, sipped, then replaced the cup in the saucer with a neat click. 'I am cognisant of the ways of servants, you see.'

'Is there one in particular whom you suspect?' I asked.

Mrs Farintosh looked coy. 'I do not wish to accuse anyone out of hand, Mrs Hudson. I would rather secure your unbiased opinion, and see whether it accords with mine.'

'Would you object if I spoke to members of your household beside the servants? Your husband, for instance?'

Mrs Farintosh eyed me over the rim of her cup. 'I would much prefer that you did not.' This time the cup clattered down.

'It may be useful to get an alternative opinion,' I said. 'I do assure you that I shall exercise the utmost discretion, and ask only necessary questions.'

Mrs Farintosh pursed her lips; she might have rolled her eyes if she had not been so refined. 'Very well.' Her dark eyes met mine. 'Could you come now?'

I drank some more tea to give myself time to consider. On one hand, I did not particularly like the feeling that I was being rushed into things. However, this case seemed to be proceeding along such narrow lines that there was every possibility of concluding it before lunch. 'Of course, Mrs Farintosh.'

For the first time, Mrs Farintosh smiled.

Her house was imposing: a wedding-cake confection of white stucco. A footman had ridden on the footplate of her carriage, and came to help us both out. The door opened as Mrs Farintosh approached it, and I noted the contrast between the imperturbable footman who answered it and the dishevelled Billy who had wrenched our front door open the day before.

'First I shall show you where the tiara was kept,' said Mrs Farintosh. She led the way up a grand staircase and passed several doors until we came to a suite of rooms: first a boudoir, then a bedroom with a four-poster bed. Mrs Farintosh walked to a large jewel case which stood on a small table between the dressing table and the bureau, and lifted the lid. The blue velvet showed a circular depression in its nap, but nothing more.

'The tiara vanished a few days ago,' she said. 'It was there at half past one in the afternoon, when I was changing my earrings ready to pay some calls. When I returned at half past five, it had gone.'

'Do you keep your jewel case locked?'

Mrs Farintosh sighed. 'I must admit that I do not,' she said. 'At least, not always. I am in and out of it quite often, you see. My maid has a key and is committed to locking it, and I'm afraid I leave it to her.'

'You are sure that nothing else has gone missing?' I asked.

Mrs Farintosh shook her head decisively. 'Just the tiara.' She moved to her bureau, took a piece of paper from a pigeonhole, and handed it to me. 'I have made a list of the servants, their positions, and the duration of their service. I thought you could interview them in descending order.' She rang the bell. 'The morning room is the best place to speak to them.'

'May I enquire as to the other members of the household?' I asked. 'Do not worry; I do not propose to interview them all.'

Her lips pursed again. 'Apart from servants, the household consists of myself and Mr Farintosh.' She looked at me with those dark eyes as if daring me to question her. 'Shall we get on?'

I took a deep breath and composed myself. I was not sure what I would encounter, but something told me that this matter was not quite as straightforward as Mrs Farintosh appeared to think. 'Yes,' I said. 'Let us get on.'

CHAPTER 14

'So you were in the kitchen all afternoon.'

'Yes,' said the parlourmaid, who according to my sheet was called Simmons. 'I was polishing the silver, as I always do on Tuesday afternoons. Cook was preparing dinner, Becky was in the scullery, and the footmen were popping in and out. When I had finished, Mr Edwards and I counted it back into the cupboard, and I remember that the clock struck six just as he closed the door. I hurried upstairs to wash and change; Mrs Farintosh doesn't like us to be in day dresses after six.'

'I see.' I sighed to myself. So far, the servants all had alibis. The cook-housekeeper had been in the kitchen, preserving pears then preparing dinner. Simmons had been with the cook. The butler, Edwards, had been interviewing the footmen in his room, since the head footman had recently left and he wished to promote an existing servant rather than bring in a newcomer. *At this rate, it will turn out that nobody did it.*

'Is that all, ma'am?' Simmons's enquiry was not curt but pleasant.

'Yes, that will do. Thank you for your time.'

'Shall I send Parsons in next? The lady's maid,' she added, for clarification.

'Yes please, but could you give me a few minutes first?' I picked up the cup of tea at my elbow and took a sip. It was lukewarm at best.

Simmons rose. 'I shall order fresh tea for you, ma'am, then send Parsons.' She curtsied and glided from the room, clearly a much better parlourmaid than I had ever been during my short time in domestic service.

A few minutes later, she brought a fresh tea tray and shortly afterwards, a pretty, petite maid entered. 'Simmons said you wished to see me, ma'am. Letty Parsons.'

I glanced down my list. *Parsons – lady's maid – five years' service.* 'Do take a seat.'

The maid looked apprehensive. 'I'm not sure I can be of much help, ma'am.'

I studied her for a few seconds. 'Why is that?'

Her hands twisted in her lap. 'Well, it was my half day, so I wasn't there.'

'Oh.' *Why didn't Mrs Farintosh mention that?* 'At what time did you leave the house?'

'I finished my work early, had some bread and cheese, got changed into my Sunday dress and hat, and left at almost one o'clock.'

'I see,' I said, making a note. 'Did anyone see you go?'

'Oh yes, I went through the kitchen. Cook was in there, of course, and Molly was having a cup of tea. She asked me to tell her whether they had any wide red ribbons at the Penny Bazaar.' She smiled. 'Molly is seventeen, and very fond of ribbons.'

I made a note. 'And Molly is…?'

'She is a housemaid, ma'am. Molly Seddon.'

'So you left at one o'clock. Do you remember seeing the tiara that morning?'

'Oh yes,' said Letty. 'I checked specially before I left, because lately my mistress has left her jewel case unlocked, as she did that day. So I locked it and took my key with me.'

'Excellent,' I said. 'When did you return?'

'I came back at half past six. Mrs Farintosh had said I might stay out until seven, as they were dining late.'

Another perfect alibi. 'And did you see any ribbons?'

For the first time, Letty Parsons looked uncomfortable. 'No, ma'am, I didn't.'

'Oh. Perhaps the Penny Bazaar was out of your way.'

'Yes,' she murmured.

'Did you have a nice half day?'

Letty buried her head in her hands and wailed. 'I knew this wasn't about the tiara! She's found me out, and she'll make an example of me!'

It was a few seconds before I recovered myself enough to come round the table and press my handkerchief into Letty's hand. 'I don't know what you mean, Letty.'

'No followers or – spooning, on pain of dismissal,' muttered Letty, and I understood.

'Has this been going on long?' I asked.

'I met Jim at the draper's,' she said, 'the one I always go to for Mrs Farintosh. He is the assistant there; he works for his father. We've been walking out for the last two years.'

'Did you go somewhere together, Letty?'

She nodded. 'He had the afternoon off too, so we went to the music hall.' She gazed at me, wide-eyed. 'It was wonderful.' She scrubbed her eyes with the handkerchief. 'Will you really not tell Mrs Farintosh?'

'I don't see why I should,' I said.

'Thank you,' she whispered. A pause. 'Do you want to ask me anything else?'

'Just one thing,' I said. 'Is Mrs Farintosh normally a careless sort of person?'

Letty's eyes widened again. 'No, not at all. But lately, she's seemed . . . preoccupied. I don't know why; she wouldn't tell me.'

I smiled; I doubted Mrs Farintosh would seek a confidante in Letty. 'That will do, Letty. Could you send in Molly next, please.'

Letty managed a wavering smile and left my handkerchief on the table in a crumpled ball.

A couple of minutes later there was a gentle tap at the door, and a face peeped round it. Molly Seddon's abundant brown hair escaped from under her cap in loose waves. She had a pink-and-white complexion which was rather more pink than white at the moment, possibly from nerves. Her blue eyes were fringed with long lashes, and her mouth was a little rosebud. Her hands, though, were as rough and red as any housemaid's. 'Letty said you wanted to see me, ma'am.'

'That's right, Molly. Do take a seat.'

Molly sat down and looked me straight in the eye. 'I know you'll think it's me,' she said, before I had the chance to ask a question.

I regarded her for a few seconds while considering how to reply. 'Why do you think that, Molly?'

'I was in Mrs Farintosh's boudoir practically all afternoon.' She shrugged, her mouth screwed up tight.

'I assume you were meant to be there,' I said.

'Yes, though I wished I wasn't.' Her nose wrinkled. 'We were clearing lunch when her bell rang, and as Letty had gone out it was my job to answer. So I went, and she had a big basket of stockings ready. "All these need mending," she said, "and I expect you to stay until they're done. You may have a cup of tea, then come up and get started."'

'Surely mending stockings is Letty's job.'

'It is,' said Molly, 'and I hate it. I'd rather scrub floors any day. But Letty was out, so it fell to me.'

I was sincerely sorry for her; I hated mending myself. 'How long did it take you?'

'Three and a half hours. The clock was right in front of me, ticking all the time. Some of the heels were practically out, you know. I swear she'd worn them to death.'

I thought of Mrs Farintosh's neat clothes and her pristine boudoir. 'So you went downstairs at about five.'

'I did, and Mary hadn't straightened the rooms, and there wasn't time to stop until dinner was over. Their dinner, I mean.'

'When you were upstairs in the boudoir, Molly, did you go into the bedroom? More specifically, did you go near the jewel case?'

Molly snorted. 'No fear. The bedroom is out of bounds

to everyone except Letty.' She giggled. 'And Mr Farintosh, I suppose.'

I considered my next question carefully. 'How do you get on with Mrs Farintosh normally, Molly? Is she a kind mistress?'

'She has been very kind,' said Molly. 'I first came when I was nine, as a scullery maid, and I missed my home – not that it was much of one. Cook caught me crying into the sink once and she must have said something. Mrs Farintosh came all the way to the scullery just to see me, and she told me things would get better, and that if anyone was unkind then I should tell her.' She smiled warmly, recollecting. 'Sometimes I found little things under my pillow: a spinning top, or a twist of sweets, and I never found out who put them there.' Then her smile faded. 'But when I moved up from under-housemaid two years ago, things changed. I do as I'm told, and I don't stop and talk to men when I'm running errands, or anything like that, but she gives me a hard look now when it was a soft one before.'

'I'm sure you're doing your best, Molly,' I said, studying her heart-shaped face. 'Molly, if I asked you to swear that you had nothing to do with the disappearance of this tiara, could you do it?'

'Of course I could. If you brought me a Bible I'd put my hand on it and swear just like that.' She laughed. 'What would I do with a tiara, wear it to scrub floors?'

'In that case,' I said, 'I have nothing more to ask.' Molly got up. 'Oh, one more thing. Could you tell me where I might find Mr Farintosh, if he is at home?'

'He's at home and he's in the study,' said Molly promptly. 'He rang earlier for someone to fetch his favourite briar pipe, then to find his newspaper.'

'Could you show me to the study, please?'

Molly's streamers and skirts flew as she whisked along the passage. I could barely keep up with her. She tapped at the study door and a deep voice called 'Come.' Molly opened the door, and I saw a cheerful man of perhaps thirty-five, with dark curly hair. He was sitting at his ease in an armchair, his feet on a footstool and a novel on his lap. He seemed rather pleased to see Molly.

'Mr Farintosh, sir, Mrs Hudson asked me to bring her to you.' Molly bobbed.

'Thank you, Molly, you may go.'

She bobbed again and withdrew, and I noted that Mr Farintosh's gaze followed her, instead of moving towards me.

Our interview was brief. He had been out on business then at his club on the day in question, returning just in time to dress for dinner. 'Don't ask me to tell you what the tiara looks like,' he said, with a smile. 'I must have seen it a hundred times, and I can't tell you a thing about it. Except that it's insured.'

'Was your wife distressed when she told you that the tiara was missing?'

He considered. 'No, if anything she seemed calm. I thought she might be in shock, but Diana bears things very well. I wanted to call a policeman at once, but she wouldn't hear of it. I don't know why not.' He frowned. 'She gets funny notions sometimes.'

'Have you been married long, Mr Farintosh?'

'Twelve years in July. Though I don't know what that has to do with your investigation.'

I rose. 'If you'll excuse me, Mr Farintosh, I shall take a walk to think over the case so far. I shall return within the hour.'

He looked astonished. 'Is that what a lady detective normally does?'

'I do not know,' I said, 'for I'm sure I never met one.'

CHAPTER 15

Luckily I knew Mayfair and the surrounding area, and found what I sought in ten minutes. The pawnbroker's shop was nestled in a maze of side streets which led into a less salubrious neighbourhood. I examined the window display, then entered.

A man in a grubby brown apron stepped out of the back room and came to the counter. 'Have you brought something for me to, um, value, ma'am?' He took in my smart clothes. 'Or perhaps you might be interested in viewing my stock. We have some lovely rings.'

'I am seeking an opal tiara,' I said. 'Would you happen to have one?'

The man looked wary.

'It is not a police matter,' I said. 'Or not yet. I do number various inspectors from Scotland Yard among my personal friends.'

'A woman came in a couple of days ago,' the shopkeeper said. 'She was wrapped in a big black cloak, with the hood pulled so far over her head that I could only see her mouth, and she shoved a bundle of hankies at me. I nearly fainted when I unwrapped it. "Take good care of it," she said, and snatched the ticket from my hand. She'd have forgotten the money, too, if I hadn't called her back. I'm nothing if not honest.' He gave me a triumphant look.

'I'm sure you are honest,' I said. 'Could she have disguised her voice?'

The man grinned. 'Worst Cockney accent I ever heard. Didn't match her cloak, which was super-fine. Her gloves were best-quality kid: the sort I could have sold on in a twinkling.'

'Where is the tiara?'

'In a safe deposit box at the bank,' he said. 'What do you take me for? I don't want no robberies.'

I took a crown from my purse and slid it across the counter. 'Thank you very much. You've been extremely helpful.' And with a considerably lighter heart, I made the return journey to Mrs Farintosh's house.

Ensconced in the morning room with yet more tea, I made short work of the rest of the servants, and was especially kind to Becky the scullery maid, who cried the whole time she was in the room and barely managed to choke out a word. I returned her to the care of the under-housemaid, and when I emerged into the hall, found Mrs Farintosh waiting for me. She stood there: composed, elegant, unshakable. 'Have you reached a conclusion?'

I studied her for a moment. I had expected to have a few minutes' solitude after the interviews to think things through. Then I remembered Mrs Farintosh's keenness to begin the case; she would not be satisfied until she had an explanation. I doubted my solution to the case would be what she wanted. However, I had decided when I took my first case that I would put helping my clients before everything else. And sometimes that meant telling them things they did not wish to hear.

'I have reached a conclusion, Mrs Farintosh.'

'Good.' Her expression was hard to read. On one hand she looked eager, on the other, slightly apprehensive. 'Should we summon the servants?' She eyed the nearest bell.

'That will not be necessary at this stage,' I said. 'I would prefer to share my conclusions with you first, Mrs Farintosh.'

'Yes, of course. Perhaps we should go to my boudoir.' She led the way upstairs. 'Shall I ring for tea?'

'Not on my account, thank you,' I said. Truly, I did not think I could manage another cup of tea for anything.

We settled in armchairs in front of the fire. 'So,' said Mrs Farintosh, making a steeple of her fingers rather as Sherlock did. 'What is your conclusion, Mrs Hudson?'

'The first thing to note,' I said, 'is that most of the servants have perfect alibis, since they were working together. Your lady's maid, Letty Parsons, is the obvious suspect, as she has a key to your jewel case—'

'No!' cried Mrs Farintosh, her eyebrows drawn together.

'But she left the house at one o'clock,' I continued, 'and I know from you that the tiara was still there at half past one. Obviously Parsons had nothing to do with it, since she was out all afternoon.'

Mrs Farintosh visibly relaxed. 'Yes, that is correct. Parsons is innocent.'

'Having ruled out Parsons, the next obvious person to look at is Molly Seddon, your housemaid. She was mending stockings in this room for most of the afternoon, alone and unsupervised.'

'Yes,' said Mrs Farintosh, leaning forward slightly. 'She was.'

'She had the perfect opportunity.' I smiled. 'All she had to do was go into your bedroom next door, take the tiara from the unlocked case, hide it about her person, then slip out of the house and obtain money for it.'

'Indeed,' said Mrs Farintosh. 'It seems obvious.'

I paused. 'May I ask whether Molly Seddon is the person you suspect?'

Mrs Farintosh smiled. 'You may.' Then her face became serious. 'It is a sad business; she is so young, and I daresay it was a foolish impulse. Perhaps I should not have trusted her alone in here, but she has been with us so long that the thought never entered my head.'

I leaned my chin on my hand. 'What course do you wish to take?'

Mrs Farintosh was silent for perhaps a minute, but her face was calm and untroubled. 'The best thing to do,' she said at last, 'is to ask her to leave. I could demote her to kitchen maid, I suppose, and she would be below stairs and away from temptation, but I would never be easy in my mind. No, I shall ask Cook to write her a brief character relating to her service as a scullery maid and under-housemaid, which was very good, and she may obtain a post elsewhere.' She sighed. 'I do not think it would do anyone any good to have her arrested, and no doubt the tiara is far away by now, if it has not been melted down.'

'A most practical solution,' I said.

Mrs Farintosh acknowledged my compliment with a smile.

'How odd that Molly was in your boudoir, though,' I said. 'Surely it would be your maid's job to mend your stockings, and there was a whole basket of them.' I paused. 'Almost as if you had been saving them up.'

'I don't know what you mean,' said Mrs Farintosh. 'That sounds as if you think I was punishing the girl.'

'It does, rather,' I replied. 'Molly saw it in that light, too. One of the things she told me was how kind you had been when she was a little girl, and that now she didn't seem to be able to do anything right.'

'She was a perfectly good housemaid,' said Mrs Farintosh. 'I had no complaints, until this happened.'

'That is the problem, isn't it?'

Mrs Farintosh stared at me. 'I beg your pardon?'

'That homesick little girl has become an attractive young woman. She is hardworking and diligent – perhaps a tiny bit rebellious, as girls can be at that age – but as yet she has no idea of the power she could hold over men.' I paused. 'I understand you forbid your maids from spooning or having followers.'

'Yes, I do,' Mrs Farintosh snapped. 'Mooning about, sneaking off, giggling in corners…'

'So none of them may ever marry, because you do not approve.'

'It isn't like that,' she said. 'Please come to the point, Mrs Hudson. If there is one.'

I found myself gripping the armrests of my chair, and put my hands in my lap. 'Very well, Mrs Farintosh. Here is my solution. Firstly, allow your maids to have followers within reason, and to walk out with men during their days off, if they wish. Then they will find a release for their bottled-up feelings, and be less likely to succumb to temptation closer to home. I trust you understand me.' I looked her straight in the eyes. She held my gaze for a moment, then looked away.

'Your other task, Mrs Farintosh, is to search carefully amongst your things.'

'But the tiara has always been kept in my jewel case—'

'I do not want you to search for the tiara, Mrs Farintosh. You must search for the pawnbroker's ticket.'

She gasped, and put a hand to her throat.

'Go to the pawnbroker's shop, reclaim the tiara, announce that there has been a mistake, and put this behind you.' I was startled by the force of my speech, but my feelings were entirely genuine. Mrs Farintosh might be my client, but I had the interests of the whole household at heart.

I gathered myself for a final effort. 'I doubt this is the advice you wish to hear, Mrs Farintosh, but you need to hear it. Do not let jealousy, suspicion, or resentment get the better of you. Perhaps you do not have everything you desire, but behaviour such as this may mean that you lose what you *do* have. At present, I am confident that you have your husband's affection.' Mrs Farintosh bit her lip. 'I have no doubt you thought you were acting for the best, but if you had followed through on your plan to frame Molly

111

Seddon it would have come back to haunt you. At the very least.'

Mrs Farintosh swallowed. When she spoke, her voice was hoarse. 'Don't tell Edwin,' she said. 'Please. I'll double your fee. I'll do anything—'

'What I want you to do, Mrs Farintosh, is be kind to your servants. You have their loyalty, and they deserve your respect.' And with that, I rose to take my leave. I felt for the woman who had comforted little Molly Seddon, and who, perhaps, had hoped for children of her own, but I could not condone her actions. I might seem much closer to Mrs Farintosh in my appearance and manner, but my heart and my sympathies were with the staff who lived under her rule.

CHAPTER 16

I looked at the notes in my hand. 'I can't possibly take this. It's far too much.'

'Take it. Please.' Mrs Farintosh took a step back. 'I give it to you willingly, but there is one condition.'

'And that is?' I hardly needed to ask.

'That you don't breathe a word of this to anybody. You may mention that I was a client of yours – and I shall willingly recommend you as an excellent and reliable detective – but if you tell anyone…' She put her face in her hands. 'I shall kill myself.'

'It is not so very bad.' I took a step towards her and she flung out a hand.

'No! Don't come near me. What I did was wrong, and I'm ashamed. I am ashamed that you know, and the thought that anyone else would learn of it…' Her lips trembled. 'I am buying your silence, which probably makes me even worse. What else is money for? It doesn't buy happiness, Mrs Hudson.'

'I am sorry,' I said. 'I did not wish to distress you, simply to protect your household. I cannot take all this.' She had given me ten pounds. I doubted little Becky made much more than that in a year for slaving in the scullery sink. I counted out five pound notes and put them on a nearby table before I changed my mind.

'I can well afford it,' said Mrs Farintosh. 'Some lessons come at a higher price than others.' Then I understood that she wanted me to take the money; it was a punishment for herself, not a reward for me.

'As you said, Mrs Farintosh, you can well afford it. I suggest that you give the money to a charitable cause, or better still, buy home comforts for your servants.'

She studied the floor for perhaps half a minute, then met my eyes. 'Remember, Mrs Hudson, not a word.' Still watching me, she rang the bell. 'Mrs Hudson is just leaving,' she said, when Parsons appeared. 'Would you mind showing her out, please. Then I have a call to make, so I shall need you to help me dress.'

'But lunch is in fifteen minutes, ma'am,' said Parsons, with a slight frown.

'Then I shall have mine on a tray when I return. I shan't be long. Please apologise to Mr Farintosh for me.'

I followed Parsons downstairs to the front door. I could tell that she wanted to ask me what had happened, but professionalism forbade her. 'I hope it went well, ma'am,' was all she said.

'Goodbye, and thank you for your time.' And as the door closed I wondered if I would ever encounter such a case again, or such a woman.

Once I was clear of the house I looked at my watch: a quarter to one. I had asked for our lunch to be later that day, partly so that Sherlock might have a chance of

114

developing an appetite for it, and partly so that I would be home in time. A branch of my bank was no more than five minutes' walk away. I thought of the five pounds burning a hole in my purse, and began walking.

Ten minutes later, I left the bank feeling lighter both of purse and of heart. But what to do now? I still had time to spare. I smiled, and turned my steps towards Debenham and Freebody.

'Good afternoon, Mrs H,' said Alf, giving me an approving glance. 'You're very smart today.'

'Why, thank you. I have been out on business, and decided to call in on my way home.' He held the door open for me, and I wandered into the store.

I felt like buying something, but I was not sure what. Then I caught sight of a counter draped with neckties and cravats. I had everything I wanted, but a gift for Sherlock might cheer him after his difficult evening – and, more than likely, a morning of indisposition. I approached the display and spent some time choosing a necktie he would wear in his own person, and which might also suit his disguise as a wealthy man about town. In the end I settled on a tie of sky-blue silk patterned with small navy diamonds.

'That's nice,' said Frances as she took it from me. 'Is it a present for Mr Hudson?'

'In a manner of speaking, yes.' I watched her make a parcel. 'Is Evie in today?'

Frances looked around, then leaned forward. 'She's in, but she spent half the morning in the stockroom, counting everything up and checking it. She volunteered because she can sit down.' She handed me the parcel and took my money.

I put the small package into my bag. 'Thank you, Frances.' But Frances was looking not at me, but over my shoulder. 'Is everything all right?' I asked, for her face wore a puzzled expression.

'Oh yes,' she said. 'I thought I saw a customer, but I must have been mistaken.'

I gazed in that direction, but saw no one. A thought occurred to me. 'Have you seen any more of the golden-haired shopper who likes gloves?'

'Not since she came in and bought a pair. I think she's finally got what she wanted.'

I grinned. 'A satisfied customer, then. I'll see you next week.'

I left the shop and turned towards home, my smart heeled boots clicking on the paving stones. *A good morning's work*, I thought to myself. *I have earned my lunch.*

The streets were comparatively quiet; perhaps everyone was eating lunch, at a restaurant or at home. Then I heard an odd sound, like a pair of hobnailed boots with one boot louder than the other. *Clack*-click. For some reason, it made the hairs on the back of my neck stand up. I moved to the kerb, on the pretence of crossing the road, and glanced behind me, but saw no one whose appearance corresponded with that noise. I crossed the road, and continued on my way. *Just a silly fancy.*

But a couple of minutes later, there it was again. *Clack*-click. *Clack*-click. I could not look round: then whoever it was would know I had seen them.

It's broad daylight, I told myself. *You're imagining things.* I stepped into a side street, out of my way, and after a slight pause, *clack*-click, *clack*-click.

It could be a coincidence. It's only a person with one odd boot, walking the same way as you. I turned right, then right again to return to the main road. I kept my pace steady, brisk rather than unhurried, and still the *clack*-click, *clack*-click followed me.

Don't run. I kept walking, and was rewarded after a minute or two with the sign for an underground railway station. I took a ticket and went to the platform. When the next train came I got straight on, then jumped off just before the doors closed. No one else left the train, and I watched it pull away with a sense of relief.

I went to the opposite platform, took the next train, changed to a different line at the next opportunity, and disembarked at the station closest to Baker Street. I ran up the steps, listening all the while, but I did not hear that odd, uneven gait. I should have felt safe, but I did not. I emerged into the street and went to the cab rank, promising the driver double his fare if he would drive like the wind. The destination I gave him was not Baker Street, but a road perhaps a quarter of a mile away. The cab driver was almost certainly trustworthy, but what if I had not shaken off my pursuer with the odd boots, and they had handed the chase to someone else? They could easily have followed the cab.

Eventually we reached my supposed destination. I had my money ready, jumped down and handed it over, and to his credit the cabbie was away at once, keen to earn his next fare. No other cab was near.

The address I had given was next to an alley which led into a maze of other alleys and passages: eventually, it would take me home. I picked up my skirts, cursed my fashionable boots, and hurried in, slipping on the damp, uneven cobbles.

Once I was fairly in I stopped and listened for the *clack-click* of my sometime pursuer, but there was silence. I sighed out a breath, and carried on. When I was but a minute from home I stopped and listened again, but the alleys were quiet. *It is now or never*, I thought, and plunged on until I found myself hammering at my own back door. I remembered a time around a year ago when I had made the same journey, petrified that I would be taken up and arrested – or worse – before I could reach safety. I had been dressed somewhat differently, but my heart pounded just as it had then.

After what seemed an age, a key rattled in the lock and Billy pulled the door open. 'What do you— Oh.' He stared at me. 'Why have you—'

'Let me in and lock the door,' I muttered, stepping forward, and Billy moved back to admit me. The kitchen was the same as ever, and as I took in the well-scrubbed table, the bright pans, and the smell of cooking, the thought of what might have happened overcame me. I made for the table and sank into the nearest chair, shaking. The room was beginning to spin. I put my head in my hands, closed my eyes and took deep, slow breaths until the feeling subsided.

'What has happened, ma'am? Are you all right? We thought it was odd that you weren't home for lunch.'

'What time is it?' I consulted my watch and answered my own question: almost two o'clock. I had spent an hour dodging my shadow.

'Martha waited lunch for a quarter of an hour, ma'am; she's just gone to see if Mr Holmes has finished. You could still go up.' I raised my head and saw Billy's anxious face. 'Or – or you could have it on a tray in your room, if you'd rather.'

'Thank you, Billy. I'll go up.' I swallowed, then rose slowly. I ascended the kitchen stairs, gripping the handrail as if I might be washed away.

Was someone following me?

Did I shake them off?

Do they know where I live?

I clenched my teeth: no good could come of such thoughts. I gained the hall and ran the fingers of my right hand along the wall as I made my way to the dining room, as if losing contact with the house would catapult me outside.

Don't be so ridiculous, Nell.

I took a final deep breath as I arrived at the dining-room door, lifted my chin, and entered.

119

CHAPTER 17

As I came into the room, Martha's eyebrows drew together slightly. 'Ma'am, you have time to get changed before you have lunch. I will go downstairs and fetch your plate from the oven.'

I looked at Sherlock, who was absorbed in a copy of the *Financial Times*. 'Thank you, Martha. I shall go and change, then.' I knew her suggestion was not out of any solicitude for me, but because she disliked waiting on me when I wore any form of disguise. Then again, perhaps I would feel more myself when I was not dressed as someone else. 'I shall not be long.' As I turned to leave the room, Sherlock's head lifted, but I was fairly on my way.

I hurried upstairs, removed my wig and stocking cap, cleaned off the slightly darker eyebrows I had assumed to match the wig, and did my hair in a simple plaited bun. It had grown considerably since its shearing the previous year, but its tendency to curl remained, making it more difficult to tame than it had been previously. Five minutes later, I re-entered the dining room.

This time Sherlock looked up. 'Good afternoon, Nell. How was your morning?'

I was about to reply when Martha re-entered with my plate. 'It is corned beef hash today, ma'am.' She went to the sideboard and retrieved a covered dish. 'Shall I serve?'

'Don't worry, Martha, I can serve myself.' She nodded but did not withdraw, moving to the window to adjust the curtains. Suppressing a sigh, I went to the sideboard with my plate. As I passed Sherlock, I noted that his food was untouched. 'The newspaper must be interesting today,' I remarked.

He tore himself away from it. 'I am following the stocks of the various businesses in which Humphrey Montagu has an interest,' he said. 'I would have done it earlier, but my brain was not in the best shape.'

I served myself a large portion, glanced at Martha, and sat down. 'No riddles in the post today?' I knew there could not have been, but I couldn't help asking.

'No, no more riddles,' he replied, immersed in the newspaper. I could feel my certainty ebbing away the longer I waited.

Suddenly, he glanced up. 'So, how was the case?'

I stopped pushing food around my plate. 'It is resolved.'

He smiled. 'What is resolved?'

I remembered the fear in Mrs Farintosh's eyes. 'I cannot give specifics, but something which was missing has been found.'

The corner of Sherlock's mouth moved up still further. 'That is cryptic, Nell.' He broke into a grin. 'Have you been sworn to secrecy?'

I gave Martha's back a look which she must have felt, since she stopped fiddling with the curtain and left the room. 'As a matter of fact, I have,' I said. 'But I am more concerned about what happened afterwards. I think I was followed.'

Sherlock put the paper down and stared at me. 'Followed? By whom?'

Now I had his full attention. 'I don't know: I didn't see. But I heard an odd noise, like a pair of uneven boots, and when I took a diversion, it continued. I went to the nearest tube station and managed to lose them there.' I sighed. 'At least, I think I did. The boots stopped.'

Sherlock frowned. 'You didn't come straight home, did you?'

'Of course not,' I said, shortly. 'I took two tube trains, then a cab, and made my way to the back door via the alleys.'

'Good.' He picked up his fork. 'But why would someone follow you? You were in disguise. It is not as if someone would be watching for a person fitting your description.'

'I don't know why, either,' I said. 'But I was followed after I left the department store. I'm certain of it.'

Sherlock scooped up a forkful of corned beef hash and meditated as he ate. 'Well, I do not think there is much you can do but be careful.' He considered. 'It is probably a coincidence. You didn't see anyone.'

'I heard them!' It was all I could do not to bang my fist on the table. Tears sprang to my eyes and I blinked them back, hard.

'Then maybe there is something in it,' Sherlock said, looking rather worried. 'Did you see the telegram for you on the tray?'

I ran my hands through my fringe, glad that the wig was off. 'No, I didn't. Thank you.' I went to the hall and retrieved it, then sat down and opened it. 'It is from Mr Poskitt,' I said. 'He asks whether I can visit the Stanleys for lunch tomorrow.' I let the telegram fall on the table and put my head in my hands. 'Today, of all days…'

A chair scraped, and Sherlock's arm encircled my shoulders. 'You will go, won't you?'

'I don't know,' I said miserably. 'I agreed, and I have been paid my fee already, but—'

'Then you should go,' Sherlock said gently. 'I know you are worried, but you can paint yourself an inch thick and travel by cab the whole way, if that makes you feel safer.' I almost managed to smile at the thought of myself disguised as heaven knows what and travelling in state.

Sherlock moved a chair to sit beside me and took my hands. 'You have had a scare, Nell, but the longer you leave going out, the worse it will be.' He stroked my thumbs with his. 'Do you remember how it was when you came back from – from Chambers Hall?'

I closed my eyes, and a shiver ran through me. I recalled the first day I had stepped out of the house into London bustle, and how overwhelmed and distressed I had felt after being shut away in a country house for so long. Slowly, I let out a breath. 'You are right. I cannot stay in the house for ever.' I reached for my fork. 'I just wish it had not been tomorrow.'

Sherlock smiled. 'You are a detective in demand, Nell,' he said, and patted my shoulder. 'Your clients need you.'

He returned to his place opposite me.

'What of your clients?' I asked. 'Will you be waiting on Humphrey Montagu again tonight?'

Sherlock, chewing, shook his head. 'I shall let him socialise in peace this evening; Wiggins and his associates may take the lead.' He grimaced. 'Apart from anything else, my liver will thank me.'

Once I had replied in the affirmative to Mr Poskitt's wire and sent Billy to the telegraph office, I busied myself with domestic tasks for the rest of the day. I planned menus for the next few weeks and submitted them to Martha, then took an inventory of the linen cupboard and noted what needed replacing. Finally, I looked in my own drawer and made a small pile of stockings to darn. *I can work on them an hour at a time. But perhaps not today.*

Dr Watson arrived home earlier than usual that evening, and seemed in a much better mood at dinner. He was most interested that I would be visiting the Stanleys the next day, and was full of questions I might ask and observations on the probable health of Emmett Stanley. 'I wish I could accompany you and provide my medical opinion,' he said, spooning an extra potato onto his plate. 'Alas, work will not permit.'

'We are all busy,' I said. I was a little put out that Dr Watson was casual in his manner towards me. However, I had not mentioned my suspicion of being followed that day. Dr Watson was always solicitous of my safety – much more so than of Sherlock's – and he would have counselled me to put the meeting off or decline the assignment. Having escaped from Inspector Lestrade's idea of suitable constraints for a woman in potential danger, I had no mind to submit myself to Dr Watson's notion of the same. *I am perfectly capable of looking after myself*, I thought, cutting a neat piece of Dover sole.

At the end of dinner, Sherlock announced his intention of retiring to his consulting room. 'I have research to do,' he said, 'and I may as well do it while I am unencumbered by other commitments.'

I imagined him dressed in what I called his Criterion outfit, and smiled. 'That reminds me: I have something for you. I bought it today.'

'Something for me?' His brow furrowed. 'You will have to reveal the mystery.'

'It is still in my bag upstairs,' I said, 'if you would care to join me for a few minutes.'

'I shall read through my notes of the Stanley case,' said Dr Watson. 'If I come across anything of use, I shall make a note of it for you.' He pushed his chair back and left the room. Sherlock and I exchanged amused glances, then went upstairs together.

I had left my bag on the dressing table. I extracted the neat parcel Frances had made and handed it over. 'I saw it, and thought it would suit you.'

He took the parcel and looked at it with that same half-pleased, half-puzzled air. 'But it is not my birthday.'

'Presents aren't just for birthdays. Come on, Sherlock, open it.'

He undid the string and folded back the tissue paper. 'A necktie!' He smiled. 'Thank you, Nell.'

'I hoped you would like it,' I said. 'It might be suitable

for the Criterion, too.'

'Oh, most definitely.' He pulled off the tie he was wearing, then, bending to see in the mirror, knotted the silk around his neck. 'There. What do you think?'

I turned him towards me and adjusted the tie slightly so that it lay straight. 'On reflection, it suits you far better than the fool who frequents the Criterion. Perhaps you should not let him wear it. I suspect he will only spill whisky down it.'

'Perhaps you are right.' He inspected my dress. 'If I may say so, that dress is far too nice to be wasted on clients who insist that their cases remain private.'

'That's hardly fair—'

Sherlock put his finger on my lips, then bent and kissed me. 'Perhaps we should both remove all our fine garments and save them for best.'

'Perhaps we should,' I murmured. I worked the knot of his tie undone, and the silk slithered away.

Sherlock put his arms round me. 'Now I am stripped of my smart attire, I should do you the same service.' He began to kiss me, and with every kiss another button loosened, until my dress joined his necktie in a heap on the floor.

CHAPTER 18

At breakfast Dr Watson handed me some closely written pages. 'I have summarised the salient points and added questions you could ask.' His eyes met mine. 'I hope you find it useful.'

'I am sure I shall. Thank you, John.'

'No trouble at all,' he said, rather gruffly. 'When do you leave for Ealing?'

'I have plenty of time. Lunch is at one, and Mr Poskitt advised that I arrive at noon, so that I may speak with Mrs Stanley first.'

'Ah, very wise. Very wise.' Dr Watson wiped his mouth with his napkin. 'I must be off; it promises to be a busy day. I shall see you both later.' He halted at the door. 'A wire will find me at the hospital, if necessary.'

'I shall bear it in mind,' I said, and he left.

I buttered another piece of toast, then turned my attention to Dr Watson's papers. He had summarised the events of the case, as far as we knew them. On another page were his recollections of Emmett Stanley's state of health at their last meeting, with suggestions for modifying his anxiety, and finally a list of questions on topics relating to the case.

'It appears you have an assistant,' remarked Sherlock. His tone was light, but when I glanced up he looked rather put out.

'At present, yes. I am sure that when Dr Watson can help you, he will be happy to assist.'

'We shall see.' Sherlock reached out with his fork and speared a rasher of bacon from the dish. 'Anyway, enough of him. Who will you be for your trip to Ealing?'

I ate perhaps half my slice of toast before responding. 'I shall go as I am.'

Sherlock's eyebrows drew together. 'Why, Nell, after yesterday? Surely it would be safer to—'

'Perhaps. Or perhaps not.' I took another bite of toast. 'I have deceived Mrs Stanley twice, and I do not wish to do it again.'

I had woken early that morning, the question of what to wear and what to do repeating itself in my head. I could follow Sherlock's half-serious advice and make myself appear completely different, but such a disguise was unlikely to deceive the Stanleys at close quarters, and might imperil the success of my visit. And different clothes and hair had not stopped my pursuer yesterday.

'At least take a cab,' said Sherlock. 'Watson would agree with me if he knew what had happened yesterday.'

'Yesterday you thought I was imagining things.'

'And have you changed your mind since yesterday, when you were sure someone was following you?'

We gazed at each other in silence, neither willing to look away and give the appearance of conceding. 'The tube station is a short walk from here,' I said. 'I doubt anyone will manage to kidnap me. I shall take a cab at Ealing.'

Sherlock finished his bacon, then rose and kissed the top of my head. 'There is no point in trying to persuade you once your mind is made up. Please, be careful.'

'I shall.' I kissed him and he smiled at me, but I saw the worry behind that smile.

And now I was on my second tube train, and approaching Ealing. I had brought Dr Watson's questions with me, but I planned to let the Stanleys talk and see what arose. Mr Poskitt had chosen me because I was not a policeman or a conventional detective, and I did not wish to betray his trust.

My stop approached and I got up. I was the only passenger to leave the train, which pleased me. I could not deny that the short walk to Baker Street station had seemed filled with monsters on every side. It had been all I could do not to run, but somehow I had managed it and taken a ticket without giving the impression that I was out of my wits. *Perhaps it was a coincidence*, I thought, as I gave my ticket to the platform attendant.

I passed through the gate, and a coachman stepped forward. 'Mrs Hudson? I have been sent to collect you.' I looked closer and recognised Mrs Stanley's footman, John, whom I had met briefly before. *There is nothing to worry about.*

He led me to a light gig, rather than the closed carriage I had expected, and soon we were bowling along the street. We arrived at gates I recognised, and made our way down the sweeping drive to the manor house I remembered, though the grounds were less neatly kept. When we entered the house, things were different again. The grandeur of the huge hall had been softened with bright rugs scattered over the marble floor, and there were fewer paintings than before.

The butler came forward. 'Mrs Hudson? I shall take you to Mrs Stanley.' He did not show me into the parlour, but a cosy sitting room. Sofas and chairs were scattered with cushions and afghans, the walls were lined with bookshelves, and Mrs Stanley herself was engaged in knitting what looked like a sock.

She stood up at my entrance. 'I'm very pleased to meet you, Mrs Hudson,' she said, putting down her knitting and giving me her hand. 'Thank you for coming all the way out here.'

'It was no trouble,' I said. 'I travelled on the underground, and it was a pleasant journey.'

Mrs Stanley made a moue. 'Oh, I hate the tube,' she said. 'I know I should embrace the modern world, but I do not wish to sit crammed together with it.' She laughed. 'But you have not come to listen to my moaning. I understand you are here to speak to Emmett.'

'And to you,' I said hastily, since Mrs Stanley looked as if she might summon him then and there. 'I am sure your recollections will be extremely valuable, especially of those times when Mr Stanley was less able to appreciate what was happening.'

'That's putting it mildly,' said Mrs Stanley. 'He is much better now, and quite chatty when he is in the mood, but there were days when I doubted he would ever speak again.' She fiddled with her cuff. 'Anyway,' she said brightly. 'You have come a long way. Would you like a cup of tea?'

I assented, and soon we were making small talk as if I were a new acquaintance paying a call, which in a way I was. I was taking a sip of my tea when I noticed Mrs Stanley regarding me curiously. 'Excuse me for asking, Mrs Hudson, but have we met before? You seem familiar.'

I had wondered what I would do if Effie Stanley recognised me, but her question still took me by surprise. I had arrived at the house determined not to lie, but could I reveal that I was the person who had begun this whole sorry chain of events?

I met her eyes. 'Perhaps we have met briefly at a social function. One meets so many people.'

Her face cleared, and she laughed. 'You are right, it will be something of that kind.' Then she looked thoughtful. 'Normally I have a good memory. Perhaps it is advancing age.'

I smiled. 'I know you are not one of my clients.'

Effie Stanley giggled. 'That must be so interesting. What is it like being a lady detective? Do you have to follow people? Have you ever arrested anyone?' Her eyes sparkled with mischief, and more than ever I was glad that I could meet her as myself, more or less.

Eventually the gong sounded and we went through to the dining room, where Emmett Stanley joined us. He was plumper than I remembered, but seemed younger. The lines of tension and worry which had seemed etched on his face had faded, and he was simply dressed in a loose shirt with a cravat at his neck. Mrs Stanley, likewise, was wearing a day dress of burgundy cotton. If anything, I was overdressed.

The butler served a simple lunch of potted-shrimp salad followed by a fruit tart with cream, nothing like the grand meal I had expected. 'We live quietly,' remarked Effie Stanley, putting her spoon and fork together on the plate. 'Now that Emmett has retired from business, we would rather be comfortable than impressive.' I smiled to myself: Mr Stanley's business had been fraud. It was hard to imagine the meek, quiet man in front of me as a master criminal.

'I believe you want to talk to me about what happened when I was kidnapped,' said Mr Stanley suddenly. 'I don't mind, but perhaps we should do it without Effie. It does upset her so.'

'Well, obviously,' said Effie. 'I didn't know if you were alive or dead.'

'Neither did I, much of the time,' her husband replied.

Mrs Stanley rose with a show of reluctance, but was not slow in whisking out of the room.

Emmett Stanley turned to me. 'This will not take long, Mrs Hudson, for much of my brain refuses to think of those times. Mostly I was tied up alone in a dark room. On the few occasions when I was taken from it I was hooded, so I cannot describe the people who kidnapped me.' He shrugged. 'The worst part was that I knew nothing. I could not have given them any useful information if I had wanted to. I considered inventing something, but what if they knew it to be false? No doubt they would have carried out their threats then and there.'

'You may not have seen them, but do you remember anything about their voices?'

'There were two men and a woman,' he replied immediately. 'One man had a low, rumbling sort of voice, and his speech had a Cockney intonation. I think he was a servant of some kind. The other man's voice was high and harsh, and he was well spoken. They asked me the same questions over and over again. Sometimes they threatened to kill me if I could not answer them. The woman was the worst, though; I dreaded hearing her voice.'

'What sort of things did she ask you?'

His face clouded. 'She asked me no questions. Instead she described, in great detail, the things that they would do to me because I would not give them what they wanted. She always smelt of the same perfume, and sometimes she would lift my hood enough to press a cloth scented with it over my nose and mouth. "This is jasmine," she would whisper. "Learn to fear it." And then she would talk of the weather as if we were acquaintances who had met in the street.' He put a hand to his brow.

'I'm sorry to bring back these memories, Mr Stanley,' I said. 'Could I perhaps ask one more question?'

He sighed. 'One more.'

'What exactly did they ask you?'

He shook his head. 'That was the strangest part. It was nothing exact, only questions like "What do you know? Who told you? How did you find out?" I racked my brain for knowledge, and tried everything I could think of, but none of it was right. In the end, as far as I could think straight, I concluded that they were trying to drive me insane.' He gave me a rueful smile. 'For a time, I believe they succeeded.'

'Thank you—'

We both looked up as Effie Stanley re-entered the room, and I saw immediately that she had changed. Her face, so open and friendly earlier, was a closed mask. 'Emmett, you must be tired with all this talking. Why don't you go and rest? Otherwise you will be fit for nothing.'

Mr Stanley gave his wife a surprised glance, but rose meekly to his feet. 'As you wish, my dear.'

Once he had left the room, Mrs Stanley turned to me. 'I hope your conversation was useful, Mrs Hudson,' she said. 'However, you must return to London now, before it gets late. I have spoken to John, and he will have the carriage ready in a few minutes.'

'That is kind of you, Mrs Stanley,' I said, after a pause. 'I do sympathise with Mr Stanley's suffering, and of course you have suffered too.'

'I have,' she said. 'When he lapsed into convulsions at the slightest word, I feared the man I had married would never come back. And in some respects, I was to blame.'

She looked me in the eyes and my heart beat faster. 'I am sure that is not the case, Mrs Stanley,' I said. 'Mr Stanley determined his own actions.'

'He did. But he relied on me for help, and I failed him.' Again, that direct look.

I fought the urge to wriggle under her gaze. 'If you don't mind, I shall wait outside for the carriage,' I said. 'It is good weather.'

'Or an ill wind,' she replied. 'Goodbye, Mrs Hudson.' And this time she did not offer her hand.

How did she know? The words rang in my head all the way to the station, and throughout my train journey home. What had betrayed me? A mannerism, a phrase, an expression?

The train arrived at Baker Street and I disembarked, my head still full of questions. I sighed. I had spoken to Emmett Stanley and discovered there was little to learn, and in that respect I had done my duty. *It would have made no difference if you had gone in disguise, Nell*, I told myself. *You will never know what made her recognise you.* Shaking my head, I climbed the steps to the street and turned in the direction of home.

'Excuse me!' called a deep male voice behind me. I considered looking round, but who would seek me out?

'Nell!'

I froze. I knew that voice only too well: a voice I had never thought I would hear again. Footsteps approached me, but I could not turn. I could not do it.

'At last.' I felt a hand on my arm, and looked into the face of my husband, Jack Villiers.

CHAPTER 19

'It's me, Nell,' he said, as if I wouldn't recognise him. 'Jack.'

'I know it is,' I muttered. I took him in. He wore a smart new overcoat and a hat to match. His face was thinner than I remembered, and burnt browner than it could ever have been by an English sun, but he appeared well.

'Is that all you're going to say?' he asked, with a smile.

I thought of all the things I could say. *Why were you so stupid? Why did you marry somebody else? Why have you come back?* But those questions would reveal that I knew what had happened, and in doing that I might reveal things about myself that I did not wish him to know. I looked up at him. 'I would rather not talk in the street.'

'No, of course not,' said Jack. 'I thought we could perhaps – I don't know where you live, but—'

'I would like some tea,' I said. 'I know a place nearby.' Without waiting for his response, I walked to an expensive tearoom which I never usually patronised. So much the better. The last thing I wanted was to take Jack to a place where I was known.

We sat down at a table. 'This is nice,' he said, taking off his hat and stretching his legs. 'It may surprise you, but it is a while since I had an English afternoon tea.'

A waitress approached. 'May I take your order?'

'Just a pot of tea for me, please,' I said. 'Nothing else.'

'Do you mind if I have something to eat, Nell?' asked Jack. 'I have been waiting for some time.' He addressed the waitress. 'Tea for me too, and a Welsh rarebit, please.'

The waitress repeated the order and hurried away.

'So, won't you ask me?' Jack said, looking rather amused.

'What do you wish me to ask you?' I pulled at a finger of my glove, then stopped. If I took off my gloves, he would see that the ring I wore was not his.

'I am glad you are managing well,' said Jack. 'You would hardly come to this sort of place otherwise.' His eyes moved over me, taking in my hat, my jacket, my dress, and I wanted to swat him away like a fly.

'I get by,' I replied.

'I looked for you in Clerkenwell,' he said. 'I didn't think you would have moved.'

'I had to give up the house in Clerkenwell when you went missing.' My jaw clenched.

He had the grace to flinch. 'I'm sorry about that. I didn't know—'

'You didn't think,' I snapped.

'It wasn't my fault!' All conversation in the room ceased, and I felt people's eyes on us. Someone tittered.

'Very well,' I said. I leaned across the table and lowered my voice. 'Tell me what happened. Tell me why you

137

disappeared for four years and never sent a word.'

He swallowed, and redness crept up his neck. 'It was a misunderstanding,' he said. 'A terrible misunderstanding. But it is over.'

The waitress brought a tray, set out the tea things, and left before we could embarrass her.

I inspected the tea in my pot, stirred it and poured myself a cup. 'So, what happened?' I added milk to my cup, and waited.

Jack looked at his cup then at me; he was waiting for me to pour his tea. I remained still. 'I will not speak of the details,' he said. 'Certainly not in public. I became aware six months ago that things were – not as I had thought, and immediately took steps to return and seek you out.'

I sipped my tea and set it down. 'Return from where?'

He met my eyes. 'I was in Tasmania. It's an island south of Australia—'

'I know where it is.' I knew all too well; and in consequence, I had thought I was safe.

'I bumped into an old policeman colleague in Hobart. As you may imagine, he was surprised to see me, and shared the rumours he had heard about Napper Jenkins. Including the circumstances surrounding his death.' He poured his own tea and put in two sugars. 'Once I realised the mistake I had been labouring under, I resolved to return home as soon as I could.'

'Did you have nothing to keep you in Tasmania?' I closed my eyes for a moment, remembering the announcements I had read in the *Mercury* newspaper. Of a birth, and a wedding.

Jack studied the tablecloth. Then he looked up at me, and I saw the pain in his eyes. 'Until recently, I did. But there was an outbreak of typhoid fever, and…' He closed his eyes and pinched the bridge of his nose. 'All you need to know at this time is that I hired a manager to oversee my business. Once I was satisfied he could take care of things, I booked my passage home.'

I longed to shout at him, to push my chair back and say that I never wanted to see him again. But in the face of his misery, I could not. Clearly Jack believed he was acting for the best. How could I explain a tenth of what I felt without giving myself away?

'What is your business?' I asked, in an attempt to reach neutral ground.

That drew a rueful smile. 'You will find this hard to believe, Nell, but I am a farmer. I bought out my – the previous owner when he wished to retire, and the business has thrived.' He studied me. 'It is like you, Nell, to ask about money matters. You were always so careful with money.'

'I had to be,' I said, quietly.

That made him look away. 'I have not touched a drop of alcohol since I left England,' he said. 'I understood the harm it had done me, and swore I would never touch it again. You have nothing to fear in that respect.'

At least he has learnt something. 'How did you find me?'

He stirred his tea, thinking. 'It was harder than I thought it would be. When I got off the boat two weeks ago I went straight to Clerkenwell, but you were not there, and no one knew anything of you. I considered visiting your mother' – I stared at him in horror – 'but I thought the shock might be too much for her.'

'Thank heaven you did not,' I muttered. I dreaded to think what my mother would have said to him. Or, indeed, to me, as I had never told her the true story.

'Then I called on Inspector Lestrade at the Yard. He was astonished to see me, but once he had recovered himself he told me that you did not write reports for him any more, and that you had left the house in Clerkenwell years ago.'

Silently I thanked the inspector for his circumspection. Now his determination to keep me out of the newspaper report about the attempted bombing made complete sense.

'As I had no word of you, I took matters into my own hands. I arranged for a search to be done at Somerset House and found that you had not married in my absence, or – anything else.' He looked at me earnestly. 'I did think of you many times while I was away.'

I thought of how happy and busy Jack must have been in Tasmania, and it was all I could do not to snort. 'And what then, when you discovered that I had not died or remarried?'

Jack winced. 'Knowing that you were always very sharp in police matters, and that you did not work for the inspector any longer, I thought you might have gone into business on your own account.' He smiled. 'I could not imagine you returning to schoolteaching. So I combed the street directories and the newspapers for a Mrs Villiers engaged in any kind of detective or investigation business.

140

I found no Mrs Villiers, but I did find a Mrs Hudson, and the wording of the newspaper advertisements reminded me of you.' He gazed at me, puzzled. 'There is no Mr Hudson, is there?'

I met his gaze full on. 'There is no Mr Hudson,' I replied. 'The name is a matter of convenience.' *And I thought myself so clever, so well hidden.*

'I thought so,' he said. 'It would be like you to engage in business discreetly. As the advertisement said to write to Marylebone post office, I hired a man to watch for someone answering your description who visited the post office more than once. He described someone who resembled you, and I set him to a more general observation of the area. He wired me this morning to say that he had seen you enter Baker Street station. All I had to do was go there and wait for your return.' He grinned. 'I thought that was rather neat.'

Oh, how I cursed my decision not to visit Ealing in disguise! *It is no use regretting it*, I told myself. *He would have tracked you down eventually*. 'And so you found me,' I said. 'I am sure Inspector Lestrade would compliment you on your detective skills.' The Jack I knew would never have been so clear-minded.

The waitress brought the rarebit. 'Sorry for the wait, sir,' she said, but I could tell from her manner that she had been waiting for a lull in the conversation.

Jack picked up his knife and fork and set about his meal. 'Excuse me, Nell,' he said. 'I have not eaten since breakfast. I couldn't leave my post in case I missed you.'

'That is quite all right,' I said, and watched him eat. His

table manners were perfectly correct, but he was completely focused on his food. Not like Sherlock, who would often lapse into thought at the table and enter a sort of trance, only coming to when the rest of us had finished eating.

What on earth shall I say to Sherlock?
What shall I do?

A few minutes later, Jack's plate was clear. 'Are you sure you don't want anything to eat?' he said.

I shook my head. 'I had lunch two hours ago.' Two hours ago, my main worry had been whether Effie Stanley would recognise me. How I wished I could turn back the clock, and do something to ensure that Jack could never find me.

The waitress came for Jack's plate. 'Would you care for anything else?'

'Just the bill, please,' said Jack. When she brought it he glanced at it, pulled out his wallet, and put down a ten-shilling note. It was far from the only note in his wallet. 'There,' he said, and drained his cup. 'I am ready when you are, Nell.'

I poured the last dregs of tea into my cup and met his eyes. 'Ready for what, exactly?' I spoke as smoothly and calmly as I could, but my brain was screaming at me to get out, to run away and never return.

Jack drew back and looked puzzled. 'I know this is sudden, Nell, but now that we have found each other, we can pick up where we left off. I am currently staying in a hotel, but it will not take me long to find a suitable house.'

I stared at him in utter horror.

Jack's eyebrows drew together. 'What is it, Nell?' He took my hand, and I was too overwhelmed to pull away. 'I made a terrible mistake, and I'm very sorry, but I shall do my best to make it up to you. It will be difficult to explain to people, but we shall have to bear that. You are my wife, Nell, and your place is with me.' He squeezed my hand, and the gentle pressure felt like a weight crushing me into dust.

CHAPTER 20

'No.' The word came out as a croak, and I had to repeat it. '*No.*'

Now it was Jack's turn to stare. 'What do you mean, Nell?'

I swallowed. 'We can't just pick up where we left off. You abandoned me four years ago; you have no idea how I have lived since then.' I wrenched my hand away. 'How dare you think that you can come back and pick me up like a dropped toy when it suits you?' People murmured around me, but I did not care.

'Nell, I didn't know what to do. I was in a position I couldn't get out of.'

'Really? And what sort of position do you think you left *me* in?' I rose abruptly.

'Please let me try again, Nell.' Jack looked up at me miserably.

'If you must contact me, you may write to me at Marylebone post office – but you knew that anyway.' I glared at him. 'And call off your man immediately, or I'll do something about it that you won't like.' I hurried out of the tearoom as quickly as I could.

Once outside, I walked in the opposite direction from home. I turned into a quiet side street, then an alley, and waited. No footsteps followed me, and when I peeped out the road was empty. I left it a few minutes longer, then made my way through the streets until I was in the alley which led to home. The back way, of course: I would not risk walking in at my own front door. I snorted to myself. What a world, where a woman could no longer reach her own house without taking precautions.

Martha opened the door to me. 'What has happened, ma'am?' she said immediately, her eyebrows lifting at my expression.

I stepped inside. 'Put the kettle on, please, Martha. I barely know where to start.' I pulled off my gloves and remembered that moment in the tearoom when I had had to stop myself from revealing the ring Sherlock had given me. I touched the plain gold band with my forefinger and shivered.

'Shall I fetch Mr Holmes, ma'am?'

I shook my head. 'Not yet. I shall go upstairs and get changed. If anyone calls, anyone at all, I am not at home.' I considered making an exception for my mother, then decided against it. The last thing I wanted to do was explain the situation to her.

I climbed the stairs feeling as if my feet were weighted with lead. How confident, how foolhardy I had been this morning. And now everything had come crashing down.

I reached the bedroom, took off my boots and hat, and flopped onto the bed, careless of my dress. My mind was a miserable, empty void. I had no ideas, no plans, only the stark realisation that my life as I knew it was over, and I was about to lose everything I held dear. I felt tears well up and let them fall, too spiritless to wipe them away.

A light tap at the door roused me. 'I brought the tea, ma'am,' Martha called. 'Shall I leave it at the door?'

'No, wait a moment.' I dried my tears, then rose, opened the door and took the tray from her. 'Thank you, Martha.' She had put a plate of biscuits on the tray too, and that little gesture was almost enough to make me bawl. I turned and put the tray on the dressing table.

'Will you be down for dinner later, ma'am?' Martha seemed smaller than usual, and very worried.

'I don't know. Possibly. I'll get changed,' I said, to make her go.

Martha withdrew, and I changed into a house dress. *What would Jack have thought if he had seen me dressed like this?* My mouth twisted in a grim approximation of a smile. *Would he have bothered calling out to me, or would he have let me go?* I hung my day dress in the wardrobe, then sat at the dressing table and examined myself in the mirror. What would he have seen?

The face in the mirror was pale, and thinner than it had been four years ago. Then again, four years ago I had been pregnant with Jack's child: something else he didn't know. I remembered the day when I had been happy and busy, tidying the house and buying treats for dinner, because that was the day when I planned to tell him my great news. I dressed differently now – I could afford to – but what would he see when he looked past my smart hat and dress? I leaned closer to the mirror. I was four years older, and looked it. When I frowned, the little line between my eyebrows took a while to fade.

And what of Jack? He was more tanned and perhaps leaner, though it was hard to tell. And more serious: the ready smile and the great laugh that burst out of him when he was amused had both gone. *No wonder, if he has lost a wife and child to typhoid fever...*

I jumped at another tap on the door. 'What is it, Martha?' I called. 'I have not finished my tea yet.'

'It's me,' called Sherlock. 'May I come in?'

I closed my eyes and sighed in despair. Then I shrugged. 'Yes,' I said. All I was doing was wallowing in my own misery. Perhaps Sherlock would be able to help, and have a better idea of what to do. Despite my angry words to Jack on parting, I did not know if I could stop him from pursuing me.

He pushed open the door and his smile faded as he saw me. 'Whatever is it, Nell?'

I met his eyes. 'When I returned to Baker Street station after visiting the Stanleys, Jack was waiting for me.'

His eyebrows drew together as he took in the information. 'Jack?' He crossed the room to me. 'Jack Villiers?'

'Yes.' He put his arms around me, and I buried my head in his shoulder. 'And he expects that we will pick up where we left off,' I murmured into his shirt.

'That's ridiculous,' said Sherlock. He drew back slightly to look at me. 'As if he has any claim on you.'

'But he does,' I said. 'I told him that I would not go with him, but in law he is still my husband.'

'What about the woman he married?' Sherlock retorted. 'What will she have to say?'

'Nothing,' I replied. 'She died of typhoid fever. The child, too.'

Sherlock exhaled sharply. 'How convenient,' he said. 'He doesn't know where you live, does he? How did he find you?'

I shrugged. 'He used to be a policeman, and now that he has money, he hired someone to help him track me down. But as far as I can tell, he doesn't know my address.' My mouth twisted upwards, but it was not a smile. 'If he knew, I daresay he would have called.'

Sherlock ran a hand through his hair, then rose and began pacing. 'He's not getting away with it,' he said. 'Desertion, bigamy…' He came to an abrupt halt. 'I'll wire Mycroft and get his recommendations for a lawyer.'

I stared at him, uncomprehending.

'And if a lawyer can't find a way out of this, I'm sure there is another way.' Sherlock paced again. 'I wouldn't normally resort to violence, but if that is the only option…'

I buried my face in my hands. 'Please stop,' I said. 'This isn't helping.'

He rounded on me. 'What do you mean, I'm not helping? I'm doing my best to find an answer to a problem I never expected to have.'

'I am not a problem to solve!' I cried. 'Through no fault of my own I am in an impossible situation, and you're behaving as if I am your property! You're no better than he is!' I felt tears of vexation welling up as I ran to the door and wrenched it open. *I won't cry in front of him.*

'Nell, wait—'

I slammed my way out and ran upstairs to my sitting room. There I locked the door behind me, sank into my armchair, and wept.

What shall I do? My first thought was to run away. To withdraw my money from the bank, disguise myself, pack a bag, and catch a train to a place where Jack would never find me. But then what? Set up as a detective in another city? What was to stop Jack from tracking me down again? And this time he would be better prepared. I imagined him waving an order which would compel me to live with him. A miserable existence where I would live out the rest of my days in a sterile marriage, the wife of a reasonably well-to-do businessman, condemned to pay calls and entertain his friends at dinner.

What if he decided to return to Tasmania? What would I do then?

And what – what about Sherlock?

I dragged my mind away from that grim vision and back to the present. What sort of life could I live now? I would not be able to call at the post office for my mail in case Jack or his spy lurked nearby. I saw a world where I could never leave the house in my own person, sneaking out in disguise wherever I went, whether to visit my mother, carry out my work at the department store, or meet a client.

Would there be any more clients?

I buried my face in my hands and sobbed at the thought that everything I had worked for, everything I had dreamed of and made a reality, could slip through my fingers so easily. 'There is no way out,' I whispered. 'Life will never be the same again.' I sat in my chilly sitting room, the fire unlit, and wept for all that I had lost.

CHAPTER 21

Eventually I cried myself out and sat, silent and miserable, in the armchair. As usual, crying had not helped; all I had done was make myself feel worse. *You should know better, Nell. Do something.* I moved to the bureau, uncapped my pen, took a piece of paper and stared at it.

I was no further on when someone tapped at the door. Probably Martha, to ask whether I would require a dinner tray. 'Yes?' I said.

'I have tea,' said Sherlock. 'Fresh tea. And an apology.'

I got up and unlocked the door. 'You may come in so long as you don't talk about violence and lawyers.'

'I'm sorry, Nell,' he said, and he did actually look contrite. 'I panicked. I don't want you to run away again. I couldn't bear it.'

I bit my lip to keep it from trembling. 'I'm not sure I have a choice.'

He crossed quickly to the bureau, set down the tray, then took me in his arms. 'Don't say that, Nell. There must be something we can do.'

'I hope so,' I whispered. 'But perhaps the first thing to do is pour the tea.'

He managed a shaky laugh at that. 'Always so practical.' He poured us both out a cup, then closed the door and sat down. 'May I ask how much you have told him?'

'As little as possible. He has worked out that I am Mrs Hudson, and that I work for myself as a detective.' I paused, not sure how he would take my next words. 'And no, I didn't mention you.'

A wry smile. 'Should I be pleased about that?'

'I don't want to give Jack any ammunition against me,' I said. 'I have no doubt that if, heaven forbid, this matter went to court and it became known that I was living with a man to whom I am not married, it would go hard with me.'

'It's so unfair,' Sherlock muttered.

'I agree,' I said, 'but that is how things are. I have told Jack that he may write to me via the post office, but I made it clear that I have no intention of setting up home with him. I doubt he understands why – why should he? He probably thinks that he is doing me a great favour.' My lip curled.

Sherlock took my hand. 'You're sure about that, Nell?' His eyes searched mine. 'You definitely don't want to go back to him?' My heart went out to him, and I had never loved him more than in that moment when he put my happiness before his own.

I kissed him, and stroked his cheek. 'How could I, when I have you?' Immense relief spread over Sherlock's face. 'He may be well off, and possibly a better man than he was when he left, but I feel nothing for Jack.' I thought for a moment. 'No, that is not true. I am sorry that he lost a wife and child' – I still couldn't bring myself to say *his* – 'but the thought of living with him, of any kind of intimacy, utterly repels me.'

Sherlock smiled. 'I should probably be ashamed that I am glad.' He kissed me very gently. It was like a first kiss – though not the first kiss we had shared. Then he moved my cup towards me. 'What do we do?' His eyes seemed to cloud as he looked at me. 'And I said we, not you. The one thing I can't bear is when you push me away. You are independent, and I respect that, but that doesn't mean you have to do everything alone.'

I sipped my tea, considering his words. 'You are right,' I said, and put my cup down. 'I was so driven to manage everything myself when I was with Jack, and so frustrated when others took the credit for work I had done, that I believed I could only trust myself.' I thought of the inspector's promises of work, which had come to nothing. 'Often, I was right,' I continued. 'But never about you.'

'Good.' He took my hand. 'So shall we try to work together on this matter, on the basis that you are not a problem to solve?'

I nodded, barely able to speak. 'Yes, Sherlock.' I swallowed. 'I shall try not to let my pride get in the way.'

'I shall do the same,' he murmured. He turned away and wiped his eyes. 'What a conversation to have. And what a situation we are in.'

'I know.' I grimaced. 'The Case of the Reappearing Husband.'

'Oh don't, Nell.' But he couldn't help laughing, and somehow, I felt a little better.

Sherlock drained his cup. 'We are still not addressing the question of what to do.' He took my hands. 'What are your thoughts, Nell?'

'I was too angry and upset to think earlier,' I said. 'The one thing I do know is that violence is not the answer. I understand that you are angry with him, as I am, but even so...'

'I had a feeling you would say that,' Sherlock replied. 'Like you, I spoke in the heat of the moment.' He paused, thinking. 'Could he be bribed? We could pay him to go back to Australia, or Tasmania, or wherever it is—'

'I doubt it,' I said. 'He isn't in need of money, and I suspect it would make him more determined to remain here and attempt to wear me down.' I paused. 'Perhaps you were right about a lawyer.'

'It is worth trying,' said Sherlock. 'He has stayed away and sent no word for four years.' He glanced at me. 'Not to mention marrying another woman.'

I winced. 'I suspect he regards that merely as part of his mistake.' I thought for a while, then faced Sherlock. 'In his mind, I truly believe that he thinks he is doing his duty and putting things right.'

Sherlock grimaced. 'People who are convinced they are in the right are always the worst to deal with. It is settled, then. I shall call in at Mycroft's club tonight and see what can be arranged. He will know of a suitable lawyer.'

I should have been glad, but a chill ran through me. I folded my arms to mask the trembling. Sherlock was doing his best, I knew he was, but I wanted to scream at the thought of my life – *my* life – being discussed without me, by men who dwelt behind closed doors that I could never open. I met his eyes. 'I would like to come,' I said quietly.

Sherlock frowned. 'It is a gentlemen's club, Nell.'

'I know. But this is my business – my life and my future – and I wish to be part of the discussion. I would prefer it if we visited Mycroft together.' I paused. 'Besides,' I added, hoping this argument would have some weight, 'surely you have to go out and get drunk with Humphrey Montagu again tonight.'

'Never mind that,' said Sherlock, waving a hand. 'This is far more important.'

'That is exactly why I wish to be present,' I said. 'In any case, I must report to him on my visit to the Stanleys.' I sighed. 'Not that it was successful. The reverse, in fact. I don't know how, but Effie Stanley found me out. She didn't say it in so many words, but she did.'

'It was always a risk,' said Sherlock. 'I doubt you could have done anything to stop it.'

'I know, but it still annoys me. If I possibly can, I intend to keep working. If I let Jack disrupt our lives, I shall feel as if he has won.'

'Perhaps we can talk over your case and mine after dinner.' Sherlock consulted his watch. 'We only have half an hour: just enough time to send a wire to Mycroft, then make ourselves more or less presentable.'

I picked up my pen and drew the paper towards me. 'I shall write it now.' I smiled. 'It may even be longer than twelve words.'

'I am glad to hear it.' Sherlock kissed my cheek.

I composed my wire and Sherlock pronounced it a

155

miracle of circumspection. 'I shall take this downstairs to Billy,' he said. Then a curious expression came over his face. 'If I do go to the Criterion tonight, Nell, do you promise to be here when I return?'

I wanted to say *Of course*, but it was not as easy as that. 'I promise,' I said, slowly, 'unless something happens to make me feel I must leave immediately. If I do go, I promise that I shall either leave word of where I am with Martha, or get word to you as soon as I can.' I looked down, then met his eyes. 'I cannot promise more.'

He gazed at me for a long moment. 'I cannot ask more.' Then he strode across the room and wrapped me in his arms. 'I hope, for both our sakes, that it never comes to that,' he murmured into my hair. He drew back, studying me, and I felt as if he were looking into my soul. 'I swear that if it is in my power, he will never be able to come near you again.' He stood up abruptly, as if he had said too much, and left the room.

I stared at the door Sherlock had passed through as if it might tell me something. Not half an hour before I had felt utterly hopeless. But now – I reached out and touched the handle of the cup he had drunk from. Sherlock and I were together. Now there was hope. Now there was a plan. Now there was a way forward. And in spite of all the uncertainty, I smiled.

CHAPTER 22

Dr Watson took his last bite of bacon and egg and laid his knife and fork together neatly on his plate. 'And what does the day hold in store for you?' he asked me.

I considered replying that I was planning to go for a ramble in the park, then take in the new exhibition at the National Gallery, but decided that was too heavy-handed a response. In any case, I had ventured out twice in the preceding days: once to meet a new client, then to wrap up her case. On both occasions I had met her at a hotel different from those I normally used, and had disguised myself to such an extent that I was confident my own mother would not have known me. I had no doubt that my client thought me a strange individual, but I had found her beau, who had lost his memory after being struck by an omnibus when crossing the road, and that was all she cared about.

Dr Watson was still looking at me. 'I shall send Billy to enquire for any mail for me,' I said, 'and plan accordingly. And of course, there are our cases in progress.'

'Yes.' He drained his teacup. 'Cases in progress. I daresay you two will be shut up together in the consulting room. Well, as it is Saturday, and a fine day, I shall take a walk then lunch at my club. I believe Thurston will be there, and it is a good opportunity to practise.' He mimed aiming a billiard cue.

It was not for me to divine John Watson's feelings, but his habit of remarking whenever Sherlock and I were busy together suggested that he was nettled by our new collaboration. I had spent hours wading through facts and figures related to Humphrey Montagu's directorships, and scanning the society pages to piece together a network of his acquaintances – and in turn, their acquaintances – which was pinned to the consulting-room wall and resembled nothing so much as a giant spider or an upside-down tree.

For his part, Sherlock had carried out several tasks on my behalf, enquiring at hospitals for the missing fiancé and collecting my mail when he was near the post office. It felt strange – a different kind of intimacy – but it was a far better demonstration of his love and care for me than a more ostentatious show of affection.

Dr Watson turned to Sherlock, who was still eating his breakfast. 'What is your plan, Holmes? Will you stay at home too, or will you sally forth?'

Sherlock swallowed his mouthful of toast. 'I shall visit Wiggins first thing and see what intelligence he has for me. Then I may call on Lestrade and update him on the progress of the case so far. Not that there is much.' He made a face. 'Montagu has not mentioned business to me, much less suggested that I invest in any of his enterprises. If Lestrade were not so insistent that he is a man to watch,

I would sum up Montagu as a genial man who enjoys life and has a knack for getting on with people.'

'I wonder what his wife is like,' I mused.

Sherlock's eyebrows drew together. 'I hope you aren't thinking of forming an acquaintance, Nell. At least, not until this business with Villiers is over.' He sighed with exasperation. 'Trust Mycroft to make us wait for a meeting. I'm sure he is free before Monday morning.'

I poured myself more tea. 'To be fair, Sherlock, my telegram did not imply urgency, since I had to word it so carefully.'

'What do you think Mycroft will advise?' asked Dr Watson.

I had decided that as we all lived under the same roof, it was prudent to inform Dr Watson of my husband's return; if Jack did somehow call at the house or appear in the vicinity, I wanted to know. Dr Watson had been extremely surprised at the news, and every so often brought it up out of the blue, as if it had struck him afresh. I wished he would not: every mention of my husband brought back my dread of what might happen. But Dr Watson's simple faith that Mycroft Holmes and a lawyer would solve the problem cheered me, even as I recognised how unlikely it was.

'I have no idea what Mycroft Holmes will say,' I replied. 'To be frank, John, the advice of whichever lawyer he recommends will be much more significant to me, and I shall wait for that.' I raised my cup to my lips, then froze as Billy burst into the room.

'It's a note, sir,' he said, thrusting a white envelope at

159

Sherlock. 'And it looks like the other one that came. You know the one.'

'I do indeed,' muttered Sherlock as he ripped it open. Dr Watson and I hurried round the table to peer over his shoulder.

Dear Mr Holmes,

How clever you are! I had no doubt that you would find my little surprise; however, leaving it until the last minute was a masterstroke in building tension. Perhaps you should consider treading the boards, or at the very least penning a one-act drama. The London theatre would be in your debt.

I am even more impressed by your modesty in allowing Inspector Lestrade to take the credit for your actions. It indicates a generosity in you that I had not suspected.

This time, though, I want you to have all the glory – or should I say responsibility? To that end, if I learn that you have communicated with Scotland Yard or your brother at Whitehall before you solve my riddle, then I shall bring forward the revelation of my little joke. I'm sure you don't want that.

Regarding my latest present to you, I believe that people from all walks of life would voice their opinion on it, though whether they would be listened to is another matter. After eleven o'clock today, they may be silenced.

Yours,

An Admirer

'The scoundrel!' muttered Dr Watson, clenching his

fists.

'Undoubtedly,' said Sherlock. 'But that doesn't help us.'

'People would voice their opinion…' I murmured.

'What about the Houses of Parliament?' said Dr Watson. 'People voice all sorts of opinions there.'

'They aren't from all walks of life,' I pointed out. 'This must be a place where anyone can go and speak—'

'Speakers' Corner!' exclaimed Sherlock. 'How many times have we passed it and seen some poor soul holding forth to a pack of scruffy children and a dog?'

'That would fit with no one listening,' I said. Then I frowned. 'It seems too easy.'

'I know,' said Sherlock. 'But the bomber has not given us much time. It is half past nine now.' He sprang to his feet. 'Nell, go and put on whatever you need to, and be quick about it. Watson, if you are coming, do the same.'

Dr Watson glanced at me, then Sherlock. 'Is it wise for Mrs Hudson to accompany us?'

'Nell helped to disable the bomb last time,' said Sherlock, 'and we shall both be there to defend her.' He looked at me. 'What say you, Nell?'

'Give me two minutes,' I said, and dashed upstairs. I pulled on an old wide-brimmed hat and a voluminous cloak, and put on boots that, if necessary, I could run in.

'Excellent,' said Sherlock, as I ran downstairs. He was carrying the toolbox. 'Billy is holding a cab.'

A minute later, we were on our way. Dr Watson's eyes gleamed as he glanced first at us, then out at the street, then back to us. His face was flushed, his breathing quick. I hoped it would not fall to him to do anything with the

161

bomb.

Though the journey was short, it still seemed to take an eternity until we pulled up at Marble Arch, paid the cabman, and ran through the gate to Speakers' Corner. A man dressed in black was holding forth to a few spectators. 'The end of the world is nigh!' he cried.

Sherlock took his arm and firmly led him away. 'You don't know how true your words are, sir,' he said, 'but I must interrupt you for a few minutes. Watson, please take this man and his audience to safety.' He pointed to a distant expanse of grass. 'Nell, come with me.'

We ranged the area, looking for a box or a bundle. I noticed a small hillock behind the place where the speaker had stood and hurried towards it. Sure enough, beneath a covering of grass was a brown canvas cloth, and under that a locked metal box. 'Sherlock! Over here!'

Sherlock crouched in front of the box and applied a chisel to the lid. The box sprang open, revealing a smaller bundle of cardboard tubes and the same smouldering fuse, longer this time. One snip of Martha's kitchen scissors and the bomb was safe. Sherlock extinguished the cut fuse and pulled the rest of it away, and our shoulders sagged with relief.

We beckoned Dr Watson, and when the preacher returned Sherlock addressed him. 'My name is Holmes, and I am an amateur naturalist. I am collecting specimens for the new Museum of Natural History, and I spotted a rare bird's nest close to where you were standing.' He tapped the metal box. 'I do apologise for disturbing you.'

The man beamed at him. 'Sir, there is no need to

apologise. I am merely pleased that you acknowledged the truth of my words.' He gave Sherlock a warm handshake. 'May I continue my mission?'

'You may,' said Sherlock, and we made for the gate.

In the cab home Dr Watson was full of questions and speculations, and not at all disheartened by his position on the outskirts of the action. Sherlock answered him in monosyllables until eventually Dr Watson regarded him with a puzzled frown. 'What is wrong, Holmes? I thought you would be jubilant at having foiled the enemy once again.'

'Of course I am relieved, Watson,' said Sherlock, studying the box on his lap, 'but there is a bigger mystery to be solved.' He looked up, and seemed to be gazing at something far beyond the confines of the cab. 'Why did our adversary make this puzzle so elementary?'

CHAPTER 23

Mr Harris peered at me, his expression incredulous. 'Mrs Hudson?'

'Yes indeed, Mr Harris,' I replied. 'I could explain, but it is complicated.'

'Mr Harris, I can vouch for my companion if that will help,' said Sherlock. He looked rather amused than otherwise.

'Very well,' said Mr Harris. He knocked on the inner door of the room, entered, and returned perhaps a minute later. 'Mr Poskitt will see you now, and Mr Holmes will join you shortly.' He coughed. 'I have made him aware of your – appearance.'

'Thank you,' I said, and sighed inwardly. Would the rest of my life be like this?

Dr Watson, naturally, had been full of ideas as to how I might disguise myself for our visit to Somerset House, including padding my stomach with a small pillow, putting my leg in plaster and using crutches, and dressing as a delivery boy. I would have laughed if I had not been on the verge of tears. Luckily, Sherlock had persuaded him of the impracticality of his suggestions. 'You forget, Watson, that

Nell may need to move quickly, and also that she needs to be admitted to Somerset House with me.' Dr Watson had looked disappointed, but acquiesced.

In the end I had compromised with a smart dress and the dark-brown wig, parted in the centre and drawn back into a severe bun. Heavy dark eyebrows, pink cheeks and a set of cheek pads completed the transformation. I resembled nothing so much as a child's peg doll, but at least I had been able to remove the cheek pads surreptitiously once we were inside Somerset House.

'I still think you most attractive,' murmured Sherlock, as I wrapped the pads in a handkerchief and put them in my bag.

'I'm glad *you* do,' I retorted.

Mr Poskitt did his best not to start when he caught sight of me. He stared for a moment, then his usual bashful smile appeared. 'Do take a seat, Mrs Hudson.' Sherlock placed a chair for me. 'I shall just see whether Mr Holmes is free.'

He went to the door in the corner, opened it, and stuck his head around it. 'Mr Holmes, they have arrived,' he murmured.

'Oh good,' said Mycroft Holmes's voice. We heard a creak, then the door swung open and the man himself came in. 'Good heavens!' he exclaimed, and laughed.

'My present appearance relates to one of the matters I wish to discuss,' I said, tartly. I had already had quite enough of being peered at, stared at and laughed at, and it was not yet half past ten in the morning.

Mycroft launched himself into an armchair and

consulted his watch. 'Almost time for elevenses,' he remarked. 'Why don't you offer our guests refreshment, Poskitt?'

The bell was pressed, the order given, and we settled into our seats. 'You are here to discuss your visit to the Stanleys, Mrs Hudson,' Mycroft remarked, 'but I find myself more curious to know the reason for your get-up.'

I clasped my hands together to keep from clenching my fists. 'My husband, Jack Villiers, has returned from Tasmania,' I said. 'He expects me to go back to him; in his eyes we are still man and wife. I'm afraid that he will try and force me to obey him, and so I am doing my best to ensure that we do not meet again.'

Mycroft listened with his head on one side, like a plump bird. 'I see,' he said. 'Yes, that does explain your . . . costume.' There was a noise outside the door and he listened hopefully for a few moments, then turned to me when no tray was forthcoming. 'That is awkward.'

'We wondered whether you could recommend a good lawyer,' said Sherlock.

'Mmm,' said Mycroft. 'A couple of chaps at the Diogenes Club are experts in the, um, murkier aspects of matrimonial law. I have no doubt something can be done.' He looked severely at me. 'At all costs, it must be kept out of the courts.'

'I have no wish for this matter to go to court,' I said firmly.

'Good.' Mycroft sat back, stretching out his legs. 'I imagine the last thing either of you would want is to become a byword for, well, immorality.'

Sherlock sat bolt upright. 'Mycroft, you know that if Villiers had died then Nell and I would already be married.'

'I don't doubt it, old boy.' Mycroft waved a dismissive hand. 'But I doubt the newspapers and the general public would take such a liberal view.'

'Thank you for your advice, Mr Holmes,' I said, fighting to keep the bitterness out of my voice. 'If you could recommend a lawyer, we do not need to discuss this further today. Shall we move on?' If I had to listen to him on this subject any longer, I would burst into tears.

Mycroft studied me for a while. 'Yes indeed, Mrs Hudson.' He turned to Sherlock. 'Have you received any more communications from your adversary, the bomber?'

'I have,' said Sherlock, reaching into an inner pocket and passing Mycroft the envelope. 'He struck again on Saturday morning, but we managed to find the bomb and make it safe without difficulty.'

'Excellent.' Mycroft read the note and chuckled. 'I am mentioned in dispatches, I see.' He looked up. 'Speakers' Corner, I presume.'

'The same,' said Sherlock. 'A smaller device this time, but still sufficient to cause death or serious injury.'

'I do not doubt it.' Mycroft perused the note again. 'Have you deduced the identity of this trickster?'

'I am not certain,' said Sherlock, 'but I think it is Moriarty.'

Mycroft's eyebrows drew together. 'Professor Moriarty?' A laugh rolled out of him. 'I don't think so, dear boy.'

Sherlock's hands clenched, then unclenched. 'Please explain your reasoning, Mycroft.'

'It is simple,' said Mycroft. 'This is not Moriarty's handwriting. Moreover, he would never express himself in this manner; when working for us, his communications were brief to the point of terseness. Finally, Moriarty would never waste his time on this riddling. If he wanted to plant a bomb he would get on and do it, not write notes and give clues.' A tap sounded at the door. 'I believe that is our tea.'

Sherlock and I accepted a cup each and brooded while Mycroft examined the biscuits and petit fours, eventually selecting a small plateful. 'So, Mycroft, who do you think our bomber is?' asked Sherlock.

Mycroft held up a hand while he chewed a mouthful of pastry. 'A good question, dear boy. Possibly a frenzied admirer of yours who wishes you to gain greater glory. Although I can't say I approve of their methods.' He selected a small, round biscuit. 'I saw that Lestrade attributed the first attack to the Fenians.' He snorted. 'Ridiculous.'

'I agree,' said Sherlock. 'At the moment we are much better at deciding who it is not than who it is. But if we eliminate the impossible—'

'None of this is impossible,' said Mycroft, looking affronted. 'It is possible that Moriarty or the Fenians are behind this, but extremely unlikely.' He popped the biscuit into his mouth and pondered. 'The key is to work out why someone wants *you* to disarm bombs for them. That is why I suggested the admirer hypothesis.' He tapped the note.

168

'As this person signs themselves.' He picked up his cup. 'Keep me informed, Sherlock.' He took a deep draught of his tea and set the cup down. 'Mrs Hudson, would you be so kind as to tell me about your visit to the Stanleys?'

'Yes, of course,' I said, feeling distinctly queasy. 'I'm afraid it is not good news.' I gave a brief account of the visit. 'Mr Stanley could furnish me with no descriptions of his kidnappers, and once Mrs Stanley had found me out, she would speak to me no longer. It is regrettable, but I can be of no further use regarding the Stanleys.'

'It appears not,' said Mycroft. 'You weren't dressed like that, were you?'

'Of course not!' I exclaimed. 'I wore no disguise.'

'Yet she recognised you,' Mycroft mused. 'Peculiar.' He sat up straighter. 'Tell me again what Stanley's interlocutors asked him.'

I referred to my notes. 'The questions were along the lines of "What did you know?" and "Who told you?"'

Mycroft pursed his lips. 'Nothing definite. Mmm.' He turned to his colleague. 'What do you think, Poskitt?'

'I do not have any suggestions to offer,' replied Mr Poskitt, 'but I am sure Mrs Hudson did her best.'

'Mmm,' said Mycroft, again. 'I'm sure you did the best you could, Mrs Hudson. There is no point in sending you now that Mrs Stanley distrusts you. Perhaps you were distracted by this business with your husband.'

'Hardly,' I said curtly. 'My husband apprehended me as I was returning from Ealing. It has absolutely no bearing on the interview.'

'The whole business puts us in a bad light,' said

Mycroft, as if I had not spoken. 'To send an interviewer who is then recognised from a previous intervention where they operated in disguise.' He shook his head. 'Not good at all.'

'That was why you hired me!' I cried. 'You wanted someone who had met the Stanleys and would not employ official methods.'

'We did,' said Mycroft. 'Or rather, Poskitt did. That was an error of judgement.' He sighed. 'We shall have to consider what else we can do.'

'There is no more to do! At least, not with Mr Stanley. He was perfectly open with me, but he could tell me almost nothing.'

Mycroft leaned forward. 'Tell me, Mrs Hudson, did we pay you in advance?'

'You did,' I said, wondering whether he would ask me to return the money.

'In that case, I shall not detain you any longer.' He selected another petit four from his plate. 'Poskitt, would you mind summoning Harris? I am sure our guests could find their own way out, but we would not want any inconvenient questions to be asked.' His gaze lingered on my face, and the corner of his mouth turned up in a smirk. 'I'll wire you about that lawyer, Sherlock.'

I managed to hold my tongue until we were safely in a cab. On the way out of the building Sherlock had looked at me several times, first with enquiry, then increasing perturbation. 'The – the—' I thumped the seat in frustration. 'I know he's your brother, Sherlock, but—'

'I should have warned you,' he said resignedly.

'Mycroft's intelligence is second to none, but his capacity for empathy is somewhat lacking.'

'I can see that.' I smacked the seat again. 'Why would he understand? He is a man who does what he likes, and answers only to the highest authority. If he took a mistress, no one would say a word. Yet here am I, living to all intents and purposes as a married woman, and he speaks of me as if I were a street drab.' I sighed. 'Those poor women do not do it for pleasure, I am sure.'

'Nell…' Sherlock turned me gently towards him, careful to keep his hand from my painted cheek. 'Let's focus on the good things. Mycroft will give us the name of a lawyer, you do not have to visit the Stanleys again, and you have already been paid for your work.'

'At this rate, it will be the last payment from him that I ever receive.' I folded my arms and stared out of the window. We were already heading into Marylebone. I opened my bag, unwrapped the cheek pads, and slipped them in place. 'I assume we are going the back way,' I said, carefully.

'We are,' said Sherlock, and as he looked at me he couldn't suppress a grin. 'I'm terribly sorry, Nell, but if we can still laugh, that is something.' He leaned over and kissed me carefully on the forehead.

'I know it is no fun for you, either.' I put my hand on his cheek. 'Thank you for coming with me.'

He smiled. 'Don't worry about Mycroft. His bark is worse than his bite. He will help us, I know it.' And as the cab drove down Baker Street, then turned into a side road, I hoped with all my heart that he was right.

CHAPTER 24

I scrubbed at my face with a cloth, examined the result in the bathroom mirror, and groaned. The rouge had been easy to remove, but the thick dark eyebrows were a different matter. They had faded to a light-brown shadow of themselves, but were still most definitely present. I applied more cold cream and sat on the edge of the bath to give it time to work, making a mental note to myself to avoid such a heavy disguise in future unless it was absolutely necessary.

Five minutes later, the eyebrows were at last gone. I washed my face and went back to the bedroom to tame my hair, which had rebelled from its confinement into a springy mass of waves.

'I'm in the consulting room,' Sherlock called. 'Join me when you're ready.'

When I entered the consulting room, feeling more myself, Sherlock had pinned some sheets of paper to the wall. Roughly in the middle he had written *BOMBER*, and on the far left he had written *MORIARTY?*

'Are you thinking about what Mycroft said?' I asked as I reached his side.

'I am,' said Sherlock, 'and he has a point. The more I consider it, the more peculiar it is that someone is spending all this time in encouraging me to thwart them.'

'Indeed,' I said. 'You should write that down.'

Sherlock stepped forward, drew an arrow from *BOMBER*, and wrote at the end of it: *Provides clues*. Then he wrote *National Portrait Gallery* at the top left of the paper and *Speakers' Corner* further along, and underlined both. Under *Speakers' Corner* he wrote *EASY*, and under the first heading he wrote *INTERMEDIATE*.

'Hopefully the next one will be easier still,' I said.

Sherlock drew arrows from the name *MORIARTY*, and added the words *terse, businesslike, secretive*. From the word *BOMBER* he added *communicative, encouraging, emotional*. After the last word he added a question mark.

'I know what you mean,' I said, 'but it is not quite that. It is as if something is bubbling beneath the surface.' I took the pen from Sherlock and added *dangerous* and *access to explosives*.

'Mycroft is right, isn't he?' Sherlock sighed and his shoulders sagged. 'There is no reason to believe it is Moriarty.'

I turned to him. 'So why do you think it is him?'

Sherlock shrugged. 'It is nothing more than a feeling . . . but Mycroft does not deal in feelings.' He continued to study the wall.

I touched his arm and he looked down at me. 'That does not make Mycroft the better man.'

'Perhaps.' Sherlock grimaced. 'But it means he will not listen to anything that is not based in cold, hard fact.' He jabbed at the paper with his forefinger. 'And while I am trying to solve this, I am getting precisely nowhere with the Montagu case.' He scowled at the wall. 'I have a good mind to wire Lestrade and tell him I'm giving Montagu up as a bad job.'

'Have you found nothing incriminating?'

'No, nor even suspicious. Either Humphrey Montagu ought to be on the London stage as the premier actor of his generation, or he is as honest as you or me.' He smiled. 'Possibly more so.'

I looked at the spider diagram pinned on the wall which listed Humphrey Montagu's various friends and acquaintances. I had begun to investigate them, but so far I had come across nothing to support Lestrade's theory. A thought occurred to me. 'I wonder…'

Sherlock turned to me. 'What is it, Nell?'

'This may be nothing,' I said, slowly, 'but you have a bomber who is keeping you busy; you wait for their next letter, race to disarm their devices, and try to anticipate their next move. In addition, you and Inspector Lestrade are both heavily involved with this case.' I tapped the spider diagram. 'Despite our best efforts, neither of us can find any convincing evidence. Could both these matters be intended as a diversion from something else that is going on?'

Sherlock's eyes widened. 'It is possible, and infinitely more likely than Mycroft's hypothesis that I have an insane admirer. I do believe my only admirer is Watson.' He grinned. 'Have you read his account of the Case of Speakers' Corner, as he calls it?'

I smiled back. 'I have. As a stylistic point, I was rather concerned about his overuse of the word *elementary*. I am sure I saw it at least five times.' I looked at the paper on the wall. 'Of course I admire you too, Sherlock, but apart from your satisfied clients and Inspectors Lestrade and Gregson, I would not have thought that many other people knew of your detective skills.'

'Apart from the criminals I have apprehended,' said Sherlock. 'They will be painfully aware of my existence, and moreover they would have an excellent reason for keeping me occupied elsewhere.' His eyes gleamed. 'Nell, I think you are on to something.' His mouth curled in a wry smile. 'Sadly, I must again remove Moriarty from the running, since you have all the credit for apprehending him.'

I snorted. 'Among a very select group of people, Sherlock. I doubt my part in the case will ever become public knowledge.' I tried not to let it rankle, as I had been amply paid for my work, but the official silence on my substantial role in the case still vexed me, even a year on.

Sherlock drew me to him and kissed the top of my head. 'People who matter know, Nell.' And with that I had to be content.

'So who could it be, if not Moriarty?' I asked. 'Which criminals of your acquaintance fit with what we know of the bomber?'

Sherlock thought for a moment. 'We need Watson,' he said. 'He has far better knowledge of my cases than I do. As far as I am concerned, once a case is finished it drops out of my head to make room for the next one.' He ran his hands through his hair. 'And Watson will not return until this evening.'

'In that case,' I said, 'there is no more we can do now.'

'I agree,' said Sherlock. 'I had planned to go to the Criterion tonight—'

'Wait.' I looked at the spider diagram. 'Something is missing.'

Sherlock studied the wall. 'Are you sure, Nell? Between us we must have spent hours collecting this data.'

'We have,' I said. 'But who is missing?' I stepped forward, drew a short line to the right of Humphrey Montagu's name, and added *Eliza Montagu, née Davenant.* 'She is an important person in her own right. With whom does she associate? What would she know of her husband's businesses? How much influence does she have?' I moved back, imagining another network of people who might be involved. 'This could be another false lead, and Mrs Montagu may be as honest as her husband, but it would be prudent to investigate her too before we dismiss this matter as a waste of time.'

'How can we do it?' asked Sherlock. 'We can go through newspapers and periodicals, but they will not tell the whole story. And I can hardly befriend a married woman, particularly when I am already known to her husband. There are limits to my ingenuity.'

'You would not need to do that.' I eyed him, wondering what he would say to my next words. 'Perhaps, if we could secure intelligence from Wiggins as to Eliza Montagu's movements, I could go and—'

'Absolutely not,' said Sherlock. 'Out of the question.'

'Think about it, Sherlock. Like her husband, she will socialise in exclusive places. Ladies' clubs, and events with restricted admission. It is practically impossible that I could encounter Jack there.'

'Not impossible,' said Sherlock. 'Unlikely.'

'Don't quote your brother,' I snapped. 'One of him in the Holmes family is quite enough.'

Sherlock sighed. 'If Mycroft finds us a lawyer and he manages to remove the threat of Jack Villiers, then yes, your help would be very much welcomed. As things stand, we cannot risk it.'

'You aren't risking anything,' I muttered.

'Yes, I am,' Sherlock shot back. 'Both our reputations are at stake, in case you hadn't noticed. And I don't mean our professional reputations.'

I was ready to make a sharp retort when banging on the front door forestalled me. I jumped, and clutched Sherlock's arm before I knew what I was doing.

Sherlock's eyes met mine, and he took my hand. 'Sorry, Nell,' he murmured. 'That was uncalled for.'

'Shhh.' I heard Billy's boots, then the snick of the bolt.

'Telegram!' cried Martha's nemesis.

'Perhaps it is Mycroft's answer,' said Sherlock. He put his arm around me. 'We shall know soon.'

Billy's footsteps hurtled upstairs. 'Telegram for you, sir,' he called, 'and something else.'

Sherlock's arm tensed.

Billy knocked, then opened the door and handed Sherlock the telegram. 'There's this, too.' He held up a pale-blue envelope. 'But I don't know who it's for.' He passed it to Sherlock, and we saw that it was blank. No address, no stamp, no postmark.

'That's odd,' said Sherlock. 'Let's start with the telegram.' He ripped it open, and read out: *Sir Geoffrey Rivers best lawyer office Chancery Lane STOP Give him my name STOP M.* He smiled at me. 'I told you Mycroft would help.'

I smiled back, but I couldn't keep my eyes off the blank envelope. 'Will you open it?'

Sherlock raised his eyebrows. 'You may, if you like, Nell, since it could be for either of us. Or not.' He studied it. 'At least it is not from our friend the bomber. The envelope is the wrong colour.'

I went to the bureau for a letter opener. I both wanted to see what was inside the envelope, and feared it.

The envelope was not bulky. I slit it open and retrieved a single sheet of pale-blue paper with the letterhead of a nearby hotel. There was just one line, in neat large capitals. I gasped, and nearly dropped it.

I KNOW WHERE YOU LIVE, MRS HUDSON.

CHAPTER 25

'What is it, Nell?' Sherlock was at my side in an instant.

I handed him the note, unable to speak.

'This is him, isn't it?' Sherlock's jaw clenched. 'This is Villiers!' He began to pace. 'I've a good mind to hunt him down and beat some sense into him. Better still...' He opened the top drawer of the bureau and took out a pistol.

'No!' I cried.

Sherlock turned, pistol in hand. 'Don't tell me it won't solve anything. I think it would sort things out admirably.'

'And put you in prison, or worse.' I went over to him, took the pistol and replaced it in the drawer. 'Give me the letter. Please.'

He handed me the note. 'Is it his writing?'

I looked at the paper. Jack's penmanship had never been so neat, though he had had to improve it in the course of his police duties. 'Not unless he has changed the way he writes, or disguised it. I don't recognise it.'

'There is no sense in him doing that.' Sherlock sank into an armchair, then looked up and saw Billy, staring. 'Billy, go downstairs until you are called for.'

'Yessir,' Billy gabbled, and vanished. His boots

179

clattered downstairs.

'He'll tell Martha,' I said. My knees wobbled, and I sank down on the sofa.

Sherlock sprang up and sat beside me. 'I'm sorry, Nell. Are you all right?'

'I – I don't know.' I felt numb, hollowed out. 'If it is not Jack, then who is it? Who would threaten me?' I thought of the people I had had contact with recently. My clients had been satisfied with me – even Mrs Farintosh, in her own way. Mycroft Holmes and Mr Poskitt were, of course, above suspicion. I had no quarrel with anyone who worked at Debenham and Freebody. Which left… I frowned. 'The Stanleys?'

'But why? Mrs Stanley made it clear you would not be welcome if you called again, and surely that is all she would wish to do.' It was Sherlock's turn to frown. 'Unless it is a vendetta…'

'But I was trying to help them.' I rubbed my temples to release the tightness which would lead to a headache, then looked at the note in my lap: *I know where you live.* 'Whoever sent this wants me to run away, and that must be because of what I'm doing. What has provoked it?'

'Something that relates to them,' said Sherlock. 'It cannot be otherwise.' He put his arm round me. 'There is your work with clients, your work at the department store, and your recent task for Mycroft. And you help me.'

'I doubt any stocking thief would be so keen to be rid of me,' I said. 'And while I consider my personal detective work important, I doubt I have upset anybody by finding a missing fiancé or an opal tiara.'

'So it is Mycroft, or me,' said Sherlock.

'It must be,' I said. 'But what shall I do? I can't stay here and become a bag of nerves every time someone knocks at the door.' I imagined a future shut in my sitting room, scared to open the curtains in case someone was outside with a gun, never to see a play, or walk in the park, or go investigating with Sherlock. I buried my face in my hands. 'I can't live like this.'

'I know.' Sherlock rubbed my back and we sat for a while in silence. 'But what will you do?'

I took my hands away and looked at the note. 'This tells us nothing,' I said, dropping it on the floor. 'Cheap paper, cheap envelope, capital letters. All I can do is leave.' I sighed. 'But I don't want to leave you.' I remembered my guilt when I had packed in secret and written my note to Sherlock, knowing he could not stop me, since I would be long gone by the time he received it. I would not deceive him like that again.

'I don't want you to go,' said Sherlock. He kissed me: a gentle kiss, which felt like a goodbye. 'If it were not for the bomber, I would come with you, but we have no choice. Not if you are to stay safe.'

'But if I go, I am playing into their hands,' I said. 'I would be safe, but while I am gone they are free to do whatever it is they are doing. And I doubt it is good works.' I rested my chin on my hands, thinking.

'It is galling, I admit.' Sherlock sighed. 'We must get you out of the house without being seen, then to a place of safety close enough that you may be reached easily.'

'But how, and where?' I put aside the first part of

Sherlock's idea, and considered where I could go. A hotel was no good, since anyone might catch sight of me unless I stayed in my room, and that was little different from being shut up in Baker Street. 'I suppose I could disguise myself…' I made a face at the thought of the various heavy disguises I had worn recently, which had been uncomfortable and frankly unconvincing at close quarters. The thought of adopting any of them for a length of time was unpleasant.

I winced as I remembered my preparation for going undercover, when I had submitted to Evie's ministrations, and how upset and defeated I had felt when I saw myself for the first time. I heard the snip of Evie's scissors as she cut my hair, and felt the pain as she plucked my eyebrows and scrubbed my hands raw. But there was something else… I pushed those memories away. 'Evie,' I said. 'I could go to her. She is in London, and I doubt that whoever sent this would know of our friendship.'

'You are right,' said Sherlock, and for the first time he smiled. 'Now, how do we get you there?'

**

Martha giggled. 'This is very odd, ma'am.'

She was sitting in our bedroom, dressed in my clothes and a light-brown wig arranged in my usual style, watching Sherlock make me into as accurate a copy of herself as possible. I was wearing my dressing gown, but one of Martha's black stuff dresses hung ready on the wardrobe door, along with her coat and bonnet, and a pair of stout boots stood beneath.

'There,' said Sherlock, putting down the pencil he had

been amending my eyebrows with. 'That will do.' He lifted the wig from the mannequin head and settled it over my stocking cap. 'I presume you can do your own hair.'

'Of course,' I said. Taking a handful of pins and remembering the usual tight knot at the back of Martha's head, I coaxed the wig into obedience.

Sherlock looked at his watch. 'It's time to go, Martha,' he said. 'Do you have the letter I wrote?'

Martha patted my bag. 'Yes, sir.'

'Excellent,' said Sherlock. 'Hopefully you will not need to show it to anyone; it is a precaution. I shall accompany you to the train station, buy a ticket for somewhere suitably distant, and see you onto the train. You will get off at the first stop and buy a ticket to London with the money I have given you, then return by cab and enter via the back door. Is that clear?'

Martha nodded vigorously. 'Oh yes, sir.'

'Then let us go.' Sherlock turned to me. 'I am sorry to leave you alone except for Billy, Nell, but we must make Mrs Hudson's departure as convincing as possible.'

'I know,' I said, wishing he didn't have to go.

'I shall return within the hour.' He kissed my hand. Then he picked up the case we had packed together, Martha pulled down her veil, and they left.

I busied myself with putting on Martha's dress, woollen stockings and boots, which was the work of a few minutes. I thought of ringing for tea, but I did not want to appear to Billy in my current guise, and besides, drinking tea might undo Sherlock's handiwork. I sighed and took up the novel which had lain unopened by my bed for at least a week, but the words danced before my eyes and I put it down. In the end I found a deck of cards and played patience. It did not suit my mood at all, but it helped quiet the worries in my head.

It was almost an hour later when I heard the front door open. I longed to run downstairs and make certain that Sherlock had returned, but I did not want to risk being seen. The door closed, and quiet footsteps climbed the stairs. Sherlock put his head around the door. 'She is safely away,' he said. 'I did my best imitation of a dejected lover, and Martha did her best not to laugh at me.'

'Good,' I said. 'Do you think you were watched?'

'I am sure of it,' he answered. 'A man arrived in a cab perhaps two minutes after us, and loitered on the platform with his hands in his pockets. He did not board the train, and once it had gone, he vanished too.'

'Let us hope that is the end of it.'

Sherlock looked at me curiously. 'Would you consider staying?'

I stared at him. 'We have gone to so much trouble—'

'I know, and you are not going far, but…' He pushed his hair back. 'I don't want you to go. I shall worry about you.'

'I shall get word to you as soon as I can,' I said. 'I promise. But if I don't go soon, I shall miss Evie.' I stood up and took his hands. 'I would kiss you goodbye, but…'

'I would have kissed you goodbye before I started disguising you,' said Sherlock, 'but Martha was there.'

I smiled, though I did not feel like it. 'We shall save it for my return.' I put on Martha's coat and tied her bonnet over my wig.

Billy looked up from the newspaper when I walked into the kitchen, and stared. 'I knew you was doing it, ma'am, but really…' He grinned.

'I'm glad you're impressed.' I picked up the basket Martha used for shopping. I had already put extra money in her purse and written a shopping list, though I would not be patronising our usual shops. 'Hopefully the real thing will return later tonight, and it will not be too long until I see you again.'

'Right you are, ma'am,' said Billy.

'Please don't stare,' I said. 'I'm just the maid, remember.'

Billy returned to his newspaper as I took a deep breath, opened the back door, and stepped outside.

I walked to a nearby grocer's and bought things I hoped Evie would find useful. Then I moved on to a bakery, where I bought some buns. Finally I ventured further still, to a butcher, and bought pork chops. No one stared, no one frowned at me, yet still my heart thumped. I consulted my list as I stepped out of the shop, and kept walking. 'Ribbon,' I muttered, and turned my steps towards Debenham and Freebody, a short walk away.

Alf looked surprised as I approached the store; servants were not their usual clientele. 'My mistress wants ribbon,' I muttered, keeping my head down. If I could get past Alf without being recognised, I would feel safer.

'Of course, dearie,' said Alf, opening the door. As I passed I distinctly saw him catch the eye of the nearest assistant, then jerk his head at me. I felt indignant on

Martha's behalf.

The nearest assistant, luckily, was Gladys, and I marched to her with a sense of relief. No other customers were near. 'Gladys, it's me, Mrs Hudson,' I said quietly. 'Don't react.'

Gladys's eyes widened, but she said nothing.

'Thank you. Can you tell me where Evie is?'

'She's on handkerchiefs,' murmured Gladys.

I made my way towards the back of the store. Evie was leaning on the counter, flipping a handkerchief over and over with her forefinger. When she saw me approaching, she wearily drew herself up.

'Relax, Evie, it's me,' I said. 'I need your help.'

CHAPTER 26

Evie's eyes opened almost impossibly wide. 'What is it?' she muttered.

'Show me some handkerchiefs.'

Evie turned to the drawers behind her, pulled one out at random and deposited it on the counter. 'These ones are nice, madam.'

I took one and unfolded it, pretending to examine the lace edging. 'I must get away, Evie,' I murmured. 'First of all, can I stay with you tonight?'

'Yes, of course,' she said under her breath. 'What's happened?'

'I'll tell you later. For now, I have to work out a way of leaving here and getting to your flat without being seen. I don't think I was followed, but it's possible.'

Evie picked up another handkerchief and shook out the folds. 'This one has real Ghent lace, madam.' She leaned forward, took the other handkerchief from me, and laid it on the counter to fold it. 'The store closes in a quarter of an hour,' she said. 'That's when everyone will leave. If someone is waiting for you, they'll assume they missed you in the rush. We haven't much time.'

'I know,' I said, 'I'm sorry.'

'Put your hand on your heart and look pained. I'll be back in a minute.' She whisked to the next counter and had an earnest word with the assistant there, pointing in my direction. Then she returned. 'I've asked Adeline to watch my section. Don't worry, I didn't say it was you. I just said you'd had a funny turn and needed to sit down, so I'd take you in the back to avoid putting off the customers.'

'Thanks,' I said. 'I think.'

Evie took my arm and guided me towards the door that led to the offices and staff rooms. 'Slower,' she said. 'You're meant to be poorly, remember.'

'Sorry,' I said, and clutched at my heart again.

Evie took me to the cloakroom and sat me on a stool. 'What do you have in mind?' I asked, apprehensive.

'Nothing too terrible,' she said, and laughed. She went to a tall metal cupboard at the side of the room and pulled out a plain black dress with a white lace collar and cuffs already attached, like the one she wore. 'I'm afraid it's a bit long, but it'll hide those boots. Go and put it on, and I'll sort out some other things.' She gave me a sidelong glance. 'I don't suppose you have any money?'

I reached into my shopping basket and handed her Martha's purse. 'Don't spend it all,' I said. 'I may need some for travelling.'

'Don't worry, I won't. You get that dress on.' And she vanished.

I went into a cubicle and put on the dress. As Evie had said, it was too long, and the lace cuffs reached my fingers, but at least it was different. I put Martha's clothes in a neat pile.

Evie returned, out of breath, five minutes later. 'Here you are,' she said. She had a bright-red coat over her arm, and carried a matching hat.

'Good heavens,' I said, regarding them with dismay.

'If you're to be a shop girl, you can't dress like a duchess.' She grinned. 'Anyway, I have receipts, so you can return them provided you don't get them dirty.'

I reached for the coat, but Evie moved it away. 'Not yet. I need to do something with that hair.' She took a packet of hairpins out of her pocket. 'Sit down.'

I obeyed, and sat still while Evie combed, fluffed, and repinned. 'That's better.' She went to the cupboard again and returned with a pot of rouge and a box of powder in her hands. 'I won't be able to do much, but I'll try.'

I submitted to being powdered and rouged, hoping that Evie was restraining herself. 'There,' she said, after a minute or two, and pinned the hat in place. 'Put your coat on, and we can go.'

'What about the basket?' I said, getting up and taking the coat from her. 'I brought food. For you.'

Evie considered, then went out. While she was gone I put on the coat and went to the mirror. A pert, over-made-up shop girl wearing a cheap hat at a jaunty angle stared back at me.

Evie returned with a roll of the store's brown paper, with *Debenham & Freebody* printed on it, and a ball of string. She bundled my purchases together and made a parcel of them, then put on her coat and hat and tucked the parcel under her arm. 'People are starting to leave. We really must go.'

We went into the corridor and Evie strode towards the door that the staff used. 'Wait!' I cried.

Evie stopped. 'What is it?'

I moved forward slowly. 'We can't just walk out of here. We must check it's safe.'

'Which is exactly what they'd expect someone on the run to do.' Her expression softened. 'I know it's difficult, but trust me.'

I swallowed, and walked to meet her.

Evie undid the catch, pushed the door open and sailed through. 'Tomorrow, Mary,' she said, in a loud voice, 'I don't expect to see you wearing so much rouge and powder. It isn't nice. You may think it looks nice, but it doesn't.'

'Yes, ma'am,' I said in a small voice, trotting behind her.

'I know it's only your first day, but be careful about putting things back in the right place. Make sure you pair the stockings after you show them to a customer.'

'Yes, ma'am.'

Evie kept up her harangue on my shortcomings all the way to the omnibus stop, and until the omnibus arrived. We were the only people to get on, and I heaved a sigh of relief. 'Thank you,' I murmured.

'Thank *you*,' said Evie. 'You've saved me the trouble of shopping for dinner.' She studied me. 'Are you all right?' she whispered.

'Yes. No.' I shrugged. 'I don't know.'

'It's bad, isn't it?' she said, and her face was grave.

'Yes.'

***

We sat together at the kitchen table with mugs of tea. I had managed to eat perhaps half my dinner, but Evie had made short work of my spare chop and my untouched bun. Now, though, she was staring at me as if I had broken into her flat and put on one of her dresses.

Her husband had arrived home a few minutes after us. He had been rather bewildered when Evie explained that I would be staying the night, and even more so when I appeared for dinner scrubbed clean and with light-brown hair. 'I expect you ladies want to talk,' he said, as soon as he had finished his meal. 'I'll be home by eleven.' He took his coat and left.

'I always thought you'd been married,' said Evie, 'but I didn't think—'

'Who would?' I said, bitterly.

'And now he's sending you nasty notes.' Evie wrinkled her nose. 'If you don't mind me saying so, *Mrs Hudson*, you made a bad decision when you married him.'

'It wasn't like that.' I pushed my fringe out of my eyes. 'And you know perfectly well that my name is Nell. Besides, I'm not sure he wrote that note. It wasn't his writing.'

'Who else would do it? It's got to be him.' Evie sipped her tea and nodded with finality. 'Anyway, what will you do?'

'I'm not sure.' I picked up my cup of tea and under cover of drinking, looked at the small main room of the Smiths' flat. Evie was kindness itself, but I couldn't impose on them for more than a night or two. 'I should leave London, but I don't want to. My work is here. Sherlock is here—'

'Then don't go.' Evie put her cup down and clasped my hand with both of hers. 'I have an idea. I don't know what you'll think of it, but…' She gazed at me with troubled eyes.

I shrugged. 'I'll listen to anything, Evie.'

'Well.' She looked at the table, then at me. 'You know the department store, and most of the staff know you. So why don't you hide there? If anyone asks, you're a new girl learning the ropes, and I'm training you to replace me when the time comes.' She grinned. 'Mr Turner certainly won't mind another pair of hands. We can let on to the people who know you, and the new girls won't be any the wiser if we keep it up. Mr Holmes could even come in and see you, if he's careful. And we could give a description of that husband of yours to Alf and the others, so you wouldn't have to worry.' She scrutinised my face. 'You hate it, don't you?'

'No,' I said, slowly. 'I'm thinking about it.' As a short-term plan, it was better than anything I had thought of. 'It might work,' I said, at last. 'For a little while.'

'I'm so glad!' Evie jumped up and enveloped me in a hug. 'I didn't like to think of you among strangers. And you can sleep on the sofa till everything is sorted out.'

***

The little carriage clock on the mantelpiece, probably a wedding present, chimed midnight. On the sofa, wrapped in blankets, I cried as softly as I could. Evie was so pleased

192

with her plan, so convinced that it would work, and so relieved that I would be safe that I had had to hide my feelings until she eventually retired to bed.

How can you be so ungrateful, I chided myself, but ahead of me was day after day of folding handkerchiefs and serving customers and standing at the counter and no doubt making a bad job of it. And I would no longer be able to disguise myself and roam the store looking for potential thieves, because someone was looking for me.

I was the hunter, and now I am the hunted.

I allowed myself a muffled sniff and wiped a tear away. I had been a detective with my own practice, a professional who had been called in by Whitehall, and now, for the foreseeable future, I was a junior shop girl who slept on her friend's sofa because she dared not venture into the city where she had spent her whole life.

I closed my eyes and tried to visualise a way out of my predicament, but each tick of the clock seemed to mock me. In the end I gave up and stared into the darkness, willing sleep to come and take me somewhere else. Anywhere else.

CHAPTER 27

The shriek of a whistling kettle woke me with a start. I opened an eye and saw a shape moving in the tiny area that served as a kitchen: Evie, already fully dressed.

'Morning, sleepyhead,' she said, smiling. 'I thought about waking you, but I decided to let you have your sleep out.'

'Thank you.' I struggled to a sitting position. Perhaps it was the effect of having slept surprisingly well, but I felt more positive this morning. After all, this arrangement would not last for ever. I remembered the telegram Sherlock had received from Mycroft, giving the name of a lawyer. Perhaps, while I was gone, Sherlock could meet with him… 'Do you have pen and paper I could borrow, Evie?'

'Top sideboard drawer,' Evie said, as she added milk to the three mugs in front of her. Then she turned. 'What do you want it for?'

'I'm going to send a telegram to Sherlock.' I got up and padded to the sideboard.

'Oh,' said Evie. 'Is that wise?' Her mouth twitched. 'Shop girls don't usually send telegrams, you see.'

I sighed. She was right, of course, but the limitations of my assumed identity were already annoying me. 'In that case, could Mr Smith possibly take it for me?'

Evie considered.

'I only want to let Sherlock know I'm safe, and where he can find me,' I said plaintively.

'I'm sure he can,' Evie said, as if soothing a child. 'You'll have to be quick, for he leaves before we do.' She picked up a plate with a thick slice of bread and jam. 'I'll take him his breakfast and ask.' She eyed the remaining mugs and plates. 'I'm sure you can serve yourself.'

Now that I was under pressure, every word flew out of my head. I wrote out the address and recipient in clear capitals, then bit the end of the pencil stub which was all I had been able to find in the drawer. Eventually I settled on the following:

Safe with E and working at store STOP Come ASAP and ask for Mary STOP N

It did not say half of what I wanted, but I suspected Evie's husband would balk at the idea, not to mention the expense, of sending a longer wire. I scrabbled in my purse and laid a shilling on the sheet of paper.

Evie returned, looking defensive. 'You could post a letter on the way in to work, and no one would think anything of it. And it would be cheaper.'

'I don't mind paying,' I said, trying not to show my irritation. 'It's important that he gets this quickly.'

Evie blinked.

I rose. 'You said you would help me, Evie. If I can't even ask for this one thing—'

'It isn't that,' said Evie. 'He just thought it was a lot of money to spend when a letter would get there almost as soon.' She picked up the paper and the coin, went back into the bedroom, and closed the door. I heard muffled voices, neither sounding particularly pleased, then Evie came out. 'He says it's your money. Now do get on and eat your breakfast. It'll be hard enough to explain this to Mr Turner without being late.'

**

I stood at the counter beside Evie and tried not to stare at the large clock on the wall. Half past ten, and I was already bored. I was about to prop my head on my hand when I remembered how much rouge and powder I was wearing, and forbore.

Evie nudged me. 'We are allowed to talk when there aren't any customers, you know. You don't have to just stand there.'

'Sorry,' I said, pulling myself up from the slouch I was falling into. 'I have a lot on my mind.'

I knew I ought to be grateful to Evie. She had taken the lead in our meeting with Mr Turner, glossing over the circumstances which had brought me to the store and presenting my extended stay as an opportunity, since naturally I would take no salary. Even so, Mr Turner had hummed and hawed, eyed me with a speculative expression which I was sure he would never have assumed if I had been in my normal clothes instead of a shop assistant's uniform, and finally declared that he supposed he would have to agree, 'since the two of you seem set on it.' He gave Evie a severe look. 'No messing about, you

196

understand? I expect both of you to work hard and be a credit to the store.'

'Thank you, Mr Turner,' I murmured, my head bent. Under the desk, my nails dug into my palms.

He smacked the desk and Evie jumped. 'Off you go, then. You can't lounge in here all day.'

Afterwards, at the counter, I said, 'I didn't expect Mr Turner to be like that.'

'Like what?' said Evie, who was rearranging a tray of handkerchiefs into a many-pointed star.

'He spoke to me as if he didn't know me,' I said. 'As if I were really a shop girl.'

Evie snorted. 'Shows I've disguised you well. He's judging you on what he sees, as most people do.' She raised her eyebrows. 'Did you expect special treatment?'

I considered. 'I suppose I did.'

'If you were doing him a favour, you'd get it. But you've asked him to take you on, a person with no experience whatsoever in selling, and he's got his profits to think of.' She turned back to her tray, and that was that.

So I stood there, growing more and more bored. I had even offered to fold handkerchiefs, to take my mind off things, but Evie had said firmly that it would be quicker if she did it, and I could watch for customers. So I surveyed the women wandering from counter to counter alone and in pairs, but no one ever came our way.

I thought of home. Sherlock must have received my telegram by now. I imagined him reading it, his face lighting up, and making plans to visit me. I had already briefed Alf the doorman to look out for two people – a tall, dark, broad young man with a deep tan, and a tall, slim, brown-haired young man with a prominent nose – and to inform me promptly of the appearance of either. 'I may go and see if Alf—'

'Yes, do,' said Evie. 'Anything to settle you down.'

I hurried to the main door of the department store, but Alf was already shaking his head by the time I reached him.

'You're sure?' I said.

'I'm positive. No man has come in, let alone any matching the descriptions you gave me.' He smiled. 'If I could, I'd bring him to you myself, except I mustn't leave the door.'

'Thank you, Alf.'

He touched the peak of his cap. 'I'm sure I'll see you again soon.'

I returned to the back of the store much more slowly than I had left it. *At this rate, I shall be dismissed before the day is out.* I wasn't sure whether to be pleased or sorry at the prospect. I moved from department to department, not dawdling, but not moving with a shop assistant's brisk step, either.

Something caught my eye: a woman who had been meandering between departments stepped behind a pillar near the perfume counter. It was not furtive, exactly, but odd. I continued towards the counter at the same pace, but the woman did not reappear. I walked past that counter and the next and stopped at the one beyond, where Gladys was humming to herself as she tidied a tray of lace collars and cuffs. 'I don't suppose a young man has come in asking for

Mary?' I enquired.

Gladys glanced up. 'No young man,' she said. 'Sorry.'

'Or Mrs Hudson?'

She shook her head. 'No young men at all, I'm afraid. I'll let you know if one does turn up.'

'Thank you.' The woman was walking away from the perfume counter, and I saw blonde hair tucked beneath her little hat. Her business had been concluded quickly. I gave her a few more yards, then moved in the same direction, keeping out of sight as much as I could in case she looked round. But she did not. *Perhaps she is browsing. Perhaps she's imagining what she would buy if she had enough money.* That thought, in my present depleted circumstances, resonated with me, but still I followed.

She stopped at the counter which sold stockings and spoke to the assistant there. The assistant turned to pull out a tray from the rack and the customer stood, waiting. Then she ran a gloved hand over the stockings and I started – I knew those gloves. I had my own pair.

The mysterious yellow-haired woman is back.

She spoke to the assistant, who turned to the racks and paused, looking for the tray she wanted. Quick as a flash, the woman took a rolled pair of stockings from the edge of the tray, smoothing the others to fill the gap, and stuffed them in her bag. She chose another pair from the new tray, admired them as the assistant unrolled them, watched the assistant wrap them, and handed her the money. The parcel, too, went into her bag.

I thought about hurrying over and apprehending the woman there and then, but I did not. Something stayed me:

a desire not to share my discovery with the assistant, but to have this capture all to myself. Mr Turner thought I was a liability, did he? A danger to the profits of the store? *I'll show you.* So I let her wander off, then followed, not hurrying, but gaining on her.

She was moving towards the exit, glancing at the counters on either side, but not stopping. Her business seemed to be concluded for the day. I had perhaps seven yards left in which to catch up with her. If she left the store, things would be much more complicated, and I had no wish for that. I hurried after her and drew level four yards from the door. Alf had seen me, and was already shaking his head.

'Stop right there,' I muttered, in a voice only she would hear.

She started, but kept moving. She did not look round.

'I said stop,' I said, slightly louder, and tapped her shoulder. 'I saw what you did.'

'I don't know what you mean,' she said, her face still turned away, her pace quickening.

'You know exactly what I mean.' I caught her arm and pulled her around to face me.

Her mouth was already open to deny it, but her jaw dropped as she took me in. 'But you're not—'

I barely heard her words; I was too busy staring. For in front of me, looking as if she had seen a ghost, was a servant from the grand house where I had been an undercover spy.

Milady's pet: her lady's maid, who hated me.

My nemesis, Susan.

CHAPTER 28

'You're coming with me.'

Susan struggled in my grip, her expression alternating between anger at being caught and disbelief at having been caught by me.

'Stop that immediately.' I administered a slight shake. 'Either you walk with me in a civilised manner or I shall hand you over to Alf, who will summon a policeman. It's entirely up to you.'

Her struggles stopped immediately. 'Not the police,' she whispered.

'Good. I'll let go of you on condition that you don't attempt to run away. We're going that way.' I pointed to the door leading to the back offices of the store. 'You go first.'

Susan walked slowly ahead of me, head bent, as if she were on her way to the gallows. My mind was in a whirl. Susan was the last person I had expected to see in a smart London department store; and from her expression, I was the last person she had expected to see, too. I allowed myself a grim smile. But something nagged at me – something I couldn't put my finger on.

Once through the door, I led the way to Mr Turner's

office and knocked smartly.

'Come,' said an abrupt voice.

I waved Susan in, and when she did not move, took her arm and propelled her into the office. 'Good morning, Mr Turner. I thought you'd like to know that I have apprehended a shoplifter this morning.'

Mr Turner's expression changed from irritable to stern. 'What has she taken?'

I looked at Susan. 'Turn out your bag.'

Her lower lip trembled, and the hand holding the bag shook.

'Oh, for heaven's sake.' I took the bag from her, opened it, and upended it on Mr Turner's desk. A jumble of items clattered out, and I set aside the brown-paper parcel containing the stockings. 'She bought these,' I said, 'but she stole these.' I held up the other, more expensive pair that she had taken from the tray. 'As for the rest…' I sorted through the little collection of objects. 'I suspect the cologne is ours. I saw her sneaking about by the counter; that was what drew my attention to her.'

'And that pocket mirror,' said Mr Turner, pointing to it. 'That's a line we stock.' He cast a contemptuous eye over the remainder. 'Everything else is too cheap and nasty.'

Susan was crying quietly and wringing her hands. 'What have you got to say for yourself, my girl?' demanded Mr Turner. 'Tears won't help; if you didn't want to get caught, you shouldn't have done it.'

She mumbled something and Mr Turner cupped a hand to his ear. 'What's that? Speak up, will you!'

'They weren't for me,' she muttered.

'I don't care who they were for!' Mr Turner shouted. 'You've got no business stealing.' He banged the desk. 'I don't have time for this.' I raised an eyebrow at the illustrated magazine open on his desk and he glared at me. 'Take her away and deal with her. Just make sure you keep her out of the way of customers. It's bad enough losing stock, without losing business too.' He eyed Susan. 'You!' She jumped as if she had been struck. 'Pack your things and get out.' He allowed me a brief nod. 'Good work. Now, back on duty.'

Susan packed up her things, sniffling all the while, while I wondered what to do. The easiest course was to hand her to Alf and wash my hands of the matter. The kindest course was to let Susan go with a warning and circulate her description among the staff so that she was barred from the store. I already knew I would do neither of these.

I opened the door and held it for her. 'This way.'

I took her to a stockroom where spare furniture was stored: chairs, stools, mannequins. I placed chairs for Susan and myself. 'Sit,' I barked. 'What do you mean, those things weren't for you?'

'They weren't,' said Susan. 'I mean, they were for me. I got scared because he was shouting and I said the wrong thing.' She sat there, not looking at me, feet together and hands fidgeting in her lap, the bag on the floor by her chair.

'The stockings you bought were for you,' I said.

'Yes.' A quick, scared glance. 'And the other things were, too.'

I had caught her out, but I still didn't understand. 'Why

would you buy something cheap for yourself, then steal something more expensive for somebody else?'

'I didn't,' she muttered. 'I told you, I was nervous.'

'I'm sure you were,' I said. 'You could go to prison for this. But I still don't believe you. I suggest you sit there and think about your position.' I studied her, trying to work out what was going on. Every so often she glanced at me, like a child peeping to see if I was still angry, then looked away. She was a picture of cringing subservience – or was she? Was she playing a part? I recalled the moment when I had apprehended her: the way her jaw had dropped when she realised who I was. Her words: 'But you're not—' That was an odd thing to say. Of course she would be shocked to see me, but those words didn't fit. *But you're not . . . what?*

Then I grasped it. Susan had not been shocked to see *me*, as such. She had been shocked that I was in the store and able to catch her, because I was supposed to be somewhere else. *But you're not meant to be here.* I gasped. The shop assistants had told me about the yellow-haired suspected shoplifter, who never appeared when it was my day at the store. Every other day, but not *my* day. How long had Susan known of my position? And more importantly, *how* had she known?

'How do you know I work here?' I demanded. 'And how did you know that I wasn't supposed to be here today?' I thought of Sherlock escorting Martha to the train station, and the man who had watched her go, and my blood ran cold. Was *she* part of this? 'Answer me!'

Susan gazed at me with wide china-blue eyes. 'I don't

know what you mean.'

'Yes you do. I've got a good mind to shake the truth out of you.'

She whimpered and shrank back against her chair. 'Don't touch me!'

The door burst open and Evie appeared. 'What's going on?' Her frown became bemusement.

'I'm glad to see you, Evie,' I said, standing up. 'This woman has been caught shoplifting. Please tell Mr Turner that I am taking her off the premises to deal with her.'

Evie looked from me to Susan, and back again. 'Shouldn't you just hand her to the police?'

'Not yet,' I said, 'I haven't finished with her.' I took Susan's arm and yanked her to her feet.

Evie took a step forward. 'I don't think you should—'

'I'll return later,' I said. 'Maybe.' I pulled Susan towards the door.

'What will I say to Mr Turner?' Evie said.

'Whatever you like: I don't care. Anyway, he knows I'm dealing with it. Let me through, please.'

Evie stood back reluctantly, and I half-walked, half-dragged Susan to the door. 'Where are you taking me?' she shrieked, struggling more as we got closer to the outside world.

'To visit a detective of my acquaintance,' I said. 'Since you won't tell me the truth, let's see what you say to him. If that doesn't work, there's always the police.'

A low, despairing wail came out of Susan, and her body sagged so that I had to bear her weight, but I felt no sympathy for her. At that moment, if I had thought I could cut the truth out of her, I would have fetched a knife with pleasure.

I secured a cab quickly, and before long I was banging on the door of my home, gripping Susan's arm so that she could not get away. Billy answered, his face full of anticipation which vanished as soon as he saw me.

'Is Mr Holmes in?' I asked, without ceremony.

Billy's eyes widened as he took in my uniform. 'No, ma'am, he's on a case. He had a letter.'

I froze. 'A printed letter? In a white envelope?'

'Yes.' Billy glanced at Susan, then at me. 'He took the toolbox.'

'When did he leave? Do you know where he went?'

'He left not ten minutes ago, ma'am. You just missed him, and I don't know where he went. He ran out saying there was no time to lose, but he left the note behind.'

I bundled Susan into the house with such force that she almost went sprawling. 'This woman has information and we must get it out of her, but I need Mr Holmes for that. Take her down to the kitchen and watch her like a hawk. Lock her up if you must, but do not let her out of your sight. I have to find Mr Holmes.'

Billy gave me a pleading look. 'But, ma'am…'

I grabbed the note and the envelope from the hall table. 'Just do it, Billy. I don't have time to discuss this.' I hurried upstairs. 'I'll be in the consulting room.'

As I climbed the stairs, my sense of foreboding increased until the letter trembled in my hand. Was it a coincidence that Sherlock had received another letter the day after I had supposedly left the house? My head swam, and I gripped the banister for a moment. Then I took a deep breath and carried on. *I have to find Sherlock.*

CHAPTER 29

Dear Mr Holmes,

I do so enjoy writing to you. It is like penning a letter to a dear acquaintance; I know you will understand me. I feel you and I are alike – different from others, set apart.

Firstly, I must congratulate you on your swift discovery of my little gift for you at Speakers' Corner. I do hope that you and the onlookers appreciated it.

However, I note that you have remained silent on the matter. I am disappointed, since I want you to receive all the glory due to your part in the proceedings. But if that is your desire, so be it.

In accordance with your apparent wishes, I have prepared a surprise for you which is more remote, though still perfectly accessible to the public. Where would be the fun otherwise?

So far I have celebrated one of our great seafarers, and also those individuals who dare to stand up and speak out, whether anyone wants to hear them or no. This time I wish to pay tribute to one of our industrialists, who was instrumental in the growth of the textile industry. He has been unjustly overlooked; perhaps you could pay him a visit and let me know your thoughts? He keeps select hours, though, so you will need to visit him by one o'clock today to have any chance of an audience.

Oh, and as he is a private individual, you must visit alone. Not even your faithful scribe Dr Watson may attend you.

Yours most sincerely,
An Admirer

I raised my eyes from the letter and took in the mess that was the consulting room. Sherlock's index and other books were strewn over the bureau, on the low table, in the armchair, dropped on the floor—

A great industrialist in the textile industry, unjustly overlooked... I thought of Richard Arkwright and Samuel Crompton, but they were scarcely overlooked. I had no idea where to start, and so I began where Sherlock had left off, consulting the books he had pulled from the shelves. I saw volume *A* of the index – he had thought of Arkwright too, then. A biographical dictionary lay open on the low table. I sat down on the sofa.

Hudson, Jabez.

I winced, and read on.

Inventor of an early prototype of the mule. His invention was in use for a short time but was quickly superseded by Crompton's superior model. Hudson always claimed that Crompton had stolen the idea from him, but this was never proved, and Hudson could produce no evidence to support his assertion. He died in poverty in

1801. His grieving widow and the citizens of Castleford, Lancashire, where he was born, raised funds by public subscription to have him buried in Highgate Cemetery.

Hudson's legacy—

I had read enough. I glanced at the books Sherlock had left; another was open at an entry on the same man. It had to be the answer.

If only I am not too late. I consulted my watch, which I had retained despite Evie's disapproval. It was almost noon. I was sure I could reach the cemetery well before one o'clock, London traffic permitting, but then there was the matter of finding Hudson's grave.

I shook my thoughts off and ran downstairs, then made my way more sedately down the kitchen steps. I found Susan seated at the table, crying, and being watched uneasily by both Martha and Billy. They all turned at my entrance, and Susan gave vent to a despairing sniff.

'Billy, a word, please.' I beckoned him outside the door. 'I think I know where Mr Holmes is,' I whispered. 'I am going to Highgate Cemetery to find him.'

Billy appeared perturbed rather than pleased. 'What is it?' I asked.

'Are you going like that?'

I imagined how I must look – hatless, ungloved, without even a coat, and plastered in cosmetics. Sherlock wouldn't care. 'I don't have time to change.'

'What will we do with her?' Billy jerked a thumb at the door. 'She just keeps crying.'

'I can't deal with her now,' I said. 'You'll have to

manage as best you can. If you really can't cope, call a policeman, say that she was caught shoplifting, and refer him to Mr Turner at Debenham and Freebody. But that is a last resort, do you hear? I must go.' I ran upstairs and slammed my way out of the house.

***

It was only a few miles to Highgate Cemetery, and the cabbie drove quickly, but I spent the journey caught between anticipation of telling Sherlock about Susan and worry that I had made an error. What if Sherlock had jumped to a false conclusion? I might be heading for the wrong place entirely, and we would still have a bomb to deactivate with – I checked my watch – half an hour to go until it exploded. Or what if I had misunderstood the books in the consulting room? *Please hurry*, I thought, willing the cab to move faster.

At long last we pulled up. 'Highgate Cemetery, ma'am,' the cabman called.

I had half a sovereign in my hand as I jumped out of the cab. 'Won't you wait for your change?' the cabbie shouted as I dashed away.

'Hang the change!' I cried, picked up my skirts, and ran. As I did, I remembered Sherlock saying exactly the same thing outside the National Portrait Gallery, and smiled.

An attendant who was raking leaves from the lawn near the entrance paused and leaned on his rake as I approached. 'What's the hurry?' he asked.

'I need to find the grave of Jabez Hudson,' I panted.

He chuckled. 'Do you know, you're the second person

to ask me that today. You can't miss it. Go down that path' – he pointed – 'then turn right at the gravestone with a pair of cherubs on the top, and you'll see a sort of domed shape. That's where he is, in there. Although I don't know what the rush is about,' he added, as I hurried along the path.

I ran past austere headstones, elaborate monuments, and grave markers with the lettering worn away, but I had no eyes for anything except a pair of cherubs. At last I saw them, and the path which curved to the right. I took it, and before me, just as the attendant had said, was a small building perhaps a hundred yards distant, with pillars on either side of the door and a domed top. *The citizens of Castleford clearly had a penny or two to spare*, I thought, as I pelted down the path. I glanced at my watch as I ran: a quarter to one. The door stood open; he must be within. 'Sherlock!' I cried, even though I was too distant for him to hear.

The boom seemed to come from the bowels of the earth, and the ground quivered beneath my feet. I shrieked as Jabez Hudson's tomb folded in on itself and the dome, cracked in two, crashed to the ground. Dust and rubble shot from the wreckage, and smoke billowed towards me.

I ran forward, but a man caught my arm. He had been standing perhaps thirty yards from the mausoleum, contemplating a grave, and had jumped back in alarm at the bang. 'You can't go in there, ma'am,' he said, staring. 'Can't you see it's dangerous?'

'Someone is in there,' I said, trying to pull free. 'I have to get him out.'

'You can't, ma'am – look at it!' He was short, broad, smart in a frock coat, and stronger than he appeared. I tried to pry his fingers from my arm, and gently he pulled my hand away. 'But I'm afraid you're right. I saw someone go in, and he didn't come out before – before that.'

'What did he look like? Was he carrying a toolbox?'

The man's eyes met mine, and there was sympathy in them. 'My dear, I think I should take you somewhere out of the way. There are several benches near the entrance, or perhaps a tearoom…' He glanced down the path, and I saw his relief when he faced me again. 'Here comes an attendant.'

The man who had directed me to the tomb was sprinting down the path. When he got closer he skidded to a halt, his mouth an O of surprise. 'Well I never!' He turned to us. 'Did you see what happened?'

'A chap hurried in,' said my companion, 'and not five minutes later the whole thing collapsed.' He realised he was still holding my arm, and let go. 'This young, er, lady, saw it too.' He leaned towards the attendant and lowered his voice, as if by doing so I would not hear him. 'I think she knows the man who went in there.'

'Is that why you were in a rush, dearie?' the attendant asked.

Unable to speak, I nodded.

'Thank heavens you weren't any quicker,' said the attendant. 'Otherwise you might have been in there, too.' He stared at the pile of rubble and broken stones in disbelief. 'I'll have to go and fetch my boss. I hope he knows what to do, because I don't.' He sped along the

213

path, shouting 'Back! Back!' to all the visitors who were coming to see what had happened.

Spectators ventured closer and closer, and exclaimed, and conversed among themselves. Some pointed at me in the course of their chatter, and I turned my face away.

The attendant returned, accompanied by an older man with a bowler hat and a bristling moustache, who took one look at the scene and told him to go and fetch a policeman double quick. 'And whoever else is on duty. If there's anyone under there, we need to get what's left of them out for a Christian burial.'

The man who had restrained me touched my arm. 'Please come away. It won't do you any good to see this.'

Numb, I stared at the smoking ruins of the mausoleum. My companion, my lover, my husband in all but name, was dead, and I had not even had the chance to say goodbye. Our adversary, at last, had won.

CHAPTER 30

A clock chimed one.

That was when the explosion should have happened.

Had it been an accident? I found myself shaking my head. The out-of-the-way location, the instruction to come alone, the letter a day after I had apparently left – all these things pointed to the bomber's intention. He had lulled us into a false sense of security with his games, and Sherlock had rushed willingly to his death.

A pack of attendants came running, followed at a more sedate pace by a policeman who already had his notebook ready. The attendants gathered round their manager, who pointed to the pile of rubble. *What if—*

'Stop!' I cried. 'There may still be live explosives!'

The man in the bowler hat stared at me as if I had taken leave of my senses. 'Explosives?' He eyed the broken stones. 'Mausoleums don't explode. No, this tomb has collapsed, I think you'll find.'

'It exploded,' I said, quietly. 'Didn't it?' I turned to the man in the frock coat.

'I certainly heard a bang,' he said. 'But I wasn't facing that way, so I couldn't say.'

'I was running towards it,' I said, 'and I saw what happened. I *know* what happened. This was caused by dynamite, and you must be very careful.'

The policeman licked his pencil and loomed above me. 'Madam, may I ask how you are so sure that this was caused by dynamite?'

'She is obviously distressed,' said the man in the frock coat, taking my arm again. 'It would be inappropriate to cross-examine her.' He gave the policeman a significant look and tapped his head with the hand that was not supporting me.

Anger gave me the strength I needed to pull free of him. 'I know about the dynamite because I am a detective,' I said. 'The man who went into that mausoleum is Sherlock Holmes, who is also a detective. This is one in a series of bombs which have been planted around London, and which Mr Holmes was tasked with finding and disabling. Only this time – this time...'

'So you say you are a detective,' said the policeman, taking in my dress with barely concealed incredulity. He raised his eyebrows at the man in the frock coat, who shook his head sadly.

'My name is Mrs Hudson,' I said, 'and I am known to Inspectors Lestrade and Gregson at Scotland Yard. If you doubt the truth of what I am saying, you may refer to them.'

The policeman scratched his head. 'I've heard of both those gentlemen.'

'Yes, but what are we to do about this?' asked the man in the bowler hat. 'Are we to close the cemetery while we

216

clear this mess up? There will, I presume, be a body.' He glanced at me. 'This Mr . . . Mr...'

'Holmes,' I said. 'Sherlock Holmes.'

'Yes, Mr Holmes. Would you happen to know who is his next of kin?'

At that moment I would have given anything to turn back the clock, to have accepted Sherlock's proposal and entered into a marriage which, while bigamous, would have given me at least some standing in the eyes of the law. But it was too late. 'His nearest relation is his brother, Mr Mycroft Holmes,' I said, and I had to drag the words out of myself. 'You will find him either at Whitehall or Somerset House. Mr Holmes's parents live some distance away.'

The policeman wrote it all down laboriously in his notebook, then snapped it shut. 'Time enough to contact him once we have examined the site.' He took a few steps towards the ruins of Jabez Hudson's tomb. A chunk of stone fell and he jumped back. 'On reflection, best to secure reinforcements before we begin.' He looked at me. 'You mentioned Inspector Lestrade, madam. Would he have an interest in this matter?'

I nodded, still gazing at the heap of broken stones and debris beneath which Sherlock was buried. Something gleamed in the rubble. *Could it be...?* I dashed forward, knelt among the fragments, and began to throw them aside. *There it is...* My hands scraped on jagged edges and my nails filled with dirt, but I moved the obstructions piece by piece. Then I gasped, and covered my mouth with my hands.

Billy's toolbox was crushed, a newly exposed edge

gleaming bright in the winter sun. I stumbled to my feet and backed away.

The man in the frock coat hurried forward and supported me as my knees gave way. 'I'm so sorry,' he said. 'I take it he was a friend.'

'He was more than that.' I flung up my head and addressed the men standing around me. 'He was a fine man, a great man, and if I could live my life again I would ask nothing more than to have been his wife, even with such an end as this.' I wanted to cry, and yet somehow I could not. My throat was a tight knot of pain.

The policeman cleared his throat. 'I'll see to those reinforcements,' he said. 'Madam, I think it best that you go home.' He still didn't look as if he believed a word of what I had said, and I had no energy or will left to convince him. 'Let me get you a cab.'

'But what if—'

'Don't worry, madam.' The frock-coated man gave my arm to the policeman, and he patted it. 'If we find anything, we shall contact the brother of – of Mr Holmes.' And with that, he led me away. His grip was firm, he was a policeman, and there was absolutely nothing I could do to change his mind.

***

The cab driver could have taken me anywhere, and I would not have known. My mind was too full. Sherlock in the morning, waking with a sleepy smile. Sherlock bursting into my sitting room, full of news. Sherlock disguising himself for a case, wandering into the bedroom and asking me to attach a side whisker or sew on a button.

And finally, Sherlock painting me in Martha's image so that I could escape from Baker Street, neither of us able to say the goodbye we wished to.

I buried my face in my hands and felt sticky rouge and gritty powder. My hands came away a mess of pink and white mingled with grey dirt, but my appearance did not matter now. When the cabman had asked my destination, I had replied '221B Baker Street' without a thought. I did not care who knew my address. The worst had already happened, and I had nothing left to fear.

Eventually the cab drew up at the familiar front door. I paid the cabman and he drove off, no doubt chuckling over the woman in her shop-assistant's uniform who had paid him with a silver crown. The steps seemed like a mountain, but I dragged myself up them and pulled the doorbell.

Billy answered, and his expression changed from polite enquiry to wonder, then to shocked understanding. 'Come inside, ma'am, quickly.'

'I'm sorry, Billy,' I said. 'Mr Holmes is dead. Your toolbox…' A storm of weeping overtook me. I could no more have held it back than stopped a charging horse.

Billy led me to my sitting room, still weeping, and sat me in an armchair. He fetched a bowl of water and bathed my filthy, grazed hands, then brought fresh water and washed my face as gently as if I had been a child. 'I'll go and ask Martha to bring tea,' he said. 'Is there anything else I can get you, ma'am?'

I shook my head. I felt hollowed out.

Billy moved to the door. 'Shall I call a policeman about

the lady?'

The lady? Then I remembered. 'Yes,' I said, and my voice didn't sound like my own, it was so hoarse and rough. 'Thank you, Billy.' My triumphant capture of Susan at the department store that morning seemed a lifetime ago. *The department store…* 'Billy?'

He turned, half out of the door. 'Yes, ma'am?'

'Did a telegram come this morning for – for—'

Billy shook his head. 'There was no telegram, ma'am. Nothing, except—'

I banged the arm of the chair. 'If he had sent it, Sherlock might be alive now!' I sprang to my feet, snatched up the inkstand and flung it against the wall.

'I'll fetch Martha,' said Billy, his eyes wide with shock, and fled.

***

The clock chimed nine. Martha had helped me into my nightdress and brought me hot milk, and sat by my bedside holding my hand. Billy had tried to tempt me with toast and broth, and eventually, after much dispute with Martha, had measured me out a very small dose of a sleeping draught. I had floated somewhere between sleeping and waking, unsure which was dream and which reality.

Billy had broken the news to Dr Watson when he came home. I heard his cry of horror, followed by 'He can't be – he can't be!', and turned my face to the wall, feeling the pain all over again through him. Dr Watson's footsteps ascended the stairs, paused, then kept climbing. I am ashamed to admit that I was relieved that he did not wish to speak to me.

The doorbell rang and for a moment, before I remembered, my heart leapt. Martha must have felt me start, for she squeezed my hand. 'Billy will answer it,' she said softly.

The front door opened, followed by the hum of a hushed conversation. Light footsteps ran upstairs and Billy entered. 'Inspector Lestrade is here, ma'am, and he would like to see you.' His face indicated that the inspector had not brought good news.

I considered whether I was well enough to receive the inspector, and concluded that I would probably feel neither better nor worse if I waited. I sighed. 'Show him in, Billy.' With Martha's help I sat up and put on a bed jacket.

Inspector Lestrade stepped into the room, looking as if he did not know where to put himself. 'Please place a chair for the inspector, Martha,' I said.

He sat down and put his hat on his lap. 'I was at Highgate,' he said.

I closed my eyes and he was silent, waiting. I forced my eyelids open. 'Go on.'

'The police and the attendants worked for hours,' he said, 'and eventually they recovered...' He pinched the bridge of his nose. 'They recovered sufficient to suggest that one person was in the mausoleum when the explosion took place. Mr Mycroft Holmes attended the scene and it was agreed, beyond reasonable doubt, that the remains are those of his brother, Mr Sherlock Holmes.' He bowed his head. 'I am terribly sorry.'

The silence stretched until it frayed. 'If there's anything I can do, Nell, anything at all...'

I closed my eyes again. 'Please go.' I heard his footsteps, the creak of the stairs, and the soft click of the front door as it shut. I kept my eyes closed and huddled on my side of the bed, but no matter how tightly I curled myself I was still adrift in a vast, formless sea, and all I wanted to do was drown.

CHAPTER 31

EXPLOSION AT HIGHGATE CEMETERY
One man killed

Fenians may be responsible for an unprovoked attack causing the death of one man.

The explosion occurred at approximately a quarter to one yesterday afternoon. A police investigation revealed that dynamite had been planted in the tomb of Jabez Hudson, an industrialist.

The deceased was identified as Mr Sherlock Holmes, an amateur detective who occasionally assisted the police. His brother, the senior civil servant Mr Mycroft Holmes, made the identification.

The reason for the attack is unclear, but Inspector Lestrade of Scotland Yard, who was called to the scene, mentioned the Fenian bombings carried out in public locations across London: 'Given the similarity of this attack, and the lack of warning,' he told a reporter, 'it is foolish to discount the possibility.'

Inspector Lestrade also urged members of the public to be cautious, and report any suspicious devices to a *policeman immediately. 'Untrained citizens should not attempt to do the job of the police, however good their intentions. We shall be vigilant, and aim to apprehend the culprit as soon as humanly possible.'*

Mr Holmes's family was unavailable for comment.

Dr Watson threw down the newspaper. 'It's a travesty!' he cried. 'What does Lestrade think he's doing, misleading everyone like this? We know full well that this was a personal vendetta!' He took another piece of toast from the rack and gave me an accusing look. 'You don't seem particularly bothered, Nell.'

'That is because I read the article two hours ago,' I replied. 'I don't believe Inspector Lestrade is misleading the public. I suspect he doesn't know what to do.'

I had lain awake, staring into the darkness, until I could bear it no longer and rang for something to make me sleep. Billy came, as I had suspected he would, and looked apprehensive as I made my request.

'I don't think that's a good idea, ma'am,' he said.

'Nor would I, usually,' I said. 'But it isn't every day that the man you love is murdered, is it?'

Billy sighed. 'We shall all miss him terribly, ma'am.' I saw how haggard he was. He had not slept either.

'Perhaps you should take some too,' I said, half joking.

'No, ma'am: I've seen what it can do.'

My mind flashed back to the dark days following Jack's disappearance, when I had been prescribed laudanum to numb the pain. I would have done anything to get hold of it – and Billy had cared enough about me to wean me off

224

the drug. My face flushed with shame. 'I shall try to manage without, Billy,' I said. 'Please could you bring me warm milk, and have some yourself if you think it will help.' The relief on his face was indescribable.

Eventually I drifted into an uneasy sleep. At least I did not dream of Sherlock – that would have been too much to bear – but each time I woke, I realised anew that he was gone. As the first suspicion of light coloured the sky I stretched out a lazy hand, expecting to find him there, and almost cried out with the shock of it.

But even that meagre sleep had effected a change. The day before, I had been sorry for myself and angry at the whole world. Now I felt cold fury not just that Sherlock had been taken from me, but that he had been killed so young, and not had a chance to reach the height of his powers. If I could bring Sherlock's killer to justice, and in doing so avenge him, I would.

The paper boys began crying the news early. 'First edition! Local man killed in bomb attack!' At first I buried my head under the pillow; then my curiosity grew.

I pulled the bell and Martha appeared a few minutes later. I hoped that meant Billy was sleeping at last. 'Good morning, ma'am,' she said. 'It's early for tea.'

I glanced at my watch, which sat on the bedside table. 'Sorry, Martha, I was calling you for something else. Could you go out and buy newspapers? The paper boys are near, and I can give you the money.'

Martha's face was a picture of distress and worry. 'Why don't I bring you tea first, ma'am? You'll feel better when you've had tea.'

'You may bring me tea when you have bought the papers, Martha,' I said, in as level a tone as I could manage. 'Please do as I ask.'

Martha pursed her lips and made for the door.

'I expect to see at least three newspapers,' I called after her. 'If I don't, I shall send you back out.'

When Martha returned, looking mutinous, I ordered tea and spent an unpleasant quarter of an hour reading the coverage of the incident. One newspaper had interviewed the cemetery attendant, who described in detail the moment when the mausoleum had exploded even though he had not been there. I was not mentioned in any of the accounts; perhaps to spare my feelings, or because I was considered insignificant.

I threw the papers aside when Martha brought the tea and she looked relieved. 'Nasty things,' she said, putting the tray down. 'Shall I throw them away?'

'No, thank you.' I got out of bed and poured myself a cup. Martha stood, fidgeting. 'What is it, Martha?'

'I wondered . . . I wondered what you wanted me to do about your clothes.'

I thought of the black crape I had been forced into when Jack vanished, folded in the bottom of a trunk, and a shudder ran through me. 'I shall wear my black cotton. It is in the wardrobe; it won't need pressing.'

Martha frowned. 'But that's not—'

'I don't care. It's black, and that will do. Do you think Sherlock would want me to hide myself in a shroud of crape and bombazine? What good would that do him? You may do what you like, Martha, but I shall mourn him in my own way.'

Martha sniffled, and her eyes filled with tears. I went to her and gave her an awkward hug. 'I'm sorry, Martha. I am not myself, but I didn't mean to hurt you. I shall organise my own clothes, and ask for help if I need it.'

She nodded, and bolted from the room.

And now here I was, dressed in black which was neat rather than funereal, facing Dr Watson at the breakfast table.

He ate his toast thoughtfully, as if chewing over a plan. I tried not to glance at the place where Sherlock always sat. 'I plan to go away for a few days, Nell,' he said.

'Oh?' This was not the breakfast conversation I had expected, if any.

He looked shamefaced. 'I correspond with an old friend who lives in Hertfordshire, and he has been asking me to visit for a while. This morning I have written to accept his invitation. When I go to work today, I shall let the hospital know that I am taking a few days' leave.' He swallowed. 'I hope it will help. I see him everywhere…' His expression was a mixture of fear and sorrow. 'I shall give you the address, and of course I shall write, and if you need me—'

'I shall let you know about the funeral.' I had already found that if I said such things quickly, it hurt a little less.

He looked at me curiously. 'What will you do, Nell? You could go and stay with your mother, perhaps?'

I took another piece of toast. 'I shall stay here. It is my home, and I must get used to it without him.' I took a large bite of toast and chewed vigorously to suppress my feelings.

Dr Watson got up, approached me timidly, and laid his hand on my arm. 'You are so brave, Nell.'

I crammed more toast into my mouth to keep from crying.

He patted my arm. 'I shall go and pack.'

After breakfast, I went down to the kitchen. 'Billy, when you fetched the policeman yesterday to deal with the shoplifter, did you catch his name?'

Billy swallowed his mouthful of bread and jam. 'Constable Adams, ma'am, from Marylebone police station.'

'Thank you. Did she go quietly?'

Billy shook his head. 'He had to prise her fingers off the kitchen table and threaten her with the cuffs to make her go with him. I think she knew the game was up.'

'Good. I am going out, but I should return well before lunchtime.'

Billy's jaw dropped. 'Going out, ma'am?'

'Yes, going out. I could stay in my sitting room and feel sorry for myself, but this will do me more good.' I closed the kitchen door more firmly than I had meant to and went upstairs for my hat and coat.

Marylebone police station was a short walk away. I was not known to them, except as someone occasionally present when they dealt with Sherlock, who lived at the same address. He was an old friend of theirs, since they had nearly arrested him many times when he had been seen loitering in disguise during a case. They had become quite familiar with his various incarnations.

I approached the desk and asked the policeman on duty

for Constable Adams.

'You'll find him on the beat, ma'am. He's usually to be found somewhere on Baker Street or Blandford Street at this time.'

'Thank you. Did he bring a young woman into the station yesterday? Is she still here?'

The officer's expression was blank. 'You'll have to ask Constable Adams that, ma'am.'

I hurried off to find the constable in question, and discovered him standing on the corner of Baker Street and Blandford Street, apparently watching a crossing sweeper. 'Constable?'

He started guiltily. 'Yes, ma'am?'

'My name is Mrs Hudson and I live at 221B Baker Street. I believe you were called there yesterday, and removed a young woman accused of shoplifting.'

'So I did.' He laughed. 'She was a piece of work, right enough.'

'I'm sure she was,' I said. 'Did you take a statement while you were there?'

'Oh no,' said the policeman. 'I do that sort of thing at the station, if needed. No, the young lad I spoke to said she'd been caught stealing at Debenham and Freebody, and I was to take her to Mr Turner to find out what was to be done.' He chuckled. 'I had to keep tight hold of her hand to stop her running off. It's a good job the shop isn't far.'

The image of Susan wriggling as she was marched along by a large policeman almost made me smile. 'What happened when you took her to Debenham and Freebody?'

'It's a nice shop, isn't it?' said the policeman. 'I haven't been in before. My missus would love it. So many nice things, it's better than a day at the races. I might take her this weekend, just to look.'

'I'm sure she'll be delighted,' I replied, 'but please tell me what Mr Turner said.'

'Well, first off he said, "Not you again!" The lady cried fit to bust and said she'd been dragged out of the shop and locked up in a kitchen for hours and she was very sorry. So Mr Turner said he thought she'd learnt her lesson and if he ever saw her in the shop again he'd give her what for, and she wept with joy and said she'd be grateful to him for ever, and he told her to get out, and that was that.' He sighed with relief at having got the story out in one piece. Then he glanced at me, and his expression changed. 'Are you all right, ma'am?'

I walked away without another word. Susan and her secrets had been within my grasp, and this set of fools had let her go. I began to walk home, then stopped, turned, and made for Debenham and Freebody. Unlike Mr Turner, I was in no mood to let the matter go.

CHAPTER 32

As I approached the department store, Alf was standing in front of the doors. He smiled when he first recognised me; then he took in my black clothes and his face became grave. 'We weren't expecting you today, ma'am.'

'I don't suppose you were,' I replied. He opened the door for me and I passed into the store.

The shop was the same as always. Women of various degrees of smartness drifted from counter to counter, chattering, comparing, and sizing things up. Sizing each other up. A few looked at me, then away, as if I were some sort of bad-luck charm. I lifted my head and walked towards the door that led to the back offices, conscious of being watched. Once or twice a former colleague moved uneasily, as if not sure whether to approach me, but nobody did. I did not see Evie anywhere, and for that I was glad.

I knocked smartly at Mr Turner's door, barely waiting for a response before entering. He made a strange noise when he saw me, somewhere between a gasp and a hiss. 'Mrs Hudson,' he said, when he had recovered himself. 'Please take a seat.'

I sat opposite him and his eyes took in my attire, no doubt noting its deficiencies as mourning garb. 'Before we begin, Mrs Hudson, I have seen this morning's paper and I would like to say that I am very sorry. I'm sure we all are.'

'Thank you.'

'Of course, you may take as much time away from the store as you need.' He sighed. 'It will be difficult, but we shall have to manage.'

I could wait no longer. 'Mr Turner, why did you let her go? What were you thinking?'

He spread his hands wide. 'What was I supposed to do? A policeman hauls her in, sobbing her heart out, and she tells me that she's been locked up in your kitchen! The poor thing was scared out of her wits.'

I glared at him, barely able to get the words out. 'The stealing was incidental. If you knew what I know—'

'But I don't, do I? All I knew is that she got caught pilfering, we got the goods back thanks to your prompt actions, and she swore never to do it again. As far as I'm concerned, that will do. Every assistant has her description, and if she tries to come in she'll get escorted out quick sharp.' He clapped his hands together. 'Job done. Case closed.'

'The case is not closed!' I cried. 'She is implicated in a far bigger matter. That's what I wanted her for, not stealing. I was in hiding because I had received a threatening message, and she knows something about it. If you had thought of anything besides the shop and your merchandise, I would be taking her to Scotland Yard right now.'

Mr Turner shifted guiltily in his chair. 'That's unfortunate, but how was I to know? It isn't my job to know. You came barrelling in here with her, and to me, well, it was shoplifting.' His defensive expression softened to sympathy. 'Now we've cleared the air, Mrs Hudson, would you like a cup of tea?'

It was fortunate that nothing breakable was within reach. 'No, Mr Turner, I would not like a cup of tea. I am far too busy trying to repair the damage you have caused by letting that woman go. Good day to you.' I got up and made for the door, my jaw clenched to hold in my angry tears.

I strode down the corridor, fuming, and was about to re-enter the store when the door opened. Evie stood before me. 'Nell,' she said. 'Gladys said she thought she'd seen you come this way. I'm so sorry.'

I glared at her. 'Stand aside, please, Evie.'

Evie drew back as if I had slapped her. 'I really am sorry,' she said, a note of indignation in her voice.

'Sorry doesn't mend things,' I snapped. 'Sorry didn't get my telegram sent, did it?'

Evie gasped. 'He didn't mean to forget. He met a friend on the way to work and got talking, and by the time he remembered—'

'He never wanted to send it in the first place, and neither did you! That's why you tried to talk me out of it. If he had sent that wire and Sherlock had come here to meet me, instead of being at home when the letter was delivered, he wouldn't have gone to the cemetery. He'd be alive now.'

'You don't know that,' said Evie. She looked dazed.

'I know he would have had a chance. Thanks to you and your husband, I'll never know for sure.'

Evie opened the door for me and stood back, keeping her head turned away. I could tell that she was close to crying, but I did not care. Indeed, I was glad she felt a fraction of the distress that I had gone through. I walked past her into the store without a backward glance.

Once out of the department store, my pace slackened as I realised I had no idea what to do next. Going home was out of the question; I had not achieved what I had set out to do. Besides, the thought of being cooped up in the house with Martha and Billy offering me tea every half hour was more than my patience could stand. I wanted to walk and to think, so I made my way to Regent's Park and marched around the paths.

The vigorous motion helped me to sweep the jumble of angry recriminations from my mind, and soon I was able to think more clearly. Through a series of unhappy events Susan had escaped from my grasp, but that did not mean she could not be found. Then I let out a huff of frustration. What was I saying? I did not even know her surname. She could be anywhere by now, living under an assumed name, and no doubt laughing with glee at the thought that she had thwarted me and escaped punishment.

Wait. I stopped abruptly and an elderly gentleman tutted as he made his way round me. *She was stealing those things for somebody. Therefore she is not alone. She has at least one associate, and possibly more.* I started to walk again, more slowly. Of course she would not be alone. Someone like Susan needed a companion or confidante, someone to dare her and to egg her on. In service she had been friends with my predecessor, the parlourmaid, and when she left Susan had focused on her mistress, seeking to win her favour and satisfy her whims. Then I frowned; I was misremembering. It had not been quite so straightforward. Susan had worked well when it suited her, and been capricious and lazy when it did not. But then her mistress had not been a straightforward character, either…

I stopped dead. I was by the Serpentine, but the water, the park, the sky were gone. Instead, in my mind's eye, I saw a well-dressed, self-assured woman standing in the middle of Debenham and Freebody, amused that I had caught her stealing.

Susan's mistress, and for a short time, mine.

A woman who would stop at nothing.

Lady Sophia Chambers.

Milady.

Who else would Susan steal for? Who else would ask her – who else would dare her? I began walking, too agitated to stay still. *How did Susan find her?* Through my undercover assignment the year before as a maid in the Chambers household, I had exposed Milady as a spy leaking government secrets to Professor Moriarty, and she had been confined in a private nursing home to escape the publicity of a trial. *Are they corresponding? Has Susan seen her?* And how had Susan come to know what she did about me?

Now I had a lead; now I had a course of action. I strode

to the nearest gate and headed in the direction of the telegraph office. A wire to Inspector Lestrade would get things moving. It was all I could do to stop myself from running.

As it was, I arrived at the telegraph office panting for breath. The clerk gave me a disapproving look as I gasped out a request for pencil and paper, but I did not care. I retreated to a quiet part of the counter and composed my message:

Suspect Lady Chambers in contact with former servant STOP Also behind threatening message to me STOP Please advise STOP Hudson

I handed the message in and paid my money. 'Will you wait for a reply, ma'am?' asked the clerk.

I considered; I suspected Inspector Lestrade would need time to think my message over. However, at least I had set matters in motion. In any case, the inspector could always wire me at Baker Street. 'Not this time, thank you.'

The clerk nodded, and took my message to be sent. On his way back he reached into pigeonhole H, sorted through the contents, and handed me a small pile of letters.

I stared at them, then at him. 'Thank you,' I said.

'You're welcome, ma'am,' he said, and climbed onto his stool.

I put the letters in my bag. I would look at them at home, when my head had ceased spinning. Anything to keep me from the emptiness of having nothing to do, nothing to occupy me, nothing to stop me dwelling on the events of the previous day and the horrible fact that Sherlock was gone.

I shook the thought away yet again as I opened the door and stepped into the street. I was still so preoccupied that I did not notice the man in front of me until I almost collided with him. 'I'm so sorry,' I murmured, looking up.

I gasped, and recoiled.

There, smiling, was Jack.

CHAPTER 33

'Good morning, Nell.' Jack raised his hat. 'I didn't mean to startle you.'

'Please let me pass,' I muttered.

He stood aside, then fell into step beside me. 'I'm sorry if this isn't a good time, but you haven't answered my letter.'

I stopped dead and stared at him. 'Your letter?'

'Yes, I wrote to you. You told me not to watch you or follow you, so it was the only way I could communicate with you. You see, I've been thinking…'

I reached into my bag and drew out the bundle of letters. The second from the bottom was addressed to *Mrs H Hudson* in a careful, roundish hand I remembered well. I looked at him, and ripped it open.

Dear Nell,

I am very sorry for jumping out at you at the tube station, so to speak. Perhaps I should have written, but I was not sure if you would reply.

I have been thinking about our meeting and I suspect you have, too. In the emotion of meeting after so long, we were perhaps a little hasty. I know I was. My suggestion that you leave your new life to come and live with me was a silly idea; I should have known better.

Could we start afresh? Perhaps we could meet for lunch, or dinner, or go to the theatre together, and get to know each other again? I have lived a whole other life since I left England, and I am sure you have also had experiences which have changed you. Yet I still love you, Nell, and I hope you feel the same.

Please consider my suggestion.

With all my love,

Jack

I folded the letter into its envelope. I didn't know what to say. In truth, I felt several emotions. Anger that Jack had somehow become a reasonable, thoughtful man who was prepared to give me time, and that he had not become that man sooner, before he had left for Australia. Bound up with that was guilt, and sorrow that despite what he had learnt, there was no hope for us.

'That letter took me a long, long time to write,' Jack remarked, with a wry smile. 'I should have expected that you would read it in under a minute, Nell. You were always so quick.'

'I am sorry,' I said, 'but the answer is no. We cannot try again.'

'Why not?' Now he looked more like the Jack I remembered: quick to anger and peevish when his will was denied.

'I can't.' I turned and walked away.

'What do you mean, you can't? You can't just go with no explanation!' His footsteps were growing louder. In seconds he would catch up and take my arm, and I would be unable to escape.

I wheeled round and faced him. 'Because I love someone else, and I always will.'

Jack gaped. 'Who? You never said that when we last met! Who is he?'

'His name is Sherlock Holmes, and he is a better man than you will ever be.'

'Sherlock Holmes? But he's—' Jack took in my black dress. 'I read it in this morning's paper.' Another pause. 'That isn't full mourning.'

I drew myself up. 'Do you know how long I wore mourning for you, Jack? Two whole years of black and crape, locked away in case someone tried to make away with me as they did you. I was trapped in my own home. No, not even that: in a house and a neighbourhood entirely strange to me, cut off from my family and my friends.'

Jack looked shamefaced. 'I'm sorry about that.'

'You should be, but that isn't the worst of it. On the day you vanished, I had bought a special dinner. I was going to tell you that evening that I was expecting a child.'

Jack gasped. 'Why did you wait to tell me?' He stared at me, horror-stricken.

'I wanted to be sure,' I said. 'But the shock of your disappearance meant that I lost the baby.'

Jack stumbled to a doorway and leaned on the post, as if he could not hold himself up any more. 'If I had known – if I had known…' He reached for me like a

240

drowning man. 'Nell, I am so, so sorry.'

I took a step back. 'I'm sure you can imagine how I felt once we had tracked you down to Tasmania, and I read that you and your wife had had a son.'

He winced, and looked away for a moment. 'I have no son now, and no wife. I am alone in the world but for you. Please, Nell, I can protect you – I can care for you. You would never have to work another day, never have to worry about money…' He raised his eyes to my face, and his expression was utterly wretched. 'I don't know what this Mr Holmes was to you, or how you lived, but he's gone.' He eyed my dress again, clearly puzzled by my lack of formal mourning attire and my presence in the street. 'I understand that this is not the right time, but perhaps in the future, with our shared sorrow, I could dare to hope—'

'There is no hope,' I said.

'You were going about your business as if nothing had happened!' he cried. 'What was I to think?'

I drew myself up and faced him. 'I am going about my business, as you put it, because I am trying to discover who planted the bomb that killed Sherlock.' Jack flinched at my use of the first name. 'I went to the post office to send a wire to Scotland Yard; the clerk gave me my letters as an afterthought.' I glared at him; if I could have turned him to stone, I would. 'If you are wondering why I did not collect your letter sooner, I have been in hiding since someone sent me a threatening note. For all I know, it was you.' I flung out an accusing finger. 'You who sent me into hiding, so that I wasn't there to help Sherlock when he needed me most.'

241

'Me?' Jack appeared completely taken aback. 'Why would I do that?'

'Why would you run off to Tasmania and abandon your pregnant wife? Why would you get so blind drunk with your friend that you were incapable of knowing what you had done? Why would you marry for a second time, knowing full well that you already had a wife in England? See, Jack, you are not the only one who can ask questions.' I walked away, not caring if he followed me or not. *I will do anything to be rid of him.*

I looked back once as I rounded the corner into Baker Street. Jack stood where I had left him, his face a mask of uncomprehending pain, and my mouth twisted with grim pleasure. *Let him feel a little of what I have felt. Let him lie awake at night thinking of what might have been.* It would solve nothing, it would make nothing better, but I was too angry to care. Jack had turned my life upside down and caused me misery and heartache, and now it was his turn to suffer.

I let myself in, too impatient to wait for Billy. Martha had occupied herself while I was out by putting a black crape bow on the door knocker. I wanted to pull it off and throw it away, but I had hurt Martha enough for one day, and it was not even lunchtime.

Billy hurried up from the kitchen, and his face fell when he saw me. 'Did you find her, ma'am?'

'Find her?' Then I realised whom he meant. 'No, Billy. Between them, that dolt of a policeman and Mr Turner at the department store let her go.' I sighed. 'But I have had an idea and wired Inspector Lestrade. Perhaps something

242

will come of that.' I glanced at the salver on the hall table. There was no telegram. No post, save for a dirty, cheap, unstamped white envelope with *MRS HUDSON* inscribed on it in shaky pencilled capitals. 'When did this come?' I picked the envelope up between thumb and forefinger and inspected it.

'I don't know, ma'am. It was on the mat when I came upstairs on an errand, not half an hour ago.'

I considered it. 'Perhaps it is a message of condolence from someone fallen on hard times who knew Mr Holmes.' I wrinkled my nose. 'Or perhaps a message from a criminal who is glad he's gone.'

Billy winced. 'Don't say that, ma'am.'

'I shall say what I like,' I remarked, in a light tone that did not invite further comment. 'Please ask Martha to bring tea to my sitting room; I have correspondence to attend to. If anything comes from Inspector Lestrade, bring it to me at once.'

'Yes, ma'am.' Billy disappeared, and I suspected he was not sorry to be out of my presence. I shrugged; I was not fit company for anyone, and I knew it. *Perhaps that is why widows are shut away for so long*, I thought as I climbed the stairs, *so that they don't alienate all their friends and relatives.*

I reached my sitting room, took off my hat and coat, and hung them on the back of the door; I would deal with them later. With another sigh, I took the bundle of letters from my handbag and laid them on the bureau, then put the dirty, crumpled envelope on top. I had already decided that I would only take small cases, to allow me time to investigate Sherlock's death. That had to be my priority; everything else could wait. If it couldn't, they could find another detective.

I picked up the first envelope with its dirty fingerprints, and looked at the small fire which Martha had left burning in the grate. I contemplated throwing it in unopened, then shrugged and reached for my silver letter opener. Hopefully the sender's words would be more impressive than their hygiene. At least those shaky letters were not the cramped print of the bomber, or the rounded script of Jack.

Inside was a single sheet of paper, similarly finger-marked around the edges, with a rusty brown smear on it that might have been blood. But I stared at the scrawled words as if they had been an alchemist's secret.

Back door 9 pm. Burn this. Tell no one. S

CHAPTER 34

I read the note over and over, and a myriad of questions filled my mind. *How has Sherlock escaped? Surely it isn't possible. Where is he? How is he?* I wanted to laugh, to cry, to run to the kitchen and tell Martha and Billy my good news – but of course I could not. I could tell nobody.

That brought more questions. *How can I get Martha and Billy out of the way this evening? What if Dr Watson's friend does not answer his wire, and he returns to Baker Street?* And perhaps most urgently, how would I get through the next nine hours or so without someone guessing my secret?

A tap at the door. I scrambled the note, the precious note, back into its filthy envelope and composed my face in what I hoped was an expression of gravity. 'Come in.'

Martha entered with a tea tray. 'Lunch will be ready at one o'clock, ma'am. Cottage pie.' I noticed that she had put a plate of biscuits on the tray, though lunch was only an hour away.

My brain flipped through various scenarios. Could I suggest that Martha and Billy both took a half day, or the evening off? No: they knew me too well and would immediately suspect something. That in itself would make them refuse to go.

'Is everything all right, ma'am?' Martha's expression was concerned.

I sighed. 'I would prefer lunch at half past twelve, Martha.'

Martha opened her eyes wide. 'I can't get it to cook any faster, ma'am.'

'Try your best,' I said shortly. 'Take my hat and coat and hang them up downstairs, please.' I managed to make it sound as if she were at fault, not me.

'Of course, ma'am,' said Martha, and her face wore the blank look of a professional servant. 'If you are hungry, ma'am, perhaps you could have a biscuit with your tea.'

'I don't want a biscuit,' I said. 'I would like lunch at half past twelve, please, or as close as you can manage.' I was actually hungry – the note had had a miraculous effect on my appetite – but I would never have dreamt of asking Martha to move a meal at such short notice. 'What vegetables are you serving with lunch, Martha?'

Martha gave me a wary look. 'I thought some nice carrots.'

'I would prefer cabbage.' I picked up my letter opener to indicate the conversation was at an end.

Martha muttered to herself as she stormed downstairs. I gave her five minutes before ringing again and saying that actually, I would prefer the carrots after all. I felt terribly guilty, but I hoped Martha would forgive me in due course.

I am ashamed to say that when Martha called me for lunch I kept her waiting for ten minutes, on the pretext that

I was finishing a letter, then told her that my cottage pie was not warm enough and demanded that it be reheated. I prepared myself for a well-justified telling-off, but unfortunately Martha was made of sterner stuff and merely took my plate away with her mouth in a thin, straight line.

While I waited for her return I touched the bodice of my dress, where Sherlock's note was hidden, and heard it rustle. I longed to draw it out and reread it, but the fear of discovery was too great. *I must burn it, but not yet.*

I made a brief, surly meal, snapped at Martha about the lack of a dessert though we never had dessert at lunch, and rose to go. 'Martha, I shall need your help this afternoon,' I said. 'I must decide what to wear for the funeral.'

Any discontent in Martha's face was replaced by sorrow, and I could have slapped myself. 'Of course, ma'am. Just ring for me when you are ready.'

Upstairs, I forced myself to write out two telegrams to my mother and to Sally, both with the same wording:

Mr Holmes dead STOP Please don't visit STOP Will write when ready STOP Nell

I strewed my still-unopened letters over the bureau and rang the bell. 'Two telegrams,' I murmured, when Martha entered. 'Please make sure Billy sends them at once. I don't want visitors.' I gave her the sheet of paper and put my hand to my brow.

Martha glanced at the addresses. 'Are you sure you wouldn't like your family, ma'am?'

'I don't want anyone,' I murmured. 'Close the curtains, please; the light hurts my eyes. And turn up the lamp; I have letters to answer.'

Poor Martha's eyes were full of sympathy. 'If you don't mind me saying, ma'am, I think you should leave the letters. You aren't well.'

I rubbed the space between my eyebrows and winced. 'I have to go on. It's what Sherlock would have wanted.' It was true, but at the same time I felt terrible for deceiving Martha. 'Tell me when Billy has returned from sending the telegrams, and then we can look at dresses.'

Martha departed. I drew out Sherlock's note and read it one last time, kissed it, then threw it in the fire. As it left my hand, a horrible thought occurred to me: could this be a trap? The writing was nothing like Sherlock's usual firm hand. *What if this is a ruse to kidnap me, or worse?*

Flames licked the letter, catching the edges until tongues of flame consumed it from the outside in. No, that made no sense. If someone wished to lure me away they would choose a deserted warehouse or a quiet park as a meeting place, not my own back door. I was reassured, yet doubt still nagged at me. I was tempted to snatch the letter from the fire and see if I could detect any similarity between the shaky letters and Sherlock's handwriting, but there was only a fragment left. It curled and vanished, and sparks danced up the chimney.

I took my pocket mirror from my bag and spent a few minutes loosening hairpins and disarranging my hair. Anything which might persuade Martha of my distress would help my cause. 'I am so sorry, Martha,' I whispered.

***

'Oh, ma'am…' murmured Martha, gazing at the black clothes strewn around the room. Mourning covered it like a

248

lowering black cloud. I knelt by the bed in my petticoats, beating my fists ineffectually on the counterpane.

'I *can't*!' I wailed.

Martha placed a timid hand on my shoulder, but I shook it off. 'I don't think this is the right time, ma'am. Shall I put all this away?'

'Yes,' I sniffled. 'You're right, Martha, I should never have tried. It's too soon.' I lifted my head and watched Martha setting the room right in her usual quiet, efficient way. 'I'm so tired,' I whispered.

Martha laid a hand on my shoulder, and this time I let her keep it there. 'Didn't you sleep well, ma'am?'

I gazed up at her. 'I barely slept,' I muttered. 'I wish I could. I miss him.'

'We all miss him,' said Martha. 'Dr Watson, too. He may be staying with his friend for a while, but I know he'll be thinking of Mr Holmes.'

A wire from Dr Watson had arrived after lunch: *Visit confirmed STOP Address Fairacres Ferndene Hertfordshire STOP Please stay in touch STOP Watson.*

'And you'll be thinking of him, too.' I sniffled. 'I'm sorry, Martha. I've been very selfish, only thinking of myself when you and Billy must be grieving. Would you like to go and see your families?'

Martha looked at me doubtfully. 'But it isn't my half day.'

'That doesn't matter.' I sniffed and wiped my eyes. 'I'd feel better if I could help you and Billy. I had a big lunch; all you would have to do is put up something for dinner – perhaps cold meat and pickles…'

'That's kind of you, ma'am, I shall go and speak to Billy. Can I get you anything, ma'am?'

'Perhaps some warm milk,' I quavered. 'I shall lie down and try to sleep.'

Martha duly returned with a glass of milk to find me weeping as I struggled with my corset. 'Ma'am, you're far too tired. Let me look after you.'

I submitted to being dressed in my nightgown and having my hair plaited, and Martha helped me into bed. 'Thank you, Martha,' I said, leaning against my pillows and taking a sip of milk. 'What did Billy say?'

'He's worried about you, ma'am, just like me.' Martha smoothed the pillow.

'I don't think anyone can help me,' I said miserably. 'I'm sure I'd feel better if I could sleep.'

'Well, drink your milk and try. I shall come upstairs in an hour or so and check on you.'

I am afraid that I waited for the milk to go cold before drinking it; my plan might fail if I actually fell asleep. Half an hour later Martha found me sobbing in a tangle of sheets, my plait half-undone. 'I just want to sleep!' I moaned.

'I'm fetching Billy,' she said, and bolted from the room.

***

'One dose, ma'am, and that's all.' Billy measured the drops carefully into a glass of water. 'I'll pour the rest of the bottle away and wash it out.'

I nodded, meekly.

'I'll leave a note to say where we are and when we'll be back, in case you don't remember when you wake up.'

Billy crossed to the bureau, wrote a few lines, folded the paper in half and propped it on my nightstand. Then he gave me the glass. 'I'll come and check on you in an hour. We'll both return by eleven o'clock at the latest.' He spoke slowly and clearly, as if I were already drugged.

'Yes, Billy. I understand.' I took a small sip from the glass and he looked away. I knew he hated to see it.

'We'll go now, ma'am.' He ushered Martha from the room.

I waited until they had gone downstairs, then quietly got out of bed and poured the contents of the glass into the vase of flowers on the dressing table. I imagined the flowers drooping as the laudanum took effect. 'I'm sorry,' I whispered, and tiptoed back to bed.

Just over an hour later footsteps came upstairs, and I arranged myself artistically in the bed. 'You go in, Martha,' Billy whispered outside.

An exasperated sigh from Martha, and the door opened. I strove to breathe regularly and keep my body relaxed as the floorboards creaked. I could feel her peering at me. Then the door closed, and I heard her whisper to Billy, 'She's sleeping like a baby.'

'Good,' said Billy. 'Though I wish we hadn't had to give her laudanum.'

'But if it helps—'

'I still don't like it.' A sigh. 'At least she can't get any more. The druggist will be closed by the time she wakes up. Otherwise I wouldn't leave her.'

I winced, and promised myself that when all this was over I would reassure Billy that I had poured the drug

251

away.

I lay in bed stiff as a statue, scared to move in case the creak brought Billy and Martha upstairs and stopped them leaving. But eventually I heard Billy say goodbye to Martha, and a few minutes later a second click of the back door, followed by the key turning in the lock.

***

Ten to nine. I tucked my hair under the dark-brown wig, pushed more pins into the tight knot, and settled one of Martha's caps on top. I had put one of her aprons over my own black dress; it felt wrong to borrow Martha's clothes without her knowledge, and it was dark enough to make a lighter disguise convincing.

I had lived a lifetime in the last few hours. A jumble of incoherent thoughts and questions had whirled through my mind. *It isn't a trap, is it? Surely it can't be. What if one of the servants comes back early?* In the end I had given up trying to make sense of anything, fetched wool and knitting needles, and begun a scarf sufficiently difficult to keep my hands and brain busy, which helped to calm my nerves.

But now it was time. I went to the kitchen, turned the gaslight up a little, and set the full kettle on the stove. The spare key was already in the lock. I took an earthenware mug from the dresser and measured tea leaves into the pot, then sat down to wait. My stomach rumbled; I had fetched my supper tray at seven o'clock, but taken it back after a couple of mouthfuls, too agitated to eat. I forced myself not to look outside, not to appear to be waiting. I was a servant making herself a cup of tea in a welcome lull,

252

nothing more.

A tap at the door. I rose swiftly, opened it, and peered out. The light from the kitchen was not strong enough to illuminate the shadows.

'Please ma'am,' said a reedy voice, 'would you have any scraps for a poor hungry man?' The voice sounded nothing like Sherlock, yet…

I folded my arms to keep myself from embracing him. 'I might have,' I said roughly, 'if you come into the light and show me you're not a robber or worse.'

A stick thumped and a figure shambled forward. His trousers were torn at the bottom, his workman's shirt and waistcoat worn and patched. He leaned heavily on a stick and shivered – I could not tell whether from cold or pain. Brown hair straggled from under his cap, and what I could see of his face was covered in cuts, bruises, and dirt. But beneath it all…

'Please ma'am, let me come in for a warm.'

I sighed. 'Not for long, mind you. If my missus hears…' I opened the door wider and Sherlock shuffled forward. 'I suppose you want tea,' I said, as I closed the door and locked it. 'You'd better sit down.'

The kettle whistled. I went to the stove and filled the pot, my face turned from the glass panel in the door. 'Oh my darling,' I murmured, 'I thought I had lost you.' It was all I could do not to cry, not to gather him in my arms and kiss him. I took my supper plate from the oven and put it before him, then cut a hunk of bread and put it on the plate. Moving between him and the door, I brushed his cheek with my hand. My heart was too full for speech.

253

'Oh, Nell,' said Sherlock. He stared up at me, and he looked more weary and dejected than I had ever seen him.

CHAPTER 35

'Where are Billy and Martha?' he muttered. 'They aren't in the house, are they?'

'Visiting their families; I managed to persuade them earlier. Don't ask me how.' I fetched a knife and fork from the drawer, then went to get another mug from the dresser. 'We have at least an hour.'

'We haven't. I can stay for as long as it takes me to eat this and drink a cup of tea.' He glanced around nervously. 'If I am being watched, I can't afford to let them suspect anything.'

'Eat slowly, then,' I said, and took a seat opposite him while I waited for the tea to brew. 'How did you escape? I still can't believe it.'

'I barely believe it myself,' he said. 'When I got to Jabez Hudson's mausoleum, I found a young man inside. I think I had arrived earlier than planned, for when I entered he was shoving a wrapped bundle behind a piece of statuary. He saw me and began to edge towards the door. Then I knew the fuse was lit, and I did not have long. I dived for the bundle, he dived at me, and we wrestled for possession.'

'Oh, Sherlock…' I stared at him. 'What were you thinking? Why didn't you run?'

He shrugged. 'I don't know. That would have been the sensible thing to do, but I knew what the bundle was and I wanted to beat it. I couldn't let it get the better of me.'

I shook my head. 'Go on.'

'The cloth fell away from the bundle, and I could see the fuse burning down. We had minutes left, if that. It was plain that the man's design was to blow me up even if he died in the attempt; he had the look of a fanatic. And no, I didn't recognise him. He landed a punch which almost sent me to the floor, and I knew it was a fight to the death. I punched him in my turn, intending to stop the struggle, and I am afraid that I knocked him out cold.' He shook his head. 'I am not proud of myself, Nell.'

'It was self-defence,' I said. I ached to touch his hand, to console him, but the thought of spies outside held me back.

'Perhaps.' He sighed. 'I tried to revive him, but I heard a fizz from the bundle that suggested a change. *Then* I ran. I dived out of the back door of the mausoleum, and I was a few steps clear when the force of the explosion knocked me off my feet.'

'There was a back door,' I said, slowly. If I had known, I might have saved myself a day of heartache. I could have found Sherlock and taken him to a place of safety . . . but how could I have known?

'I managed to crawl to some nearby bushes and take cover. In truth, I did not know what I was doing; my only thought was to stay out of sight. My ears were ringing, my head was banging, and all in all I was rather out of sorts.'

'You were probably in shock.' I imagined Sherlock lying there, half-deafened, frightened and confused, and shuddered.

'Luckily I do not remember much; I must have fainted.' He tapped his leg. 'I did something to my ankle when I landed after the explosion. Not a break, but it hurts to walk. That's one reason why I took so long to reach you: that, and keeping out of sight. I do not intend to lose the advantage of being dead.' His mouth twisted in a wry smile. 'Pour the tea, Nell, and don't cry at me. I know I am a pathetic spectacle.'

I swallowed the lump in my throat and rose. 'I'm just glad you're alive.'

'So am I. I managed to reach Wiggins earlier today, and I have been laid up there. He managed to procure pencil and paper, and was kind enough to deliver my note earlier.' He frowned. 'Where is Watson?'

'Staying with a friend.' I said, setting a mug of tea in front of him.

'Poor Watson.' Sherlock took a sip of tea and grimaced, since I had loaded it with sugar. 'I wish I could put his mind at rest. My parents, too, and Mycroft. But it is impossible.'

I sat down opposite him with my own mug. 'Does it have to be this way, Sherlock? Do you have to hide?'

'I have had the dubious pleasure of reading the account of my own death,' said Sherlock. 'It would be a terrible shame to waste it. Besides, the bomber may show his hand; I do not think the young man in the mausoleum was more than an assistant. If whoever is behind this thinks that I am out of the picture, perhaps they will get on with whatever made them plot to get me out of the way.'

'Speaking of being got out of the way…' I watched him over the rim of my mug. 'Why do you think they drove me away? Wouldn't it have made more sense for me to go with you?'

'I thought about that,' said Sherlock. 'There wasn't much else to do when I was lying on a straw mattress at Wiggins's digs, keeping out of sight. Assuming that last note to you was from the bomber, or someone connected with the bomber…' He paused, thinking. 'Unless the note was from your – from Villiers.'

'It wasn't Jack,' I said. 'I have seen him. He denies it, and I believe him.' Sherlock frowned again. 'I don't have time to explain,' I said firmly. 'Tell me what you think.'

'Very well. If the bomber wanted to get you out of the way while he killed me, I can only presume that he has other plans for you.'

'What does he know about me?' Then I gasped as I realised how much Sherlock had missed. 'I must tell you what has happened.' Briefly I told him of my encounter with Susan at the department store, her blunder, her subsequent escape, and my hypothesis that somehow she was in contact with Lady Chambers, the woman who had been Moriarty's sidekick.

Sherlock whistled. 'Whatever I expected, Nell, it was not that.' A quick, appraising glance. 'Have you told anyone?'

'I wired Inspector Lestrade this morning,' I said, 'but I

have not received a reply. That was how I met Jack; he was waiting outside the post office.'

'Was he,' said Sherlock. He took a bite of bread and regarded me thoughtfully as he chewed. 'Was he pressing his suit?'

'He tried.' My cheeks burned at the memory of it. 'I would rather not discuss it.'

'I am glad he did not succeed,' said Sherlock. 'I am so sorry to have put you through this, Nell. Especially after what happened.'

It was all I could do not to reach for his hand. 'I understand, Sherlock. But what do we do?'

'The obvious thing is to find out what has been taking place with Lady Chambers. If she is involved…'

'Yes, but will she talk?'

Sherlock snorted. 'I doubt it. If you haven't heard from Lestrade by mid-morning tomorrow, I suggest you call on him and impress upon him how urgent this is. Because if Lady Chambers is involved…'

'Then Professor Moriarty may be involved too.'

'He may. I find it hard to believe that any sort of correspondence between them would be permitted, given what we know about Lady Sophia Chambers, but it is possible. And the thought that it is possible chills me.'

More than ever, I wanted to hold Sherlock in my arms and kiss away the doubt, the pain, the fear. His plate was almost empty; soon he would have to leave. 'What else can I do?' I asked.

A spark of merriment danced in his grey eyes. 'Are you finding bereavement dull already, Nell?'

259

'It is much better now that I know you are alive,' I said, 'but if I have to sit indoors all day playing widow, I shall be in danger of spontaneous combustion.'

'The main thing is to get Lestrade moving,' said Sherlock. 'Normally I would suggest going straight to Mycroft, but that is hardly practicable at present.'

'I shall do my best,' I said. 'And I may try to discover more about Eliza Montagu.'

'I thought we agreed the Montagus were a distraction,' said Sherlock.

'Perhaps they are,' I said, 'but I need a distraction. The busier I am, the less I worry.'

Sherlock laughed. 'That's the spirit.' He wiped the last scrap of bread around his plate, popped it into his mouth, and washed it down with the remainder of his tea. 'You had better throw me out of your kitchen before I get too comfortable. And before the servants return, of course, or they will think they are seeing a ghost.' Then his face clouded. 'I hope I can keep myself hidden and help to clear up this mess. Wiggins is a generous host, but I miss my consulting room.' He smiled. 'And you, of course.'

'I should hope so.' I bounced to my feet and pointed at the door for the benefit of anyone who might be watching. Sherlock got to his feet slowly, took his stick, and limped to the door. 'Move out of the light,' I murmured.

He grinned and moved past the glass of the door towards the curtained window. I did the same, then flung my arms round his neck and kissed him. 'Marry me,' I murmured. 'When this is over, no matter what it takes.'

'Really?' he murmured, his expression a mixture of

surprise and pleasure.

'Really.' I kissed him again. 'Now that I've seen you all dressed up, you're irresistible.'

'Maybe it's Martha's cap and apron,' he replied, 'but so are you. Now I must go. Remember, not a word to anyone. I only went to Wiggins because I needed a bolthole. I'm relying on you, Nell.'

'I'll do my best,' I said. 'If I have to get word to you…'

'Try not to,' said Sherlock. 'I know it's tempting, but it isn't safe.' He kissed me once more, then unlocked the door. 'Time to throw me out.'

I flung the door open. 'Get out!' I bawled. 'You've had a good meal, and that's your lot.'

'You can't blame a man for trying,' said Sherlock, with an indescribable leer which almost convulsed me.

'If I see you again, I'll call a policeman. Now shoo!' I adjusted my cap with angry defiance, slammed the door, and locked it. I took a deep breath, then washed Sherlock's mug and put it away, poured myself more tea, turned the gaslight down and hurried upstairs to change into my nightdress, ready for the return of Martha and Billy. The whole episode had taken less than twenty minutes, and yet my life had never seemed so vivid, so real.

Halfway up the stairs, I stopped dead and nearly spilled my tea. 'I asked him to marry me…' I said, out loud. Then I shrugged, and kept walking. Sherlock was alive, somehow he was not seriously injured, and we had a plan. That was more than enough.

CHAPTER 36

The morning brought no telegram from Inspector Lestrade, and there was no missive from him in the first post. There were, however, several black-edged envelopes. I picked out two. One was addressed in Mycroft's distinctive, expansive hand.

Dear Mrs Hudson,

I am sorry it has taken so long for me to write and express my condolences. The loss of Sherlock has hit me hard.

My parents and I have arranged the funeral. It will take place next Friday at 2 pm, at the church of St James near the family home, and he will be laid to rest in the family plot. Please do come; you will be very welcome. There is an inn close by, or my parents have plenty of spare rooms.

I shall write at more length soon.

Yours sincerely,

Mycroft Holmes

The other letter I opened was postmarked from the village where Sherlock had grown up.

Dear Nell,

Mycroft is writing with the funeral arrangements, but we wanted to send a line to express how sorry we are. We have lost our dear boy, but we know your loss is something very different.

Please do not be a stranger; you are welcome in our home at any time.

With much love,
Louisa Holmes

I put my head in my hands, almost knocking my plate to the floor. Martha dashed forward and moved the plate out of the way as I fought back my tears. 'Can I get you anything else, ma'am?'

I let out a shaky breath. 'No, Martha, thank you. It was just— People are so kind.'

'Of course they are,' said Martha, looking puzzled. 'Why wouldn't they be?'

I shrugged. 'I don't know.' I recalled the complete lack of support I had experienced when Jack was missing, presumed dead. That had been no one's fault, since I had been spirited away where no one could find me. I could have smiled at the irony that I received so much heartfelt sympathy for the loss of a man I was not married to, and who was not dead.

'What do you propose to do today, ma'am?' asked Martha. Her sharp eyes had already taken note of my black dress and my good stockings.

'I was expecting a communication from Inspector Lestrade,' I said. 'As I have not heard from him, I shall pay him a call at Scotland Yard.'

Martha's eyes widened. 'You're going to Scotland Yard?'

'Yes,' I replied, pouring myself another cup of tea. 'Mr Holmes called on the inspector there often, and I do not see why I should not do the same.'

Martha gave me an odd look. 'Is it so urgent?'

'Of course it's urgent; I want to find out who planted that bomb. The inspector spent time at the crime scene and knows about the other bombs, so he is the obvious person to speak to.' I sipped my tea, then put the cup down. 'What would you have me do, Martha, sit at home and cry?'

'I didn't say that,' said Martha, taking a step back. 'But you must admit that it is odd for a newly widowed woman to be chasing up to Scotland Yard.'

'If that is what it takes, that is what I shall do,' I said. 'If it makes you feel better, I shall wait until the second post has come before I set out. Does that meet with your approval?'

'It isn't my place to say, ma'am,' said Martha, stiffly. 'You looked so much better when we came back last night, and I don't want you to get upset.'

I sighed. 'Thank you for your concern, Martha, but I shall grow miserable if I sit and do nothing.' A thought popped into my head. 'Can you ask Billy to go and buy the *Daily Chronicle*, the *London Messenger*, and the *Illustrated London News*, please? Perhaps some light reading will take my mind off things.'

'Yes, ma'am. Shall I clear?'

'Yes please, Martha. I shall be in my sitting room.'

In due course Billy delivered a bundle of reading material to me. I turned straight to the society pages, looking for any news of the Montagus or of people connected with them. Eventually I found, halfway down the *Messenger*'s society page, a small paragraph:

Tonight at 8 o'clock, at the Musgrave Hotel, a musical soirée in aid of the Society For Distressed Gentlewomen. Guests include the Society's patron, the Marchioness of Parcester, the celebrated soprano Livia Ricci, and Mrs Humphrey Montagu, formerly Miss Eliza Davenant of the West End stage. We are sure that a good time will be had by all for a very worthy cause. Tickets obtainable from the Musgrave Hotel, or from the Society upon application.

That was enough to set my mind racing. I crept to my bedroom and then the dressing room, taking an inventory of gowns which would suit such an occasion. Indeed, I was so taken up with what I might wear and what identity I could assume that the rattle of the letterbox made me jump. I thrust the gown I was considering into the wardrobe and fairly ran downstairs.

A black-bordered envelope lay on the mat. Even without picking it up, I could see that it was not Inspector Lestrade's writing but Dr Watson's neat hand. The letter bore a Hertfordshire postmark.

Dear Nell,

I am writing to let you know that I have arrived safely. I am taking walks with my friend, and fishing. I fear I talk of

265

Holmes a great deal, but my friend does not seem to mind.

I hope you are as well as you can be, and finding consolation in your family and friends. Quiet reflection is a great healer, and I hope to return with a greater equilibrium of mind and more resignation to the workings of circumstance than I had when I left London. I still do not understand – but perhaps, in time, I may accept.

Yours sincerely,

John H Watson

I held the letter to my heart for a moment. Poor Dr Watson. I wished I could tell him, but the thought of John trying to act as if his great friend were still dead would have made me laugh, had it not been so loaded with danger. I went upstairs, locked his letter up with the others in my bureau, and prepared to set off for Scotland Yard.

***

Inspector Lestrade was not pleased to see me. I suspect that if I had written or wired first then he would have pleaded a prior engagement, which was exactly why I had not done so. As it was, he faced me across his desk with barely concealed irritation. 'I did not expect you here, Mrs Hudson.'

'Did you get my wire, Inspector?'

'I did, and I'm not sure what you expect me to do about it. I am attempting to get to the bottom of who is planting these bombs, and you want me to go on a wild-goose chase to a nursing home in the middle of nowhere.'

'There is a connection; I am sure of it.' I gave him the facts of the case: the threat I had received, the man who had followed my presumed self to the railway station, Susan's surprise at seeing me, her admission that she had been stealing for somebody else, and the obvious link to Lady Chambers.

Throughout my explanation the inspector frowned as he tried to follow me, and he was silent for some time afterwards, thinking. 'I'm still not convinced, Nell,' he said at last. 'But I don't suppose it can do any harm to send someone to speak to the lady in question. Or better, to contact the local force and get one of them to do it. Yes.' He rubbed his hands, clearly relieved he would have to do no more than send a missive. 'What questions should we ask?'

'If you will let me have paper and pen, Inspector, I am happy to write you a list.'

When I handed the paper to the inspector, his brow furrowed. 'None of these are questions for Lady Chambers.'

'Well, no,' I replied. 'If she is up to something, she will lie. It makes much more sense to question the staff about any correspondence she has received or sent and any visitors she has been allowed. Once we have that information, we can investigate further.'

Inspector Lestrade ran his hands through his short dark hair. 'You're right, of course. I swear I have so many irons in the fire that I am in danger of getting burnt.' He gave me a suspicious glance. 'You're not planning to go down there, are you?'

'Nothing could be further from my mind,' I said, and I meant it. I would let the police do the investigating, and in

267

the meantime see if I could get close to Eliza Montagu.

'Good,' said the inspector. He leaned back in his chair. 'Given your lack of formal mourning attire, Nell, I thought you might be up to something.'

I strove to look innocent. 'It has not come from the dressmaker yet. I would have waited, but I felt I should make you aware of this information in case it is useful to you.'

The inspector exhaled forcefully. 'We shall see. How I wish Mr Holmes were here.'

If you only knew. 'I am afraid that you will have to make do with me.'

'Oh no, I didn't mean— You are an excellent detective in your own right, of course, but I'm more used to Mr Holmes. I mean, I was.' The inspector seemed so helpless that my heart went out to him.

'I shall leave you to get on,' I said. 'Please let me know what comes of your enquiry about Lady Chambers, Inspector, and if there is anything I can do to help…'

'I will be sure to ask.' He came round the desk, took my hand as I rose and patted it awkwardly. 'I am sorry, Nell. I should have offered you my condolences on your loss, but I was so absorbed in my work when you came in that I forgot. I do apologise.'

'It is quite all right, Inspector; it is not an easy time for any of us.'

'Indeed, but you bear your loss with such fortitude.' He looked at me earnestly, and I felt an utter wretch.

I sighed. 'I shall bid you farewell, Inspector. Please keep me informed. Don't worry, I can find my own way out.'

I pulled down my veil to ensure uninterrupted passage through the corridors, and emerged into the chilly greyness of London. A cab approached, and I hailed it. 'Where to, ma'am?' asked the cabbie.

I lifted my veil. 'The Musgrave Hotel, please.'

***

I gave a final pat to my chestnut-brown chignon, settled a silk shawl around my shoulders and walked downstairs, holding the banister as I accustomed myself to the high-heeled evening slippers I had not worn for months.

Seconds later Martha was in the hall, staring up at me. 'What on earth are you doing, ma'am?'

'I am going out,' I replied. 'Kindly ask Billy to summon me a cab.'

'But – but you can't! What will people think?'

'I am not going out for pleasure, Martha.' I pointed to my wig. 'As you see, I am not going out as myself; this is work.'

Martha snorted. 'Work, work, always work.' She rubbed an eye irritably. 'I wish you'd tell us what's going on.'

I descended the remainder of the stairs. 'If I did, Martha, you would only try to stop me.'

'Maybe I'd be doing the right thing,' Martha said darkly.

'Or maybe you'd be stopping me from finding out why Mr Holmes was killed.'

We were on a level now, and Martha stared into my eyes. 'I'm glad you can say it so calmly, ma'am.' She made for the kitchen steps. 'I'll tell Billy to get you that cab.'

I waited, thoroughly rebuked in my own hallway. A bang at the door made me jump, followed by a cry of 'Telegram!'

I hurried forward and opened the door. 'Telegram for Hudson, ma'am,' said the boy, tipping his cap to me. I gave him a penny, closed the door, and ripped open the envelope.

Wire from Buckinghamshire police STOP Lady Chambers discharged to care of husband STOP Catching next train down STOP Lestrade.

CHAPTER 37

I read the telegram over and over again, as if by doing so I would achieve clarity. How had Lady Chambers been discharged from the nursing home? How could Sir William Chambers have taken her away with him? She was under a strict order. Then a horrible thought occurred to me: had the person who took her really been Sir William?

'Martha says you want me to call you a cab, ma'am,' said Billy. I almost jumped out of my skin, having been lost in my thoughts.

'Yes, but wait a moment.'

Billy looked at the telegram in my hand. 'Do you still wish to go out?' he asked, casting a doubtful glance at my wig.

I collected myself. The inspector had said he was catching the next train. There was no sure way to reach him, and nothing I could do. 'Just something unexpected, Billy. Please hold a cab for me; I shall be down directly.' I locked the telegram in the consulting-room bureau, then appraised my reflection in the dressing-room mirror. Despite my attempts at disguise, I looked what I was: a woman not sure if she were under or overdressed, and

271

anxious at the prospect of an evening in an unfamiliar place. But the main thing was that I did not look very much like myself. I nodded at my reflection, and went downstairs.

***

The doorman read my ticket. 'Mrs Moncrieff?' He flicked a glance at me. 'Just you, madam?'

'I am meeting a friend inside,' I said.

'Straight along the passageway and downstairs into the ballroom, madam.' He handed back my ticket.

'Thank you,' I said, but he was already turning to the next guest. Presumably I had passed muster, but why should I not? I had paid five pounds to attend a charitable event, and I doubted anyone present cared who I was.

I reached the ballroom, waved on by a small army of white-jacketed flunkies, and was offered a glass of champagne by an obsequious waiter. 'The entertainment will begin soon, madam, so if you would find a seat... Programmes are on the chairs.'

At least I shan't have to make conversation. The chairs had been set out in rows with an aisle down the middle, facing a raised platform on which, presumably, a band normally played. I had no experience of formal dances except in the pages of a novel; we had had scant money for such luxuries when I had been growing up, and Jack had never been a dancing man. I tried to imagine Sherlock taking me round the floor in a polka or a waltz, and gave up. He was far more likely to play music than dance to it, and music suitable for dancing was completely outside his preferred repertoire.

I found a seat in a middle row and consulted the programme.

'Deadly, isn't it,' remarked my neighbour, a middle-aged, snub-nosed woman in a blue dress. 'Hopefully things will improve after the interval.'

'This is my first time,' I said, 'so I am not sure what to expect.'

Her eyes widened. 'Your first time? How on earth have you managed to escape so long? I am always being pestered to attend this or that, or give money to indigent spectacle-makers and the like.'

I giggled. 'I am sure they appreciate it.'

'To be fair, this is one of the better outfits,' said my neighbour. 'Mrs Montagu is passionate about the cause, and sensible enough to ensure there is something worth coming for.' She fanned herself with her programme. 'Though not necessarily in the first half. I mean, they want people to stay till the end.'

The lights in the ballroom dimmed, leaving the stage illuminated. 'Please rise for the Marchioness of Parcester,' boomed a voice.

'For heaven's sake,' muttered my neighbour, as dresses rustled all over the room.

A tall, bony woman strode to the front of the stage, regarded us with an imperious eye, and motioned us to sit. 'Ladies,' she said, in rather a threatening tone, 'and gentlemen. Welcome to our soirée in aid of the Society for Distressed Gentlewomen. As you will be aware, this is a cause very close to my heart…'

After a couple of minutes, during which it became clear

firstly that the marchioness had nothing new to say, and secondly that she could talk without pausing for breath, I let my gaze wander over the people sitting in front of me. Those in the first two rows were arrayed in elaborate evening gowns, their heads topped with feathers and flowers impeding my view of the marchioness, though I was not greatly perturbed by that. Some spectators were drinking in every word, mouths open, faces rapt. Others looked frankly bored, my neighbour among them, and I assumed they too had been pestered into attending. *I hope the money actually reaches the distressed gentlewomen.*

Eventually the marchioness wound up her address, and after tepid applause a woman in a most unusual dress led a small band of people on stage. She appeared to be uncorseted, and her ankles were showing.

'That's Henrietta Hastings,' whispered my neighbour. 'Playwright and campaigner for women's issues.'

Henrietta Hastings introduced herself, then the Aphrodite Players, which consisted of three women of varying age and two meek men. 'We shall give you scenes from my new play, *The Woman Question,*' she said. 'It is a static reading, since we are currently looking for a venue to stage the play, and if anyone wishes to support us, I shall be very pleased to discuss this at the interval.' After five minutes of hesitant reading, punctuated by enthusiastic prompting from Henrietta whenever anyone missed their cue, I started to think about menus for the week ahead.

At the interval I was buttonholed by my neighbour, who introduced herself as Mrs Daisy Gibbons. She too had come alone, and was grateful to vent her feelings. I resisted the urge to accept another glass of champagne from the waiters, and presently the second half began.

Livia Ricci, the celebrated soprano, gave us a selection of operatic arias. It was certainly a great improvement on the first half, but I found myself distracted by the exaggerated movements of her mouth, and the contrast between her soaring notes and the thin guitar accompaniment from a man seated at the side of the stage.

Then a comic monologue from Mrs Humphrey Montagu was announced, and everyone sat up. Now I wished the inconsiderate women in the front rows had left off their feathers so that I could get a clear view.

Eliza Montagu bounced onto the stage, ringlets flying, and launched into a tirade which set everyone laughing. Her vitality was irresistible. Her eyes sparkled; her movements were carefree, yet graceful. She moved about the stage easily, her voice ringing out, and I wondered how anyone could sustain such a level of energy. At every moment I thought she might flag, might pause for a word, might fall out of character, but she did not. When she reached her triumphant conclusion and the audience rose to applaud her, I glanced at my watch and was astonished to discover that twenty minutes had passed in a flash.

Eliza Montagu curtsied again and again, and waited for the applause to die down. 'I am glad that you have enjoyed this evening's entertainment,' she said, and I could have sworn she was looking straight at me. 'Please, before you go, think of those poor women who cannot afford to attend such an evening, who can barely afford to eat, who through no fault of their own have been left completely unable to survive in a world such as this, and give what you can to help them.' The audience applauded all over again, and I must admit I sat down with a lump in my throat.

The master of ceremonies stepped forward. 'A light supper will now be served and our company will move amongst you. Please give generously to a very worthy cause.'

I dug in my purse; I had two pounds apart from my cab fare. I barely recalled my mission; I only wanted to get close to Eliza Montagu.

'She's ever so good, isn't she?' remarked Daisy Gibbons. 'I swear she could bring a tear to a glass eye.'

I nodded, resenting her casual words. 'I shall go and donate some money.'

Daisy Gibbons raised her eyebrows. 'She worked her charm on you, then.'

I ate a small plate of morsels from the buffet then secured another glass of champagne; I required a stimulant. Eliza Montagu would probably turn from me in contempt: a woman in last year's gown attempting to look fashionable.

She appeared a few minutes later, and a crowd of people rushed at her. She held up her hands. 'Wait a minute!' she cried, laughing. 'I am famished. Let me get a plate of food, then I shall talk with all of you.'

I was standing near the buffet table, and hastily moved towards it with my empty plate. Eliza Montagu approached and scrutinised the dishes of finger sandwiches and vol-au-vents. She looked even prettier away from the harsh light of the stage. 'What would you recommend?' she asked,

276

turning to me.

'The egg and cress sandwiches are nice,' I gabbled, 'and the curried chicken vol-au-vents.'

'Then I shall try those.' She put two of each on her plate, and after some thought added a ham sandwich. 'That will do. I always take far too much, then realise halfway through that I am full. Not that I stop eating, but I always regret it afterwards.'

I laughed. 'Your monologue was wonderful, Mrs Montagu.'

'Thank you!' She seemed genuinely pleased.

'And I was very moved by your speech. I don't know if you are accepting donations, but if you are, I would be happy to contribute.' I put my plate down hastily and took my purse from my bag.

'That is so kind, Miss, um… I don't think I've seen you at one of our benefits before.'

'I am Mrs – Mrs Moncrieff,' I said, hoping I was not blushing; my own name had been on the tip of my tongue. 'I have not been in society for a few years, since my husband – since he…'

'I understand.' She laid a hand on my arm. 'How tragic, for you are so young. I hope the first sorrow has eased, and you are able to enjoy yourself once more.'

'I am not used to events like this,' I said. 'When I was younger, I was – not a distressed gentlewoman, but times were not as easy.'

Eliza Montagu's eyes were full of sympathy. 'Fate is capricious,' she said. 'I barely see some of my friends who have fallen on hard times; their pride makes them shut

277

themselves away. I had a boon companion, but she never comes to London now. I would visit her in Ealing, but she always puts me off.'

I did my best not to stare. 'Oh, how terrible.'

'They have had to sell many treasured possessions,' she continued, 'and while Effie would never admit it, she is ashamed her beautiful home is so reduced.'

I nodded, striving to keep my face under control. Eliza Montagu knew Effie Stanley! Another connection made.

'I am fortunate, I know,' said Eliza. 'My husband is a prosperous businessman, but of course I never mention money matters in my letters to Effie.' She laughed. 'It is strange, isn't it? I have another friend who is undertaking a long rest cure in the country, and when she writes she always wants to know what Humphrey and I are doing and what his next business venture is.' She laughed. 'Perhaps when she is well she will become his business partner – or set up as his rival! That would be just like Sophia; she would love to best him.' She looked at me, and I sensed I had missed my cue.

I composed myself hurriedly; I dreaded to think what my expression had been. 'I hope she recovers soon,' I said, for lack of anything better.

'I hope so too,' said Eliza. 'She says it is nervous exhaustion. Well, that is what the doctors say; I do not think she trusts them.' She looked wistful. 'I do miss her terribly. We used to have such fun together, dashing around London like a pair of mad things.'

'To absent friends,' I said, and raised my glass.

'Yes, to absent friends,' said Eliza Montagu. 'I'm so

sorry, I am chattering on as usual.'

'It was wonderful to meet you,' I said, and I meant it. 'Before I forget—' I pressed a sovereign into her hand. 'I hope it will do good.'

'I shall make sure it goes straight to the funds,' said Eliza. She gave me a dazzling smile, then turned to the waiting throng.

I stood in a dark corner and finished my champagne while around me people chatted, gossiped, and fought to get a few moments with their heroines. A sovereign had been a small price to pay for the information I had gathered. I felt dizzy, and I could not be sure whether it was the champagne I had drunk or the ideas forming in my brain. I set my glass down, and slipped away.

CHAPTER 38

It was a short cab ride to Baker Street, and the streets were relatively clear of traffic. Even so, I had to fight the urge to leap out of the cab and run every time we slowed down or halted. At long last we stopped outside the familiar door, though I still wanted to wrench the crape bow from the knocker and toss it into the street. Instead I paid the cabbie, who looked reprovingly at my far from black gown, and let myself in.

I had barely closed the door when footsteps ascended from the kitchen. 'You've come back in one piece, then,' said Martha.

'Yes, thank you.' I took off my shawl and handed it to her. 'I would like tea, please, in the consulting room. Strong tea.'

'Haven't you done enough for one night?' asked Martha. 'It's nearly eleven o'clock. Surely warm milk would be more appropriate.'

'I'll go to bed when I'm ready, Martha,' I said shortly.

'You could at least get changed,' she said, running a disapproving eye over me.

I had almost forgotten that I was in disguise; I knew

how much Martha detested talking with me when I was not myself, so to speak. 'I shall go and change, then. But I would still like a pot of strong tea in the consulting room, please.' I went upstairs, reflecting that for someone who was supposed to do my bidding, Martha had rather a high-handed manner when it suited her.

I exchanged my evening dress for a house dress, then cleaned myself up in the bathroom; I had used minimal cosmetics to avoid detection. I removed the wig and plaited my hair. *It would never do to be discovered masquerading as someone else. Not now.*

'That's better,' said Martha, when she brought in the tea. 'Although what you're doing in here at this time of night—'

'Thinking.' I stood in front of the wall, contemplating the sheets of paper Sherlock had pinned up not so long ago. Names, characteristics, and thoughts spanned the walls, but it seemed so distant from where I now was. I sighed, fetched a fresh sheet of paper from the bureau, and pinned it to the wall. In the centre I wrote *Lady Sophia Chambers*. Then I wrote two more names to form an equal-sided triangle: *Eliza Montagu* and *Effie Stanley*. I drew lines from Milady and Effie to Eliza. Then I paused; was it definite that Milady knew Effie? 'Not definite, but possible,' I said aloud, and drew a dotted line between them.

Martha cleared her throat. 'Could I ask what you're doing, ma'am?'

I turned, and noticed that she had, as ever, put a plate of biscuits on the tray. 'Oh Martha, will you ever stop feeding

281

me?'

'There's nothing of you, ma'am. You can't blame me for looking after you, especially at the moment.'

Sighing, I poured myself a cup of tea and to appease Martha, put a biscuit in my saucer. A garibaldi, my favourite. I sipped my tea and returned to my contemplation.

'What does the dotted line mean, ma'am?' asked Martha. 'And why did you put a new sheet of paper up? Lord knows there is enough paper on this wall already.'

'Lady Chambers is friends with Eliza Montagu,' I said. 'Hence the line. Mrs Montagu is also friends with Effie Stanley. Lady Chambers and Effie Stanley may or may not be friends, but I'm sure they know of each other.'

'I'd have thought so, ma'am,' said Martha, 'but why does it matter?'

'I learnt tonight that Lady Chambers is very curious about the business interests of Mrs Montagu's husband.' I tapped his name on the bigger diagram with my pencil. 'Some of the businesses he is involved with have done well, but some have failed unexpectedly. Do you remember when Inspector Lestrade called and stayed for dinner? He engaged Sherlock to follow the Montagus because of the intelligence he had received concerning his businesses. Sherlock found nothing amiss, to the point where we thought the whole thing was a distraction.'

'But what could this Lady Chambers have done to cause that?' said Martha. 'I assume she's not a businesswoman.'

'We thought she was safely shut away from the outside

world in a private nursing home,' I said. 'As it turns out, this is no longer the case, and from what Eliza Montagu says, she was corresponding quite freely. I believe she passed on the business information she got from Mrs Montagu to someone else.' I wrote *Shared business intelligence* beside the line connecting Eliza Montagu with Lady Chambers, then drew an arrow from Milady's name, and along it wrote *To sabotage business or cause suspicion?*

'It all seems very far-fetched,' said Martha, frowning.

'On the contrary,' I said, 'it's one of the most solid leads we've had. It's just a shame that we don't know where Lady Chambers is. The inspector's telegram said that her husband had removed her from the nursing home, and I dearly hope that is true.'

'I'm not sure I do,' said Martha. 'She seems a nasty piece of work.'

'Be glad you haven't met her.' I took another sip of tea, then tapped my mouth with the pencil as I considered the paper. 'If Milady can correspond with Mrs Montagu, she can correspond with anyone.' I drew another arrow and at the end I wrote: *Moriarty?* Then I crossed to Sherlock's piece of paper and considered the characteristics and attributes he had written next to that name. 'Moriarty has connections. Moriarty has money. Moriarty could have arranged the bombs, but we don't think he wrote the letters.' I found the notes the bomber had sent and skimmed them.

Perhaps you should consider treading the boards…

My latest present to you...

I do so enjoy writing to you. It is like penning a letter to a dear acquaintance; I know you will understand me...

Where would be the fun otherwise?

'The person who wrote these sounds as if – as if they are playing a game. As if they're having fun.' I remembered Milady as I had first met her, smiling as I caught her with a stolen brooch. 'And she was.' I hurried forward and wrote *Did she send the bomb letters?* next to Milady's name. The writing was nothing like hers, but Sherlock and I had both said that the writer could easily have disguised their hand. Or she could have got Susan to write them, for all we knew....

Then another note came to mind: the missive addressed to me. *I know where you live.* The letter we had thought might be from Jack, and which he had denied. I saw Milady laughing as she imagined me hurrying to pack a bag and flee, and grinning as she drafted the letter which would send Sherlock to Highgate Cemetery. 'But why wouldn't she kill me, too?'

'Sometimes, ma'am, I wish that you would interest yourself in something less dangerous, like a charitable committee or watercolour painting,' said Martha.

'I was actually at a charitable event tonight,' I replied, finishing my biscuit and taking another.

Martha sighed. 'I declare that you could find trouble at a Sunday school, ma'am. Anyway, why didn't she kill you when she had the chance?'

'Sherlock suggested that the bomber had something

else in mind for me,' I said. 'I thought it was odd, but if Lady Chambers is behind this…' I shivered. 'She is capable of anything. Sherlock thought the bombs might be a distraction to get him out of the way, although we do not know what Moriarty's plans are. Or Milady's. But they are clearly working together.' I finished my tea and poured another cup.

'If you sleep a wink tonight, ma'am, I shall be astonished,' said Martha.

'So shall I,' I said. 'But there's no point in trying to rest until I have got to the bottom of this.' Beside Moriarty's name I wrote *Whereabouts?* and drew a circle around it. 'We have not heard directly from him; he could be anywhere. Hopefully I can get hold of Inspector Lestrade in the morning and task him with finding out where Moriarty is. I would bet a pound to a penny that Lady Chambers is not with her husband.'

'What about this Effie woman?' said Martha. 'What has she got to do with anything?'

'I was instrumental in putting her husband behind bars,' I said. 'Then he was kidnapped from prison and tortured; Moriarty and Lady Chambers were responsible.'

'Then they can't be friends,' said Martha.

'No…' I gazed at the wall. 'But Lady Chambers is meant to be Mrs Montagu's friend, and she has been passing on information about her husband's business.' I saw Milady's pen moving across the paper, spreading poison. 'She wants revenge,' I said. 'She is taking revenge on Eliza Montagu, who is free and happy, by divulging her husband's business secrets. And she even tortured her friend's husband when he was captured, though why…'

Then the penny dropped. 'He was captured to satisfy her,' I said slowly. 'The questions they asked meant nothing. It was all for her.' I shuddered, then remembered Effie Stanley as I had last seen her, her handsome, lively face twisted in contempt for me. 'Yet Effie Stanley thinks I am the villain.' But what did she think I had done? Mrs Stanley had been all affability before she had left me to interview her husband, and afterwards she had practically ordered me from the house. Something had caused that change—

'An anonymous letter,' I said. 'Or more likely, a telegram. That's how she turned Effie Stanley against me. Lady Chambers knew I was visiting the Stanleys – she was having me followed even then – and she sent a wire to expose me and make sure I could get no help from them. And the Stanleys would then also reject any support the government offered.' I stepped forward and wrote rapidly on the paper until my pencil was blunt.

'Well,' said Martha. 'Well.' She took a biscuit and ate it, her eyes fixed on the paper. 'I thought Mr Holmes did most of the brain work, begging your pardon, ma'am.'

'We both do the brain work, Martha, as you put it.' I wrote FIND THEM at the top of the paper, underlined it, then drew two arrows to Moriarty and Lady Chambers. 'We both solve cases, though not necessarily in the same way. Our skills are complementary.' I sighed, and laid the pencil on the bureau. I was glad to arrive at more or less the truth of the matter, but how I wished Sherlock could be here. I thought of him, lying on straw in Wiggins's room,

286

and rubbed my arms to disperse the sudden chill that ran through me. Then I finished my cup of tea and put it on the tray.

'Is that all for tonight, ma'am?' said Martha.

'Yes, it is.' I smiled at her. 'Thank you for helping me.'

To my surprise, she giggled. 'Oh, I didn't do anything. I just asked silly questions.'

I laughed too. 'I think Dr Watson does that sometimes. You must never tell him I said that, even though Mr Holmes finds – found it helpful.' *I must be more careful.* 'Anyway, I had better go to bed. Hopefully I can contact Inspector Lestrade in the morning and we can track these people down.'

'Hopefully,' said Martha. She picked up the tray. 'Morning tea at the usual time, ma'am?'

'Please.'

Martha left the room and I approached the sheets of paper once more, running my finger over the names. How odd, and how characteristic, that so many disparate and seemingly unconnected events had turned out to be threads in Milady's web. I saw her at the centre, receiving intelligence and spinning her lies through letters, keenly aware of all that passed when we had thought her incapable of causing harm. She was the spider, and Sherlock and I the flies she hoped to catch.

CHAPTER 39

As Martha had predicted, I did not sleep well. Milady haunted my dreams, writing letters which exploded upon touch and chasing Sherlock and me through a maze of London streets. We cowered like rats in alleys as she ran past us, laughing. I must have slept eventually, though, for I was woken by the scrape of the curtains being drawn.

'Good morning, ma'am,' said Martha.

'Good morning,' I murmured, rubbing the sleep from my eyes.

'I'm not sure if I should ask what you plan to do today,' said Martha, pouring a cup of tea and bringing it over.

'Wait for news from the inspector, I suppose,' I said. Then my face fell.

'What is it, ma'am?'

'I have letters to answer,' I said. 'About the funeral. And I must choose what to wear.' I grimaced. The thought of putting on heavy black mourning clothes repelled me, but anything else would show insufficient respect. Not just for Sherlock, but for his family and friends.

'It is hard, ma'am, but best to get it out of the way.'

'You're right.' I sighed. 'It has to be done, and the

quicker the better.'

After breakfast I found a Bradshaw and looked up trains. I would have to leave London early in the morning, but that removed the necessity for an overnight stay. Under normal circumstances I would have been delighted to spend time with Sherlock's parents, but I could not bear to maintain the appearance of a grieving widow for longer than necessary. If my mask slipped even for a moment they would think me cold, or worse. Besides, I did not want to be away from London too long.

I could put my disagreeable tasks off no longer. I unscrewed the cap of my pen and pulled a sheet of paper towards me.

Dear Mycroft…

***

An hour later, I studied myself in the glass. I was dressed head to toe in stiff black bombazine trimmed with crape. Everything was black: black boots, black stockings, black gloves, a black bonnet designed to shield me from the world, like a pair of horse's blinkers, and a thick veil that reached to my waist.

'It needs taking in, really,' said Martha, pinching the spare fabric at my middle.

'There isn't time,' I said. 'Anyway, I shall only wear this for the funeral.'

Martha sighed. 'As you wish, ma'am.' I looked at her in surprise, having expected her to argue, but I was relieved that she had acquiesced without a fight.

Just then there was loud knocking at the back door. 'That's odd,' said Martha. 'I wasn't expecting any deliveries until tomorrow afternoon.'

'I'm sure Billy can deal with it,' I said. 'Now help me take off this – this get-up.'

We had not got further than removing the veil, bonnet and boots when Billy's footsteps pelted upstairs. 'Ma'am, there is a special delivery for you.' He was grinning all over his face. 'You'll have to be quick, he hasn't got long.'

'A special delivery?' I ran downstairs in my stockinged feet. Surely it could not be Sherlock; Billy would never have been able to keep quiet.

I entered the kitchen, Martha hot on my heels, to find a short, slightly ratlike man in a voluminous white apron, a baker's cap, and an impressive beard.

I grinned. 'Good morning, Inspector.'

'Morning,' said Inspector Lestrade. 'Given how things are, I decided it was best not to advertise my presence.' He waved a hand at a large cake box on the table. 'I hope you enjoy it.'

'I'll make tea,' said Martha, moving to the stove. The inspector eyed her suspiciously.

'Don't worry,' I said, 'Martha knows about the case. She was very helpful last night, as a matter of fact. I have plenty to tell you – but first, what of Lady Chambers?'

The inspector sat down at the kitchen table. 'You will not be surprised to hear that when I arrived at Chambers Hall, Sir William had no idea what I was talking about. Indeed, he said he had never visited his wife at the nursing home, nor corresponded with her. Apparently she sent him a letter soon after her arrival that was so full of malice, hatred and viciousness that he wishes never to set eyes on her again. "That woman ruined me," he said. "And worse, she made a fool of me."'

'She did,' I replied. 'What information did you get from the local police?'

'The local chief constable telephoned late yesterday afternoon,' said the inspector. 'From what he said, it has been a catalogue of errors. Having behaved impeccably for some months, Lady Chambers was allowed to receive a limited amount of correspondence from family and friends, and to write to them, though of course those letters were inspected before posting. The staff liked her because she was an easy patient, and allowed her certain indulgences not permitted to the other residents. This even extended to short visits from her former maid and her husband, Sir William Chambers. When the staff were asked to describe him, the description matched – but it is not hard to put on a suit and false whiskers.' He touched his own chin self-consciously.

'Who do you think was the false Sir William?' I asked.

'The obvious answer is Moriarty,' said Inspector Lestrade. 'In such a lax environment, why would he not take the chance to visit his partner in crime?'

'When was Lady Chambers removed from the nursing home?'

'Three weeks ago.' The inspector's fists clenched. 'Apparently Sir William had said to the proprietor of the nursing home that he was seeking a second opinion on his wife's mental state. The proprietor was only too happy to sign a statement that he believed Lady Chambers capable of returning to society, and shortly afterwards Sir William returned with a Harley Street doctor and an order from the Home Office – both as real as my beard, I daresay. Lady Chambers left that same day.'

'What a mess.' I put my head in my hands, then took them away and faced him. 'I must tell you what I learnt last night.' As briefly as I could, I told him of my meeting with Eliza Montagu, her unknowing supply of intelligence to Lady Chambers, and her friendship with Effie Stanley.

'So she was a pawn in the game,' said Inspector Lestrade. 'Good heavens.'

'Lady Chambers is the missing part of the puzzle,' I said. 'Professor Moriarty supplied the money and the underworld connections, while Lady Chambers used her network from the confinement of the nursing home.' I frowned. 'But I still don't know why Professor Moriarty wanted to kill Sherlock and not me.'

'It does seem peculiar,' commented Martha, as she set down our cups of tea.

The inspector drank half of his in one go. 'Consider this: when government information was leaked about British movements in Egypt, who fell under suspicion?'

'Why, Mycroft Holmes.' Now I saw. 'Sherlock's brother.'

'Indeed. What would be more normal than for Professor Moriarty to assume that Mr Sherlock Holmes was behind his arrest? Mr Holmes was known to work with Scotland Yard; he was a detective; there was a family connection.'

'That makes perfect sense.' I drank deeply from my own cup. 'I can't believe I didn't see it.'

'Sometimes the spectator sees more of the game.' The inspector drained his cup and stood up. 'I had better go before people wonder what exactly I'm delivering.' He permitted himself a rare smile, which faded quickly as he noticed my dress. 'I see your mourning clothes have arrived.'

'They have,' I said. 'What do we do now? How can we find Professor Moriarty and Lady Chambers? They could be anywhere.'

'They could,' said Inspector Lestrade, 'but I doubt they have gone far. The main threat, as Moriarty sees it, has been removed, and he is free to carry out his plans, whatever they may be. The best we can do is wait. Sooner or later they will show themselves, and in the meantime, we can watch for movement from their associates.'

He walked to the door, then paused, his hand on the doorknob. 'If you don't mind me asking, Mrs Hudson, how did you meet with Mrs Montagu?'

'I happened to be attending a charity event last night, and she was also present.'

His eyes narrowed. 'Am I to assume that you were pretending to be somebody else?'

Martha snorted. 'What do you think, Inspector?'

He gave me an exasperated look. 'I suppose I ought to be thankful that you are not out chasing Lady Chambers. But listen, Nell: no more sneaking about. We've already lost Mr Holmes, and I have no desire to lose you too. Remember that.' He gave me a curt nod, tipped his cap to Martha, and was gone.

'You heard the inspector, ma'am,' said Martha. 'No

more sneaking about.'

I sighed, and drank the rest of my tea. I longed to keep busy, to advance the case and ensure Sherlock's safe return, but there was nothing I could do. My sole engagement was Sherlock's funeral in a week's time. 'The inspector is right,' I said quietly. If, as we thought, Professor Moriarty and Lady Chambers had something else in mind for me, all I could do was wait. If they wanted to find me, they would have to seek me out.

CHAPTER 40

'There, you're all ready, ma'am,' said Martha. 'I'll go downstairs and tell Billy to hold a cab for you. You must hurry; your train leaves in less than an hour.'

'Thank you.' I gazed at myself in the mirror, drowned in my black cloak. Now I was glad of that thick veil; hopefully it would hide my unease and guilt. I was going to the funeral of a man who had not died, and I would have to pretend to his parents, his brother, and his friends that I grieved as much as they. I sighed. It would have to be done, for their sake and for his. Perhaps for mine, too. I picked up my gloves from the dressing table and put them on.

I was securing the second button when I heard footsteps hurrying upstairs. 'I am coming, Martha,' I called.

She burst in without knocking, her face white as a sheet. 'It's a note, ma'am.' She put it in my hand. 'It's one of those notes.'

I looked down at the envelope. *To Mrs Hudson*, it said, in the stiff writing that Sherlock and I had come to dread.

I ripped it open.

Dear Mrs Hudson,

I hope you don't mind me writing to you. Perhaps it is not the most convenient time, given your other commitments, but I would like to say a few words.

'I don't believe this,' I muttered.

It was a terrible shame about Mr Holmes, but life must go on, mustn't it? And in the absence of the avowed star of the show, I am sure that you, the understudy, will step up to the role.

I have arranged a little surprise in memory of Mr Holmes, in a very public location. It would be most regrettable if you were to arrive late and cause any disappointment among the many people who will be there when the surprise is revealed. It is in a location you know well, and where you have spent a great deal of time. Indeed, I myself have seen you there.

As a special favour, I'm giving you extra time. We wouldn't want things to go off too early, would we? It would be much better to wait until the venue is at its busiest, thronged with people. However, I must stipulate that you go alone and refrain from contacting either the police or your acquaintances. I am watching your house, the local telegraph offices and the police stations, and any attempt by you or your servants to use them will force me to advance things.

The very best of luck, Mrs Hudson.
Yours,
An Admirer

'Oh dear God,' I murmured.

'It's him or her, isn't it?' said Martha. 'It's the bomber.'

'I'm afraid so,' I said. 'And I may contact nobody.' I flung back my veil. 'I wish Sherlock was here.'

'The swine,' said Martha. 'They've done this to make sure you miss the funeral, haven't they?'

'To be honest, Martha, I hope that's all it is.' I undid my bonnet and took it off. 'I need to think. I don't know how long I have; I hope it's long enough.'

'I'll make tea and warn Billy,' said Martha.

I sat on the bed, still clutching the letter. A place I knew well that would be busy later; somewhere I had spent a great deal of time, and where the bomber had seen me. I racked my brains. Could it be Regent's Park? I walked there often, and it grew busy after mid-morning. But where in the park? No clue was given.

I dropped the letter on the bed and put my hands to my temples, pressing on them to try and clear the jumble of thoughts cluttering my mind. Could it be one of the hotels I used in the course of my business? But there were three or four to choose from, and again, no clue to which one was meant.

A place where I spent a great deal of time... I went to the post office often to collect mail or send telegrams, but there was no particular time when it was busier.

I gasped as I realised.

A place where I regularly spent time, lately in particular, and which grew busier as the day wore on.

A place where I had seen the bomber, and the bomber had seen me. The place of our first meeting, in fact.

Debenham and Freebody's department store.

Her audacity shocked me. That, and her cold-blooded willingness to sacrifice tens or possibly hundreds of people for the chance of snaring me. 'Wouldn't it have been easier to post dynamite through my door in the night?' I said aloud.

But that, clearly, was not what Milady wanted. She wanted me to come to her, and I had no choice but to go.

I rose, put my bonnet back on, and walked to the door as if I were in a dream. But the doorknob was solid beneath my hand. It was all too real.

I went downstairs to the kitchen and found Martha setting my tea tray. 'You and Billy had better have that,' I said. 'I am going out; I hope to return later.' In the absence of Billy's toolbox, I took some cutlery, a couple of skewers and a pair of tongs from the kitchen drawer. I put the items in my bag, feeling utterly ridiculous. I did not even have a penknife, and Sherlock's pistol had gone with him to Highgate Cemetery.

'Where are you going, ma'am?' asked Martha, terror in her face. 'Please don't go alone.'

'I have no choice,' I said. 'I can't contact anyone to help, and neither can you. They are watching the house. The bomb is at the department store: Debenham and Freebody. If the worst happens, at least you can help with identification. Tell—' The next words froze on my tongue. I had been about to say 'Tell Sherlock I love him.'

'Tell who, ma'am?' asked Billy, his face beseeching.

'Tell Mycroft and Sherlock's parents that I am sorry I missed the funeral.'

They nodded gravely.

'I had better go,' I said. There were so many other things I wanted to say – how helpful and understanding they had been, how important they had become to me – but suddenly there was no time. So I said goodbye, climbed the kitchen steps, and let myself out.

***

It was still dark outside. I began walking, doubting that I would find a cab at this hour, but I heard carriage wheels behind me before I had gone far. I turned and hailed the cab. 'Debenham and Freebody, please.'

'Aren't you a bit early, ma'am?' said the cabman with a grin.

'They are having a sale on hats today,' I said. 'I wish to be first in line when the doors open.'

'I should say you'll manage that,' he said, laughing. 'Up you get, ma'am.'

It was too early even for the paper boys to be crying their wares. Here and there a sweeper plied their trade, but apart from them, the cabbie and I seemed to be the only two people in the world.

The cab drew up. 'Here we are,' the cabman shouted. 'You've got your wish.' As I got down, he gestured towards the deserted store. It felt strange that Alf was not there to welcome me, but I was very glad that he was absent.

'Thank you.' I put money in his hand.

'Are you sure you'll be all right, ma'am?' He looked both curious and concerned.

I managed to smile. 'Yes, I shall be quite all right. I think they open early today.' I walked to the doorway and stood beside it.

The cabman touched his cap. 'Good luck, madam.' He shook the reins and the horse plodded away. I imagined him later, telling his fellow-cabbies about an odd woman in deep mourning who had wanted to go to the shops practically in the middle of the night. Perhaps he would remember me when he saw the newspapers, and wonder whether I had got out safely. Or perhaps not.

Once the cab had gone, I hurried round the side of the building to the staff entrance. As I had expected, the lock had been forced – I could see the marks from the crowbar – and the door was slightly ajar. I pushed it open and hurried in, expecting at any moment to be seized. But there was no noise from the staffroom, the cloakroom, or the offices, and I gained entry into the store unchallenged.

It was still dark within: not pitch black, for faint grey light came from the skylights above, but everything was shadowy. I looked around me; where would the bomb be? And how on earth could I find it in the gloom?

It will be somewhere significant. Could it be at the glove counter where Susan had spent so much time? Or hidden among the trays of stockings that she had plundered for Milady? But no – those were more about Susan than Lady Chambers. And this, I felt sure, was all about her.

I paced, thinking, and as I walked I noticed that someone, perhaps more than one person, had been busy. Trays lay on the counters, and some of the mannequins and display models of hands or heads were bare. *What on earth has she been doing?* Speculations crowded in on me, and I walked faster to drive them out.

I myself have seen you there…

That was it! There were two places – the spot near the entrance where I had apprehended Milady, or, and I thought more likely, the costume jewellery counter where she had stolen a cheap little brooch for the thrill of it. I dashed to the jewellery counter, looked around it, then began taking out the trays from the racks, peering and feeling for the familiar cardboard tubes.

I pulled out tray after tray until all were piled on the counter. Where else could it be? I opened the drawers under the counter and rummaged through balls of string, scraps of brown paper, scissors and receipt books, but there was no bomb—

'Excuse me!'

I froze at the sound of that voice. I would have known it anywhere.

There, smiling like a hostess, stood Milady.

CHAPTER 41

Lady Chambers was not alone: on either side of her stood a man holding up a lantern, so that she was illuminated as if she were the lead character in a play. Susan stood perhaps ten feet away in the shadows, hands clasped, face expressionless.

'How nice of you to call, Mrs Hudson,' said my lady. 'Or should I say Mouse? See, I remember you very well. Come out and show yourself.' She turned to one of the men. 'Take her bag and cloak and make sure she's not armed. Oh, and take off her hat and veil. I want to see her face.'

I came out from behind the counter and suffered myself to be patted down by one of the men, who was perhaps more embarrassed than I was. 'Nothing there, ma'am,' he reported, returning to his place beside her. 'Some cutlery in the bag, that's all.'

Lady Chambers threw back her head and laughed. 'Cutlery? What are you planning to do, eat the bomb?' She smiled a superior, amused smile. 'Of course there is no bomb; I just wanted to see you one last time.'

I looked her up and down. Now I knew who had been

302

undressing the mannequins. Lady Chambers wore a navy-blue silk gown, but she had draped herself with colourful shawls and strings of beads, and her hair was a riot of silk flowers.

'Do you like my outfit?' she asked, twirling in front of me. 'I decided to do some shopping.' She assumed a contrite expression. 'I'm terribly sorry that you had to miss Mr Holmes's funeral, but at least you have come appropriately dressed.'

I remained silent; I would not give her the satisfaction of a response.

Lady Chambers waited, tapping a fan against the palm of her hand. Eventually she spoke. 'Go on, Susan, ask me why Mrs Hudson is appropriately dressed.'

Susan's expression did not change. 'Why is she appropriately dressed, milady?'

Lady Chambers laughed a tinkling laugh which set my teeth on edge, and I saw Susan wince. 'Why, because this is exactly the sort of thing that people will wear to *her* funeral.'

Don't react, I told myself. *That's what she wants. The longer you keep her talking, the more chance there is that help will arrive.*

Lady Chambers glared at her helpers. 'Don't you like my joke?' she demanded. 'Don't forget, I can always shoot you first.' She dropped her fan and took a pistol from her bag.

At the sight of it, Susan and the men nodded and smiled. One of the men even managed a laugh.

'That's better,' said Lady Chambers. She pointed the

gun at the ceiling and fired, and fragments of plaster fell to the floor. 'Just in case you thought it wasn't loaded,' she remarked.

While all eyes were on her, I turned slightly so that I could see the large clock on the wall out of the corner of my eye. Twenty past seven. I knew from Mr Turner's frequent remarks on the subject of how hard he worked that he usually arrived at a quarter to eight. I prayed he would do so today, see the lie of the land, and summon the police. *At least there is no bomb*. Then the realisation hit me that there was no bomb because I was the person Milady wanted to kill, and she had lured me there to do it. A shiver ran down my spine and I did my best to hide it.

'Not so clever now, are we, Mrs Lady Detective?' said Milady. 'Perhaps James was right, and Sherlock Holmes was the brains of the outfit after all.'

'James?' I asked, though I had a very good idea whom she meant.

'Oh, do forgive me. Professor Moriarty to you. I forgot you aren't on first-name terms. Indeed, why would you be? He is one of the finest minds of his generation. Frankly, you two had no hope against him, and even less with me as his partner.' She smiled complacently. 'Who did *you* think planted the bombs and wrote the letters?'

'I didn't know, milady,' I lied.

'Well, now you do.' Lady Chambers sighed. 'It is galling to think that James and I wasted so much time and effort in getting you two out of the way when we could probably have left you in blissful ignorance while we got on with things. But James said that we had to remove the threat of your young man before he could move to the next phase of his operations. James has rather an obsession with Mr Sherlock Holmes, you see. He thought him responsible for that regrettable business last year which caused me to lose my liberty for a while. I, however, suspected you, and some delicate enquiries proved me right.'

'Whom did you ask?' I glanced at the clock. Another three minutes had passed.

'James still has connections in government, you see,' said Lady Chambers, as if I had not spoken. 'Sad to say, they find it so hard to manage without him that sometimes they cannot resist getting in touch, even though they ought to know how unwise that is.' She smiled a smug little smile. 'That was how he learned the truth behind our arrest. James still maintained that you were Holmes's puppet, but I begged to differ. That is why I arranged for him to be killed first; I wanted to have a tête-à-tête with you on the subject of your failure.'

She took a step towards me, the gun still raised. 'Because you *have* failed. You didn't guess who was planting the bombs, and you didn't work out what was going on with poor Humphrey Montagu's businesses. Then you ran away and hid as soon as I sent you a little personal note.' Her lip curled. 'What a coward you are, Mouse.' Then she laughed. 'I grant you that going undercover here was a nice touch, and getting hold of my hapless maid should have been a triumph' – she glared at Susan, who bit her lip and looked at her feet – 'but sadly the incompetence of the local constabulary let you down. All silly little Susan had to do was cry a few crocodile tears, and they let

305

her come trotting back to me as if nothing had happened.'

'We thought you were still at the nursing home,' I said. 'Where you should have been.'

I jumped as a shot whistled past me. 'Careful,' warned Milady. 'You and I both know there was absolutely nothing wrong with me. The only reason I was imprisoned in that nursing home is because I was expendable. My dear husband had had enough of me, and unlike James I didn't have government secrets to keep, so it was easy to lock me up and throw away the key. I'm as sane as the next person. Aren't I, Susan?'

Susan started. 'Yes, milady,' she said quickly.

Lady Chambers prodded her in the ribs with the gun. 'More conviction, please, Susan.'

'Of course you're not mad, milady,' said Susan. 'You have never been mad, and you never will be.'

'There, that wasn't so hard, was it?' Lady Chambers turned back to me, shawls floating, beads rattling. She looked like nothing so much as an overgrown child who had got into her mother's wardrobe. 'Of course I'm not mad. How could I have convinced the staff to grant me so many privileges? Once I had acclimatised to my new surroundings, I spent time observing the staff and the other residents. Now, *they* were mad. Or stupid.' She giggled. 'I soon saw which patients the staff liked best: the meek ones who took what was given them without complaint. From that point I was the meekest and most compliant of them all. It crushed my spirit to play the role, but I was richly rewarded.' She shook her head, smiling. 'Poor fools. So easily manipulated.' For a moment she was in a pleasant little world of her own; then she fixed her gaze on me again. 'We had a little wager, you know, me and James.'

'Oh yes?' I assumed an interested expression.

'We did. I bet James five pounds that if he could get me out of that nursing home, I would kill you in a place of my choosing within the month, and prove it.' She gazed at the gun fondly. 'He is on the Continent, where I shall join him shortly, but I shall take pleasure in bringing a copy of tomorrow's newspaper to him, and showing him the report of your death as my proof.'

I curtsied. 'Glad to be of service, milady.'

I felt the pain before I registered the crack of the gun. 'Don't be impertinent, Mrs Hudson,' said Lady Chambers, as I clutched my upper arm. It burned, but something warm oozed through the sleeve of my dress, and my palm came away with a dark smear.

'Go and put a tourniquet on her arm,' Milady murmured to the man who had frisked me for weapons. 'I don't want her to faint until I've finished what I have to say.'

The man took a handkerchief from his pocket and approached me. 'No sudden moves,' he said, as he unbuttoned my cuff and pushed up my sleeve. He tied the handkerchief tightly just above the wound. 'It's a graze, nothing more,' he said, as he returned to Milady's side.

'Oh good,' said Milady. 'I wouldn't want to get ahead of myself. Now, where were we?'

'Just here,' said a deep voice, and Jack came out of the shadows, his gun trained on Lady Chambers. 'And this is where it ends.'

CHAPTER 42

'Good heavens,' said Lady Chambers, looking rather amused. 'Where did you spring from?'

'I have been watching out for Nell for some time,' said Jack. 'Luckily, the man who was watching the house this morning saw her get in a cab and give this address. He immediately reported it to me and I came straight here.' He turned to me. 'I'm sorry I wasn't quicker, Nell, but the hotel staff took a while to wake me, and then I had to find a way in.'

I stood silent, not sure whether I was glad to see him, angry that he had been watching my house, or aghast that he had walked into Milady's trap.

'This is an unexpected development,' said Lady Chambers, grinning. 'I thought you were devoted to Mr Holmes, Mrs Hudson. Who is your new beau?' She studied Jack and I risked another glance at the clock. It was just past the half hour: less than a quarter of an hour until Mr Turner would arrive. Unless Jack had sent his man for help?

Jack drew himself up. 'I am her husband.'

'Really?' purred Milady.

'Really,' said Jack, curtly. 'We have been married several years, and I am her husband in the eyes of the law.'

'You must love her very much to forgive her dalliance with Mr Holmes.' Milady giggled. 'Unless you were in on it too.' She turned to me with a grin. 'I'm impressed with you, Mouse. I thought you'd lost your capacity to surprise me, but it seems I was wrong.'

'How dare you!' said Jack, his face beet red. 'Do not insult the woman I love, or—'

'Or what?' asked Milady, her head on one side. 'What will you do, Mr Husband?'

'Fortunately for you, I am too honourable to shoot a woman,' said Jack. 'I shall hold you at gunpoint until the police arrive. I have sent my man to the station, and I have no doubt the police will be here soon.'

'Ohhh,' said Milady, eyes wide. 'Well, in that case—'

Jack doubled over almost before I heard the shot, then sank to his knees. Heedless of my safety, I ran to him and tried to ease his fall. Blood trickled from between his clutching fingers. 'Damn,' he muttered.

I cradled his head. 'Jack, don't close your eyes. Stay with me, Jack.'

'I'll try,' he gasped. 'I didn't think it would hurt so much.'

'Try not to move, Jack,' I murmured. 'When we're out of this we'll fetch a doctor, and everything will be all right.' I barely knew what I was saying.

Jack focused on me. 'I love you, Nell. I always did, even when I went wrong. Leaving you was the biggest regret of my life, and—'

'I hate to spoil your little speech,' said Milady, 'but I don't have time for this.' She motioned at me with the gun. 'You. Get up.'

I shot her a look of pure hatred. 'He could be dying.'

'I don't care. Get up and stand by that counter. I mean it.'

I patted Jack's arm and stood up. *What is she planning to do?* To gain time, I smoothed my skirts, then backed towards the counter. Lady Chambers wasn't looking at me, though; her attention was fixed on Jack. She raised the gun —

'Catch me if you can!' I cried, as I ran down the aisle into the shadows and dived behind a tall set of shelving racks.

A gasp, then a laugh. 'Hide and seek – what a novel idea!' A pause. 'Come on everybody, let's play Hunt the Mouse. Coming, ready or not!'

I heard stealthy footsteps as I huddled in the gloom. 'I want her alive, mind,' called Lady Chambers. 'You may shoot, but not kill.'

'Milady, we can't be found here,' said one of the men.

'We won't be,' she said confidently. 'If necessary, we can always shoot anyone who comes.'

There was muttering, then Milady's voice rang out again. 'This is an order, do you hear? Find her!'

I held my breath as footsteps came closer, and cursed the growing light above me. I longed to close my eyes, but could not. Susan rounded the edge of the racks and her eyes widened as she saw me. Then she moved on. I let out a slow breath, too relieved to wonder.

'Any sign?' called Lady Chambers.

'Not yet,' called Susan, and the men muttered a negative.

'Do hurry up. I don't wish to shoot the shop assistants. They can't help working here.' Metal heels tip-tapped as she moved towards my hiding place. 'Oh, these are pretty,' she said, and a tray slid from the rack that shielded me. I held my breath. 'One can never have too many stockings…' The tray clacked onto the counter. 'I shall take these, and these…'

I eyed the bottom of the rack. While they looked substantial, being both tall and wide, the racks were nothing more than drawer frames backed with a thin layer of painted wood, and they ran on castors to enable easy movement around the store. I could wheel one a short distance on my own, but pushing it over would be beyond me. I suppressed a sigh, then froze as footsteps approached.

'What are you doing, milady?' asked Susan, peering round the partition at her mistress.

'Waiting for you to do your job,' snapped Lady Chambers. 'So go and do it. If I did not have to save my bullets, I would shoot you too.'

'Yes, milady,' said Susan. She whisked round to my side of the rack and eyed it, as I had, then raised her eyebrows at me. I nodded, and rose stealthily to my feet. We gripped the wooden panel, one on each side. I took a deep breath, and mouthed, 'One, two, three—'

A dull thud was followed by a grunt, then the clatter of drawers falling to the floor. The next sound was a high, breathy scream.

'That's got her,' murmured Susan, satisfaction in her voice. 'She promised me the earth if I helped her, but all I've had is slaps and threats. She said it was a game, but if I'd known what she meant to do—'

'Police! Show yourselves! And no funny business – we have guns.'

Susan and I exchanged glances, then edged out from behind the counter with our hands raised. The shop floor was packed with policemen; there must have been twenty at least.

'There's a man on the floor, sarge,' called a policeman, who was kneeling by Jack. 'He's been shot in the stomach; looks bad.'

'Run for a doctor, then,' said the sergeant. He frowned at Susan. 'You told us a woman was in danger.'

'She was,' said Susan, pointing at me, 'but she is safe, though she has a minor injury.' She gestured at the fallen shelving. 'You'll find Lady Chambers here. We did it in self-defence.'

'Right, men, get that lifted,' said the sergeant, walking towards the shelves.

Another sergeant approached me. 'Mrs Hudson?'

I nodded, too dazed to speak.

'Your servant managed to raise the alarm.'

I stared at him. 'My *servant*?'

'One, two, three, heave!' The shelving rack wobbled and groaned as the policemen lifted it, and we all turned to look at Lady Chambers, who was slumped on the counter, wheezing. She glared at me and opened her mouth to speak, but the sergeant stepped forward. 'Lady Sophia Chambers, I am placing you under arrest for the attempted murder of Mrs Hudson.' He eyed the tourniquet on my arm. 'You do not have to say anything in your defence, but what you do say may be taken down—'

Lady Chambers slid off the counter into a crumpled heap on the floor.

The sergeant walked over and inspected her. 'I think she's fainted.' He grinned. 'Hopefully that will make it easier to take her into custody.'

Suddenly the store was flooded with dazzling light. Mr Turner stood in the doorway to the back offices, gaping. 'What on earth is going on in my store?' he cried. We followed his pointing finger to Milady's accomplices, who immediately dropped their guns and held up their hands.

I hurried to Jack's side. His eyes were closed, his breathing laboured. I knelt beside him. 'Jack,' I whispered, 'wake up.'

His eyelids fluttered, then opened. 'Nell,' he croaked. 'You're here.'

'Yes, I'm here.' I took his hand in both of mine.

'I tried,' he whispered. I had to bend closer to hear him, his voice was so faint.

'You did it, Jack,' I said. 'You saved me.' I wiped away a tear.

The corners of his mouth lifted slightly. 'Good,' he whispered. Then his eyelids closed and he let out a rasping breath.

'Jack? Jack!'

His hand slackened in mine.

I let go of his hand and felt for a pulse. There was nothing.

I covered my face with my hands and wept, and a few moments later a young policeman crouched next to me. 'He's dead,' I whispered.

He patted me awkwardly on the shoulder. 'Look, ma'am, the doctor is here.' He indicated a stocky man with a Gladstone bag, shifting impatiently from foot to foot. 'Let him see; it may not be as bad as you think.' He offered me a hand, and I rose unsteadily to my feet. He walked me to a pillar I could lean against. 'Would you like a chair, ma'am? I can fetch you one.'

I shook my head. 'I can stand,' I said, but he was already moving across the shop floor…

The bullet embedded itself at head height in the pillar, inches from me. Milady's head and shoulders were visible beyond the edge of the counter, the gun in her outstretched hand. 'Missed,' she said, and grimaced. 'Damn.' She inspected the gun. 'One left: I can't miss this time.' Carefully, gently, she put the muzzle of the gun in her mouth, closed her eyes, and pulled the trigger.

***

I screamed and turned away, and moments later I felt arms around me . . . arms that I knew.

'It's all right, Nell,' murmured Sherlock. 'She's gone; she can't hurt us any more.'

'She shot Jack,' I sobbed. Out of the corner of my eye I saw a movement; the doctor was shaking his head at the young policeman. 'She killed him.'

'I'm sorry, Nell.' Sherlock rubbed my back, rocking me

314

gently. 'I'm so sorry.'

I drew back and looked at him. He was even thinner than usual, and dark circles showed under his eyes, but otherwise, despite his shabby attire, he was almost his old self. 'How are you here?'

'I brought some policemen.'

I stared at him. 'What? How?'

'I helped to raise the alarm,' he replied. 'Martha sent Wiggins a signal, Wiggins reported it to me, and I raised Marylebone police station. I believe that young lady had a similar idea.' He looked towards Susan, who was talking earnestly to the sergeant.

Gasps and exclamations came from the staff doorway as the shop girls took in the scene. Evie gazed at the devastation, but her eyes grew even wider when she saw Sherlock and me. I managed a smile and a feeble wave.

The sergeant came over and cleared his throat. 'Madam, we would welcome your attendance at the station. We have much to discuss.'

'Can you manage that, Nell?' asked Sherlock.

'There is one thing we must do first.'

He raised his eyebrows. 'What's that?'

'We must telegraph your family and stop the funeral. There has been enough darkness today.'

Somehow, stumbling along pavements barely lit by an uncertain dawn, we got ourselves to the nearest telegraph office. 'I confess I'm not quite sure what to write,' Sherlock said. 'What do you think, Nell?'

I took the pencil and wrote: *Sherlock alive STOP Cancel funeral STOP Will explain later STOP.* What else should I say? The words danced on the paper and I closed my eyes to try and concentrate, but all I saw was the shredded remains of a web, and a spider dangling limp from a silken thread.

CHAPTER 43

Sherlock grinned at me. 'How does it feel, Mrs Holmes?'

I smiled back. 'I don't think I'll ever get used to it. But I thought that about being called Mrs Hudson, so we shall see.'

'I hope you do get used to it,' he said, looking apprehensive.

I laughed. 'I still don't quite believe it.' I gazed around the room, filled with friends and family.

I had held Sherlock to his promise that he would marry me when the case was over. He had been doubtful at first. 'Are you sure you wouldn't rather wait, Nell? After all, there is Jack.'

'I want to marry you, and I don't actually think Jack would mind,' I replied. 'I have already mourned him once, and I shall mourn him again in my own way, but I don't care what people think. The people who matter will understand.'

'In that case,' he said, drawing me towards him. 'I shall be delighted.' He kissed me, then knelt. 'Nell, will you marry me?'

'Yes, a thousand times,' I answered, and offered him a

hand. He accepted, but instead of rising he pulled me down and we ended up laughing on the floor, where Martha found us when she came in with the tea.

'I don't know what you two think you're doing,' she said, setting the tray on the consulting-room table, 'but at least you're happy doing it.'

Sherlock had obtained a special licence, since we did not wish to wait for banns or risk objections from prudes who thought I should wait at least a year before remarrying, and we had chosen the church in Sherlock's home village. 'That ought to be safe,' Sherlock had said.

'You don't think…'

He smiled, but there was no mirth in it. 'I don't really believe that Professor Moriarty will return from the Continent for the express purpose of ruining our wedding, but—'

'It's impossible,' I argued. 'He is a wanted man. He can never return, and certainly not to London.'

'I certainly hope not,' said Sherlock, and changed the subject.

The case had been wrapped up with relative ease. Inspector Lestrade had taken charge of it, since he had already had considerable involvement, and that saved Sherlock and me a great deal of time and trouble. Susan and the two men, in exchange for lenient treatment, told all they knew, which confirmed Sherlock's theories and was more than enough to convict Professor Moriarty in absentia, while my testimony cleared the Montagus of any wrongdoing.

However, this was overshadowed by the headline which

screamed from every newspaper the next morning: *DETECTIVE RETURNED FROM THE DEAD.* Inspector Lestrade had insisted. 'It's the least we can do,' he had said, guiding the newspaper reporter in Sherlock's direction. 'And you too, Mrs Hudson, you fully deserve the glory.'

I thought of Jack as I had last seen him, and shuddered. 'I would rather not, Inspector, if you don't mind.'

The inspector goggled at me. 'But you solved the case!'

'*We* solved the case,' I said. 'My presence complicates matters. You may mention that I was part of the investigation if you wish, but no more.'

So the account that appeared in the newspaper the next day was a farrago of half-truths and omissions. A bomb threat; a dangerous patient's escape from a secure medical facility; the involvement of Professor Moriarty; the murder of a passerby who had tried to help; the detective who led the police to the scene; the suicide of the murderer.

Sherlock read the article to me the next morning with great amusement. 'If that brings me any new clients, I shall be amazed,' he said, folding the paper and throwing it down.

'Never mind that,' said Dr Watson. 'You are both at home and safe, that's the main thing.'

Sherlock turned to him in surprise. 'What, Watson, won't you chivvy me to exploit my new-found fame?'

I half-expected John to be offended, but instead he smiled. 'Not on this occasion, my dear Holmes. I would even, as a medical man, go so far as to prescribe you a few weeks of rest and home comforts. It is not every day that a man returns from the dead.' His smile vanished. 'I'm so sorry, Nell, I completely forgot.'

I laid my hand on his arm. 'It is quite all right, John. It was a sad business, but it is over. In a strange way, it helped me to understand Jack, and why he did what he did. I do not blame him now; the bitterness has gone, and only sadness remains.'

'It is a hard lesson, though,' said Dr Watson.

'It is,' I said, 'but a lesson learnt. And we can look forward to happier times.'

I gazed around the dining room of the local inn where we had chosen to have a modest buffet after the wedding ceremony. My mother was talking to Sherlock's parents, while my sister Sally and her husband stood to the side of the room, some distance from the other guests. Sally's nose was in the air, and I suspect she thought the whole thing highly improper.

She had still not quite forgiven me for what she termed my deception. 'So this is the elderly bachelor you've been keeping house for all this time,' she observed with a sniff when we visited my mother to tell her of our approaching wedding.

I laughed. 'I never said Mr Holmes was an elderly bachelor, Sally. I merely mentioned that the gentlemen of the house were both bachelors and you assumed the rest.'

'And you said you were keeping house,' Sally continued. 'What's this about you being a detective?'

'You've always said that I should find something better to do than menial chores, Sally,' I chided, 'and when you find out that I have, all you do is gripe. I declare I don't know what to do to please you.'

Sally had retreated into her armchair, muttering, and not even Sherlock's most polished manners could bring her out of her sulk.

I looked for Dr Watson and found him chatting with Inspector Lestrade, balancing a glass of champagne and a plate loaded with cakes and sandwiches. He had returned to Baker Street in such high spirits that Sherlock and I had had to restrain him from embracing us both. Then he had swung between joy that we were both alive and apprehension that some new calamity might befall us. However, after a few days of gentle treatment he began to return to his usual equilibrium.

One day he had spent dinner in silence, his brows knitted, until I asked him what was wrong.

'I don't know how I can do the case justice in my account,' he said, giving me an aggrieved look. 'You, Nell, have falsified the record by claiming not to have been at the department store on the morning in question. It makes a nonsense of the whole thing.'

'We know the truth, John,' I said, 'and that is what matters. Inspector Lestrade does too, and the government, through Mycroft.'

On receipt of our wire Mycroft must have caught the next train to London from his parents' house, for he arrived in Baker Street later that same day. He said little, but shook Sherlock's hand firmly, and took my hand carefully in his own large one.

'It has been quite a day,' he said, 'and I am very glad to see you both.'

Some days later, when he had learnt the reason for Effie Stanley's sudden coolness towards me, he called to apologise. I took it as a great honour that Mycroft had moved outside his orbit of Whitehall, Somerset House, his club, and his apartments. 'Now that I have the full facts,' he said, 'I shall be delighted to welcome you back to Somerset House or to Whitehall whenever you choose to call. If I have any work for you, I shall be in touch.'

'Thank you, Mr Holmes.'

'Mycroft,' he replied, and wagged his head at me in such a strange yet heartfelt manner that I had to stifle a laugh.

I turned the plain gold band on my finger, which now resided there as of right, and thought of Jack. His family were deceased or scattered, and we had buried him quietly at the church where Jack and I had married, with Sherlock, myself, and Inspector Lestrade in attendance. The simple headstone bore his name and dates. I had wanted to write more, but he had led another life I knew nothing of, and I could not presume to be his chronicler. Perhaps one day I would add an inscription, but not yet.

I felt a gentle nudge and looked round to see Martha, stiff in her best frock and a hat bristling with flowers. 'They're waiting for you to cut the cake, ma'am,' she said.

I laughed. 'I take it you want a piece.'

'I made it,' she said indignantly. 'It's a good cake.'

I studied her until she reddened. 'What is it, ma'am?'

'I'm sure the cake is wonderful,' I said, 'and I'm very glad you made it, but could you tell me something?'

Martha looked shifty. 'I daresay I could.'

'How did you signal to Wiggins, exactly? And how did you know he would see it?'

'Oh, that,' said Martha. She took a tiny sip from her champagne glass. 'This stuff gets up your nose, begging your pardon, ma'am.'

I raised my eyebrows, and waited.

'Well,' said Martha, 'I sent a signal to Wiggins because that's who the master normally goes to when he's in a spot of bother. So I hung a red flannel petticoat on the washing line – red for danger, you see – and I put a loaf of bread wrapped in Debenham and Freebody brown paper on the kitchen windowsill, and Wiggins got the message.'

I stared at her. 'But you didn't know that Mr Holmes was still alive.'

'I did, ma'am. Remember that day when you – you got the collywobbles, and sent Billy and me to our families for the evening so that you could sleep?'

I felt my cheeks growing warm. 'Yes.'

'When I came back I went to make a pot of tea, as I always do, and I found enough tea leaves in there for two. I thought of how you'd been that day, and I drew my own conclusions. And I hope you don't mind me saying, ma'am, but you did slip up a good few times when you spoke about Mr Holmes, and that made me certain. So I got Billy to take a sealed note to Wiggins a while ago, proposing he watch for a signal from me each day, just in case.'

I goggled at her. 'Perhaps we should take you into partnership, Martha.' Then I laughed. 'Wait till I tell Mr Holmes.'

'Oh, please don't,' said Martha, 'I'd die of embarrassment. Anyway, you've got a cake to cut.' She grinned. 'I'll go and find that husband of yours and the pair of you can get the job done.'

'I have such a story for you later,' I murmured to Sherlock, as we made the first ceremonial cut of the cake and everyone applauded.

He looked rather surprised. 'Have you?'

'A nice story,' I said, 'and a funny one. Perhaps I am not as astute a detective as I thought.'

'Don't be silly,' said Sherlock. 'You are the best detective and the best partner I could ever have.' He took me in his arms and kissed me. 'Never forget that, Helen Holmes.'

Someone whistled, and I had a distinct suspicion that it was Evie, but I didn't care. The case was solved, the danger was past, and the future, whatever it was, could wait.

EPILOGUE: APRIL 1883

I woke early, as I generally did of late, and lay there, restless. Sherlock was still asleep beside me. I eased myself out of bed carefully, to avoid disturbing him, then wrapped myself in my dressing gown and went downstairs.

Martha was already in the kitchen when I entered, sitting at the table with her cap off and looking into a mug of tea as if she could see her fortune at the bottom. 'Good morning, ma'am,' she said, and reached for her cap.

'Don't worry about that, Martha,' I said, sitting down opposite her. 'Is there any tea in the pot?'

'There is, and it's only been made ten minutes,' she said. She gave me a sympathetic glance. 'Trouble sleeping?'

I nodded. 'I was exhausted when I went to bed last night. I woke at two in the morning, then at five, and now, at a quarter to seven, I'm awake again.' I stifled a huge yawn.

Martha rose, took a mug from the dresser, and poured me some tea. 'I put extra leaves in, in case you got up,' she said, and we exchanged a secret smile as we remembered another occasion when there had been extra tea leaves in the pot. 'Would you like a ginger biscuit, ma'am?'

My stomach growled. 'Do you know,' I said, 'I would.'

We sat in companionable silence, sipping tea. Since the adventure of Lady Chambers and my subsequent marriage to Sherlock, Martha's attitude towards me had changed. She had never been disrespectful, but she was less inclined to question my pronouncements, and generally assumed that I knew what I was doing. For my part, I was slower to order and quicker to ask, more willing to negotiate and less apt to force my will on her. At any rate, we got on better and understood each other a little more.

I had almost finished my tea when the doorbell rang. Martha and I both looked up in surprise. 'A call at this time?' I said.

'I assume it's for the master,' said Martha. 'You know how busy he is. Well, you both are, in your own ways.' She rose. 'I'll get it, as that slugabed Billy isn't down yet.'

After the newspaper reports of the strange incident in the department store, Sherlock had been very busy indeed. The newspapers, obligingly, had mentioned that he practised in Baker Street, and the local police were only too happy to point potential clients to the correct address. Barely a day went by when a visitor did not knock with some mystery or other.

I had not been idle, either. Mycroft had made good on his promise to send work my way, and the volume of letters I collected from Marylebone post office increased fourfold. I was in the happy position of being able to pick and choose my cases, and even, on occasion, refer a few of them to Sherlock.

Martha came downstairs, her face a picture. 'We have a visitor, and she wishes to speak to you about a case.'

'To me?' I eyed my dressing gown. 'I can't possibly.'

'She has come all the way from Surrey, ma'am,' said Martha. 'She looks in a terrible state.'

I sighed. 'In that case, I suppose I must see her. Please put her in the parlour and offer her tea, and I shall go and dress.'

'Right away, ma'am.' Martha bustled off. I waited until I heard voices in the parlour before getting up and wearily mounting the stairs.

I put on an everyday dress, twisted my plait into a makeshift bun, and threw a shawl over my shoulders. Given the time of day, that would have to do. I went downstairs and pushed open the parlour door. 'Good morning,' I said to the woman sitting in the window.

'Good morning,' she replied, rising. 'At least, I hope it is, for I need your help desperately. My name is Miss Stoner: Helen Stoner.'

I took her in. She was all in black, and had pushed back a heavy veil on my entrance. She reminded me of myself in mourning garb not so long ago, but she appeared terrified and exhausted beyond belief, and her hair was threaded with grey.

'How may I help you, Miss Stoner? My maid says that you have come from Surrey. How did you know to come here?'

'You were recommended by a friend of mine, Mrs Farintosh. I told her a little of my dilemma and she said that if anyone could get to the bottom of it, it would be you. She mentioned writing to Marylebone post office, but I could not wait, and having seen your wedding announcement in the *Times*, I decided to call in Baker Street.' She looked at me anxiously. 'I hope you don't mind.'

I felt distinctly ruffled, but how could I say that to such a frightened woman? 'Not at all,' I said. 'Could you tell me why you have come?'

'Of course. I live with my stepfather, Dr Grimesby Roylott, in Stoke Moran on the western border of Surrey. We live alone – my mother and my sister are both dead – and lately some strange things have happened…'

I listened in near disbelief as she told her tale. She was succinct, even in her obvious distress, and she had finished by the time Martha came in with the tea. She poured for both of us, and when she left Miss Stoner gazed at me with huge, scared eyes. 'Can you help me, Mrs Holmes? Please say you can.'

I moved my chair closer to hers and took her hand. 'I would truly like to help, Miss Stoner, and I shall do all I can, but there is a certain circumstance that prevents me from taking your case.' I moved my shawl aside and placed a hand on my stomach.

'Oh!' exclaimed Miss Stoner. 'Oh dear.' She drew her hand away and made to stand up.

'No, don't go! I am only taking cases in central London at present, without late hours or physical exertion, but I was about to say that perhaps my husband can help.'

'Your husband? Mr Sherlock Holmes?'

I smiled. 'You have heard of him, then.'

'I have, but...' She looked at her feet, then at me. 'Forgive me for asking, Mrs Holmes, but is he as good a detective as you? Mrs Farintosh was very clear as to your merits.'

I laughed. 'Some say he is even better. If you will wait a few minutes, I shall go and explain the situation.'

I mounted the stairs slowly and entered the bedroom. Sherlock rolled towards me and opened bleary eyes. 'What's going on down there, Nell? I thought the doorbell rang, but I must have been dreaming, and then you and Martha were charging around like a herd of elephants.'

'Do be quiet.' I sat carefully on the edge of the bed. 'A client is downstairs. She came to see me, but I rather think this is a case for you.' As I told the story he sat up, then rubbed his eyes, and finally reached for his shirt.

'This is exactly the sort of oddity I most enjoy.' In another three minutes he was dressed and his hair combed. He opened the bedroom door to reveal Dr Watson outside, still in his dressing gown. 'Good heavens, Watson, what are you doing up?'

'I heard a noise and wondered what was going on.' Dr Watson looked at Sherlock, then me. 'Is it a case?' His eyes gleamed.

'I should say so,' replied Sherlock. 'Our visitor came to consult Nell, but due to, um, circumstances, Nell cannot take the case. And it sounds fascinating.'

'Give me two minutes.' Dr Watson dashed upstairs and returned within that time more or less dressed, with his notebook and pen in his hand.

'Then down we go,' said Sherlock.

Dr Watson set off, but after two steps Sherlock turned. 'Aren't you coming, Nell?'

'It is your case now,' I said. 'The two of you will be quite enough.'

'But how shall I explain the beginning?' asked Dr Watson. 'She came to see you.'

'Oh, just say I'm the housekeeper or the landlady. I can give you the particulars later.' I smiled. 'Go on, you two.'

Their footsteps clattered away, on the verge of running. I took my slippers off and settled on the bed, my hands on my stomach. 'There will be plenty more cases for us,' I whispered, and pulled the bell to call for more tea.

WHAT TO READ NEXT...

If you've enjoyed the exploits of Nell and Sherlock, here are a couple of other series you might enjoy. Both are available in ebook, paperback, and on Kindle Unlimited.

Caster and Fleet Mysteries is a six-book series set in 1890s London, co-written with Paula Harmon. Meet Katherine and Connie, two young women who become friends in the course of solving a mystery together. Their unlikely partnership takes them to the music hall, masked balls, and beyond. Expect humour, a touch of romance, and above all, shenanigans!

The first book in the series is *The Case of the Black Tulips,* and you can read all about it here: http://mybook.to/Tulips.

In *All At Sea*, the first book in the Maisie Frobisher Mysteries, Maisie sets off on a cruise to India to leave her old London life behind and find adventure. When a document of international importance goes missing from an ambassador's cabin, Maisie can't help getting involved. That's if Inspector Hamilton will let her...

You can take a look at *All At Sea,* and the rest of the series, here: http://mybook.to/Maisie1.

ACKNOWLEDGEMENTS

As usual, my first thanks are for my beta readers: Carol Bissett, Ruth Cunliffe, Paula Harmon, and Stephen Lenhardt. Apologies to those of you who stayed up late to finish the book – hopefully that means I did a good job! And again, many thanks to my sharp-eyed proofreader, John Croall, who steered me away from anachronisms with his usual good humour. Any errors remaining are my responsibility.

I am, as ever, greatly indebted to the internet for all sorts of obscure information, and I really hope that no one official is monitoring my search history, what with explosives and epidemics!

If you're wondering why Inspector Lestrade was so ready to blame the Fenians for the bombs, there was actually a dynamite campaign in London and other cities between 1881-5, which led to the establishment of Special Branch: https://en.wikipedia.org/wiki/Fenian_dynamite_campaign. I should also confess that I moved the typhoid outbreak in Tasmania which killed Jack's wife and child forward from 1883. Sorry, Jack… Oh yes, and I also invented Jabez Hudson and his mausoleum.

My husband Stephen Lenhardt gets an extra thank you all to himself, for pushing me to bring Mrs Hudson book 3 into the world. His support (emotional and also culinary!) is a very important part of the writing process.

And finally, thank you for reading! I hope you've enjoyed *A Spider's Web*, and if you could leave the book a short review or a star rating on Amazon or Goodreads I'd be very grateful. Reviews and ratings help books to find their readers, and they're always appreciated.

FONT CREDIT

Title page and chapter heading font: Libre Baskerville by Impallari Type: https://www.fontsquirrel.com/fonts/libre-baskerville License: SIL Open Font License v. 1.10.

ABOUT THE AUTHOR

Liz Hedgecock grew up in London, England, did an English degree, and then took forever to start writing. Eventually, some short stories crept into the world. A few even won prizes. Then the stories began to grow longer...

Now Liz travels between the nineteenth and twenty-first centuries, murdering people. To be fair, she does usually clean up after herself.

Liz's reimaginings of Sherlock Holmes, the Caster & Fleet Victorian mystery series (written with Paula Harmon), the Maisie Frobisher Mysteries, the Magical Bookshop series and the Pippa Parker cozy mystery series are available in ebook and paperback.

Liz lives in Cheshire with her husband and two sons, and when she's not writing or child-wrangling you can usually find her reading, messing about on Twitter, or cooing over stuff in museums and art galleries. That's her story, anyway, and she's sticking to it.

Website/blog: http://lizhedgecock.wordpress.com
Facebook: http://www.facebook.com/lizhedgecockwrites
Twitter: http://twitter.com/lizhedgecock
Goodreads: https://www.goodreads.com/lizhedgecock
Amazon author page: http://author.to/LizH

BOOKS BY LIZ HEDGECOCK

Mrs Hudson & Sherlock Holmes series (novels)
A House Of Mirrors
In Sherlock's Shadow
A Spider's Web

Maisie Frobisher Mysteries (novels)
All At Sea
Off The Map
Gone To Ground
In Plain Sight

Caster & Fleet Mysteries (with Paula Harmon)
The Case of the Black Tulips
The Case of the Runaway Client
The Case of the Deceased Clerk
The Case of the Masquerade Mob
The Case of the Fateful Legacy
The Case of the Crystal Kisses

Pippa Parker Mysteries (novels)
Murder At The Playgroup
Murder In The Choir
A Fete Worse Than Death
Murder in the Meadow
The QWERTY Murders
Past Tense

The Magical Bookshop (novels)
Every Trick in the Book
Brought to Book
Double Booked
By the Book

Sherlock & Jack series (novellas)
A Jar Of Thursday
Something Blue
A Phoenix Rises

Halloween Sherlock series (novelettes)
The Case of the Snow-White Lady
Sherlock Holmes and the Deathly Fog
The Case of the Curious Cabinet

Short stories
The Secret Notebook of Sherlock Holmes
Bitesize
The Adventure of the Scarlet Rosebud
The Case of the Peculiar Pantomime (a Caster & Fleet short mystery)

For children (with Zoe Harmon)
A Christmas Carrot

WHITE
RHINO
BOOKS

Printed in Great Britain
by Amazon

13248484R00196